Praise for Sarah Price

"Sarah Price once again engages her readers in a tender drama that leaves you wondering if two very different worlds . . . the Amish and the English can collide and still leave us with beauty. After Alejandro Diaz, a famous Cuban singer, crosses paths with Amanda Beiler, an Amish girl in the middle of NYC, the beauty begins. Alejandro's world becomes Amanda's, and Amanda seeks her own path in the light of Alejandro. Fantastic and well written . . . mostly beautiful."
—Dianna Bupp, founder of All Things Amish on Facebook

"*Plain Fame* has a unique story line that will keep you up late at night hiding under your blanket with a flashlight, trying to squeeze in one last page before you head into La La Land. Yes, it's that good! I love that I loved these characters so much. They are as different as night and day . . . an Amish girl and a famous pop star brought together by an unfortunate accident involving a limo. Or was it unfortunate? Some may say it was fate pulling these two together like a magnet to metal. The only thing for certain is that their lives are about to be forever altered . . ." —Sue Laitinen, book reviewer for DestinationAmish.com

"Once again Sarah Price does not disappoint. I have enjoyed every book that I have read by her. *Plain Fame* is a little different from your normal 'Amish' novel. Readers who don't normally read Amish novels will like this one, as it, in my opinion, is more about how fame affects someone rather than being just an Amish novel." —Debbie Curto, book reviewer from *Debbie's Dusty Deliberations*

Plain Return

For a complete listing of books, please visit the author's website at www.sarahpriceauthor.com.

Plain Return

Book Four of the Plain Fame Series

Sarah Price

Waterfall
PRESS

Published by Waterfall Press, Grand Haven, MI

www.brilliancepublishing.com

Amazon, the Amazon logo, and Waterfall Press are trademarks of Amazon.com, Inc., or its affiliates.

ISBN-13: 9781503945395

ISBN-10: 1503945391

Cover design by Kerri Resnick

Printed in the United States of America

Without the gentle shove of my publishing team at Waterfall Press, this book may have remained unwritten, despite having the story already playing inside my head. I could not have done this without their encouragement and support through the lightning-paced process of editing and proofing the first three novels in the series while writing the fourth manuscript. So I thank my amazing Waterfall family for pushing me to make Alejandro and Amanda come alive once again. <3

About the Vocabulary

The Amish speak Pennsylvania Dutch (also called Amish German or Amish Dutch). This is a verbal language with variations in spelling among communities throughout the United States. For example, in some regions, a grandfather is *grossdaadi*, while in other regions he is known as *grossdawdi*. Some dialects refer to the mother as *mamm* or *maem*, and others simply as *mother* or *mammi*.

In addition, there are words and expressions, such as *mayhaps*, or the use of the word *then* at the end of sentences, and, my favorite, *for sure and certain*, that are not necessarily from the Pennsylvania Dutch language/dialect but are unique to the Amish.

The use of these words comes from my own experience living among the Amish in Lancaster County, Pennsylvania.

Then shall ye call upon me, and ye shall go and pray unto me, and I will hearken unto you. And ye shall seek me, and find me, when ye shall search for me with all your heart. I will be found of you, saith the Lord, and I will turn away your captivity, and I will gather you from all the nations, and from all the places whither I have driven you, saith the Lord, and I will bring you again into the place whence I caused you to be carried away captive.

Jeremiah 29:12–14 (KJV)

January 20

Dear Anna,

Christmas seems so long ago! Was it less than a month since I left Lancaster? With Alejandro's busy schedule, hours often seem like days and days like weeks.

While I miss all of you, I reckon the one thing I do not miss about Pennsylvania is the cold weather. For the most part, we have been fortunate to travel mostly to warmer climates during the past few weeks, and we even celebrated my birthday at a beach in Malibu. The water was too cool for swimming, at least for my taste. But it was nice to be outside during the day, even if most of the people who joined us were friends of Alejandro's.

In less than two months, we shall embark on the journey to South America for Alejandro's tour. And shortly after that tour, he has concerts scheduled in Europe. It's too much for me to keep track of, that's for sure and certain. I admit to being apprehensive about all of this travel. As I've shared with you before, there isn't much to see between the airports, appointments, arenas, and hotels. But it will be exciting anyway, I'm sure.

Please let me know how everyone is doing. I'm sure Jonas and Harvey are managing the farm just fine. From the weather reports that I've seen, I gather that you haven't had much snow in January. With February being such a short month, spring will be here before you know it. I can already see you and Mamm planning the garden at the kitchen table after supper and under the kerosene lantern.

I'm thankful to finally return to Miami. Even though it isn't Lancaster and there won't be any open fields or springtime crops, it is my home with Alejandro. It's certainly much nicer than Los Angeles! And the blue skies that drop into the sea are truly a gift from God to remind us of how he created this world with a plan for each creature, both great and small. While I hadn't expected his plan for me to take me so far away from my family, I pray each morning and each evening that I honor him in both word and deed.

I best post this letter now. We are ready to leave for the airport.

Blessings to you, Jonas, Mamm, and Daed.
Amanda Diaz

Chapter One

From somewhere in the condominium, a door shut, the sound just loud enough to cause Amanda to rouse from a not-so-deep slumber. Her loose hair covered part of her face until she rolled onto her back. As she did, the white satin sheet slipped from her shoulder and fell so that it barely concealed her chest. Filtered sunlight shone through a sliver between the drawn draperies, and she lifted her arm to shield her eyes. She heard soft footsteps and knew that it was the housekeeper, Señora Perez, beginning her daily routine. Cabinets opened, water ran. Within minutes, the faint scent of freshly roasted coffee wafted into the second-floor bedroom.

As the quiet noises of morning woke Amanda, she opened her eyes just enough to see the red lights from the alarm clock on Alejandro's nightstand. It was almost eight o'clock: too early for him to rise but quite late for her. Still, after three weeks of travel, Amanda wanted to absorb the comfort of being back in Miami at last.

Every joint and muscle in Amanda's body ached. After so many nights sleeping in different hotels and on Alejandro's time schedule, not hers, she had not slept well the previous night, even though they were home. She suspected that she needed a few days to adjust to staying in one place, and that was something she looked forward to.

With a soft, deep breath, she slowly moved her arm and let her eyes flutter open. Beside her, Alejandro slept, his head against the pillow. She smiled at how peaceful he looked with his dark hair falling over his forehead and his arm covering part of his face. Unable to help herself, she reached out her hand, hesitating before letting her fingertips brush against his bare shoulder. Alejandro's skin quivered under her touch and he let out a satisfied and sleepy groan, which escaped his throat as he exhaled. Despite the travel and the long days, his skin remained a healthy shade in contrast to her pale complexion. She wanted to trace the muscle that ran down his arm. But she also knew that he needed his sleep and decided against disturbing his slumber.

Quietly, she slipped her legs from beneath the sheet and slid them over the side of the bed. Her muscles ached from the past few weeks of travel. She wanted to stretch and work out the knots in her neck, but she feared waking him. With one last glance at Alejandro, hoping that her movements had not disturbed him, she lowered her feet to touch the soft white carpet and forced herself to stand. Careful not to make any noise, she padded over to the window.

The previous evening, it had been well after midnight by the time they'd arrived back at the condominium and everything was dark. Now, with the break of dawn, she wanted to see the sky and the sun, the palm trees and the water. The wall of windows in their second-floor bedroom overlooked the terrace and, beyond that, the ocean. She had missed that view, a realization that surprised her since she hadn't spent much time in Miami.

Amanda peeked through the gap between the curtains, giving her eyes a moment to adjust to the sunlight reflecting off the pool's surface. The crystal-clear turquoise water shimmered as if a light breeze were skimming it. Someone had already swept the patio; not a leaf or flower lay astray. The cabana drapes were open, tied back to the wooden, accordion-style doors that she'd been told were only closed during storms. So far her stays in Miami had all been brief, and she had yet to experience anything less than pleasant weather.

She could see the ocean in the distance. The rolling motion of the water looked calm and tranquil from her vantage point. She could barely make out a cruise ship on the horizon. It looked as if it was approaching the harbor just a few miles north of their building.

At the sight of the cruise ship, Amanda sighed, remembering the last time Alejandro had taken her out on his yacht: after their wedding. Our yacht, she corrected herself, and immediately felt uneasy. The idea that all of this—the yacht, the cars, the money, and the fame—belonged to her now, too, seemed foreign and unnatural. It wasn't something she wanted. No. All she wanted was Alejandro's love. With that, her life was complete. The frills and perks that came with loving him meant nothing to her.

But she knew that these luxuries were important to him.

Over the past few weeks, she'd witnessed the way Alejandro thrived on his professional life as an international sensation. When she first accompanied him on the road, she had been too distracted by all of the new places and experiences to pay much attention to the little details: the constant presence of an entourage, the white glove treatment, the VIP attention at every event. During the past few weeks of touring and traveling, especially after Christmas, she'd truly recognized that there were two sides to him: Alejandro and his stage persona, Viper. And they both enjoyed the finer things in life.

As for the two sides of him, it never ceased to amaze Amanda how effortlessly he could switch between the different identities. Although she couldn't imagine how anyone could manage living with two very different personalities, it appeared to come naturally to Alejandro. Amanda suspected that he took comfort in separating his public face from his private affairs.

When they were alone together, Alejandro pampered her with love and attention. But onstage, Viper emerged and sang his songs—often with lyrics that caused her cheeks to flush—while dancing with the six dancers who performed with him at each concert. Whether she watched his concert from the backstage greenroom or the wings of the stage, the dance troupe's suggestive gestures and choreography were enough to make her more than mildly uncomfortable. And when Viper would grab one of the dancers by the hair or pull her close to him, with his hands on her body and his mouth less than an inch from hers, Amanda felt as though her heart would burst with humiliation.

Yet when she looked around, no one else seemed to even notice. It was the same routine that Viper and the dancers had performed in all of the other cities, including the concerts that Amanda attended prior to their marriage. Now that they were married, when she saw him gyrating with one of the female dancers, she felt unbearably tense and uncomfortable.

And then there were the reporters and the interviewers.

Despite her continuous exposure to the media during the last few stops of his tour, these interactions still made Amanda feel awkward. The intrusive questions always led back to one thing: Viper. Early on, she'd recognized that the media took advantage of her shyness and inexperience in the face of the glamorous world of show business. They placed her on some sort of a pedestal, strictly because she was the wife of an international star. They expected her to play the role, but Amanda had a hard time acquiescing. All she wanted was to be herself: Amanda. But as she met with the media, she quickly learned another important lesson: the public wasn't really interested in Amanda, not as a person.

When Alejandro wasn't onstage during the preshow sound check or performing for his adoring fans, he rushed from one appointment to the next. His new manager, Geoffrey, often accompanied him, ensuring that Alejandro arrived and left on time. Amanda watched all of this with mixed feelings. The logistics behind the life of Viper amazed her.

But the intrusive idolization by endless hordes of women who seemed to follow Alejandro wherever he went did not sit well with her. Still, he was always prepared and ready to smile and pose for photos. And the lack of sleep didn't seem to bother him at all. He slept when he could, even if it was only for an hour here and an hour there.

He reminded her of a young horse with enough energy to pull a buggy from Lancaster County, Pennsylvania, to Holmes County, Ohio. He had only one speed: on. And she admitted to herself that she had a hard time keeping up with him, especially since his days often blended into nights.

Now that they were in Miami—with just six weeks ahead to prepare for the start of the South American leg of his tour—Amanda was looking forward to helping him learn how to relax . . . if he let her. She figured that if there was anyplace where he might be able to catch up on his sleep and enjoy the sunshine, it was Miami.

She pressed her forehead pensively against the cool glass of the window. How long had it been since she was last in Miami? Had it been since Thanksgiving? After all that had happened in the last few months, Thanksgiving felt like a lifetime ago. In fact, she realized, every day with Alejandro was like a lifetime. Often, as daylight dwindled and gave way to nighttime, she was left with a fading recollection of what had happened during the early part of the day. It was a strange feeling, indeed: as if they were living out separate episodes in their lives that immediately followed one another, yet were not entirely related. With the addition of each new episode, the earliest one would get erased from memory and fall into oblivion. Even during the busiest seasons of her youth on her parents' farm, Amanda's days had never contained a fraction of the activity that Alejandro had scheduled nearly every day. And without complaining or looking weary, Alejandro bore it well. She had no idea what was the source of his energy. She only knew it was consistent and contagious. He invigorated everyone around him with his strong personality and engaging conversation. When he spoke to people, his lively blue eyes sparkled, making everyone—whether fans, staff, or media—feel as if they were the most important person in the world.

One time, many lifetimes ago in Las Vegas, Alejandro had commented that he lived a *fast life*. While he often praised her for adapting so well to it, in hindsight, Amanda knew how ill prepared she had been for becoming a part of that fast life: the paparazzi, the fans, the commitments, and the travel. Always the constant travel. Why, since New Year's Eve they had crossed the country at least three times! Just last night, she teased him that their home should be aboard the jet, instead of in Miami.

Now, however, his immediate tour obligations were over. They were finally home. Gazing at the ocean, she took a deep breath. The sun lingering over the horizon and the drained feeling in her body told her she hadn't gotten enough sleep. Still, she couldn't linger in bed all day. She needed to unpack their luggage, work outside in the garden, and help Señora Perez in the kitchen. Now that they were back in Miami, Amanda wanted Alejandro to have a nice home-cooked meal that evening. His eating habits on the road left a lot to be desired.

Just as she was about to drop her hand from the drapes, she felt him standing behind her. Without even looking, she could sense his body. She smiled to herself as he wrapped his arms around her, his bare chest pressed against her back. Even though she wore a nightdress, she could feel the heat from his skin through the silk. His fingers tugged at the thin strap of her gown as he kissed the back of her neck.

"What are you doing up so early, Princesa?"

His voice sounded groggy, still thick with sleep. As she smelled the faded scent of his day-old cologne, an intense wave of warmth coursed through her body, leaving her light-headed and breathless. Being held in his arms, so muscular and strong, made her feel safe. She leaned back, her head pressing against the underside of his chin. His morning stubble tickled her skin, but she didn't mind.

"Come back to bed, Aman-*tha*," he purred into her ear, her name rolling off his tongue and his thick Cuban accent heavy with sleep. "For once, let's sleep until the sun sets. You and me. Alone with no interruptions, no cell phones, nowhere to go." He held her tighter, his embrace protective and strong.

"The sun has barely risen," she replied, her voice soft and innocent.

"All the more reason to stay together in bed. Just once, Princesa, *sí*?"

The invitation was enticing, especially since she heard the unspoken suggestion in his voice, but she knew that he needed his sleep.

She couldn't remember the last time she had both gone to bed *and* arisen with him. No, on most nights, she either fell asleep first or awoke alone, sometimes both. After his concerts, there were always places for him to go and people for him to see. She knew that his obligation to interact with his public was the driving force behind his self-imposed sleep deprivation. Most of his concerts took place back-to-back from Thursdays to Sundays, which allowed them to fly to Los Angeles so that he could work with the recording studios and meet with other artists during the rest of the week. It had been a long time since she had seen him get a full night's sleep, something that had not happened since Christmas, when they stayed at her parents' farm in Lancaster.

Reluctantly, she pulled away from him and, taking him by his hand, led him back to the bed. He followed her willingly, a half-smile on his lips.

"You need more rest," she said, helping him into the bed as if he were a child. "And I am no longer tired." That wasn't entirely true, but she wanted him to rest, undisturbed, while she took on the duties of the house like a proper wife.

He shut his eyes and relaxed as she pulled the sheet over his chest, her hand purposefully grazing his skin. When her fingers lingered by his wrist, he wrapped his hand around hers and gently pulled her to his chest, shifting his weight just enough so that her back pressed against his body once again.

"I will sleep," he whispered into her ear, "but only if you stay with me."

With his arm holding her tight, she couldn't say no, even if she wanted to. And once she felt his tight grip on her, she realized that she wanted to stay. Relaxing, she listened to his soft breath as it slowed down. She gently stroked his arm, feeling the muscles quiver beneath her touch. One of his legs was tossed across hers, another measure to ensure that she did not escape. With each breath that he took, she could feel his chest rise and fall against her back. She smiled to herself, shut her eyes, and allowed a light sleep to find her, once again.

When she awoke later, she sensed that it was almost noon. Alejandro hadn't moved; his arm was still holding her and his leg was now entwined with hers. Her body felt less weary, and she knew that with great care, she could slip from his embrace and start the long list of chores that she had planned. With gentle, deliberate movements, she slid out from under his arm and managed to escape his hold. For a long, quiet moment, she stood there, gazing down on this beautiful man that God had for some reason placed in her life. He barely stirred, his chest rising and falling in a rhythm that told her what she needed to know: he was finally catching up on sleep after those long months of eighteen-to-twenty-hour days.

Quietly, she made her way to the door that separated his bedroom from the room that had once been hers, just a few months back when she had first stayed here under his care. There, she could change her clothes without risk of disturbing him, and it was there that she still kept her increasing wardrobe, in the room's large walk-in closet. But as she turned the door handle and pushed the door open, she heard him whisper her name.

Tossing back her long brown hair, which hung in loose waves, she looked over her shoulder and saw that he was not asleep but watching her through hooded eyes. Those blue eyes! Always watching her with that look that made her feel so alive.

"Ja, Alejandro?"

"You are glad you are home, no?"

She smiled, letting her hand slide up the side of the door as she slowly slipped through the opening, pausing just long enough to answer him. "There is no place like home, Alejandro," she said softly. "But only if I am with you." She raised her finger to her lips, indicating that he should cease speaking and go back to sleep. Taking great care not to make any noise, she backed through the doorway and softly shut the door behind her. His sleepy smile was the last thing she saw, and it remained engraved in her mind as she set about creating a new morning routine that would serve them, now that they would be home for a while. Routine, she thought with warm feelings of love and anticipation, will put everything on track, at last.

Chapter Two

For most of Thursday and all of Friday, Alejandro slept, a fact that didn't really surprise Amanda. His energy and focus needed time to regenerate.

The first day, she busied herself by checking on her garden and was pleased to see that it had survived her absence. After slathering sunscreen on her arms and shoulders, she happily devoted her time to weeding and trimming back the potted plantings around the balcony on the terraced patio. Occasionally, she glanced up at the bedroom window, half expecting and half hoping that she might see him standing there. But the curtains remained undisturbed and, although she was disappointed, she knew that sleep was the best thing for Alejandro after he'd spent so much time traveling to entertain his fans.

The second day hadn't been much different. Her only companionship had come from Señora Perez and Rodriego, one of Alejandro's many assistants, who helped him at home.

On Saturday, however, he awoke shortly after she did. She was already sitting on the terrace in the shade, writing another letter to her family, when she heard him greeting Señora Perez. After a few minutes, he emerged through the kitchen door, a mug of coffee in his hands and a smile on his face. To Amanda's further surprise, he wore a light-blue short-sleeve polo shirt and khaki pants with a pair of tan leather shoes. Certainly not a Viper outfit.

"Ah, Princesa!" He set his coffee on the table and leaned over to kiss the top of her head. Before he sat down, he glanced at the paper in front of her. "You are writing a letter to your parents, *sí?*"

Delighted to see him up so early and in such a cheerful mood, she pushed the single sheet of paper toward the center of the glass table. The glow on his face and sparkle in his blue eyes, which almost matched his shirt, warmed her heart. "Why, Alejandro!" she exclaimed. "I do believe that you are relaxed!"

He laughed at her. "I am not so sure about *that*. Not yet. But . . ." He took a long sip from his coffee, as he let her hang on to every word, a technique that he had mastered when talking to his fans or being interviewed. He gave her one of his looks, the mischievous one that always made her hold her breath and bite the corner of her lip. "I do have an idea of what might do the trick."

Somehow she managed to exhale, just enough so that she could answer with a simple, "Oh?" Just a short year ago, the realization of what he meant would have left her aghast.

"*Sí.*"

From behind them, the soft shuffling of feet on the patio floor announced the approach of Señora Perez. The *señora* excused herself for interrupting them and set down a tray covered with jams, croissants, and freshly cut fruit.

"*Gracias, mamacita,*" Alejandro said, a teasing tone in his voice. The devoted housekeeper tried to hide her smile, but she was obviously pleased to see him not just back at the condominium but also looking so well rested. Amanda watched her as she hurried back to the door and disappeared into the kitchen. Alejandro, however, wasted no time in taking a plate and scooping the fresh pineapple and cantaloupe onto it. "Have you eaten, Amanda?"

She shook her head.

"Why not?" He glanced at her as he spread some jam onto his croissant. The smell alone made Amanda feel at home. "Aren't you feeling well?"

"Oh no," she said. "I'm feeling fine. Just not hungry is all."

He gestured toward the fruit. "You should have some, *mi querida.*"

But she shook her head. All of the travel had taken away her appetite. Irregularities in sleep and changing time zones had left her body confused about when to be hungry. "Tell me about your idea," she said. "My curiosity is piqued."

Placing the half-eaten croissant back on his plate, he reached for a napkin and dabbed at his mouth. "Ah, yes. You and your curiosity!" He leaned over as if he was about to tell her a secret. When she responded in kind, bending forward so that she met him halfway, he whispered, "You will have to wait, Princesa. It's a surprise."

"Oh help!" But she couldn't avoid laughing. "You and your surprises! Why, I think the last surprise you gave me was our wedding!"

He shook a finger at her. "You are wrong. Thanksgiving, no?"

"Ah yes. Thanksgiving."

For sure and certain, the Macy's Thanksgiving Day Parade had been an amazing experience. To get to see the volunteers preparing the balloons as the workers inflated them was something that Amanda knew was special. Then they had actually ridden in the parade, waving to the crowds as Alejandro sang. It was a magical day, indeed. But for Alejandro, it hadn't been special enough. He had surprised her after the parade with a private car that immediately whisked them from Midtown Manhattan to the airport, where a private plane stood ready for them. After all, he had told her, Thanksgiving was about family. They had returned to Miami for a family gathering at the condo, where the food had already been prepared and his mother, aunts, and cousins awaited their arrival.

"Ja vell," she said coyly. "I reckon that I have given you little surprises, too, *ja?*" When he gave her a questioning look, she whispered, "Kansas City?"

Now it was his turn to laugh.

Amanda had seen the photos in the scandalous tabloids, caught the entertainment television shows, and read the gossip websites. She knew that her surprise appearance at his Kansas City concert had caused an uproar with his fans. Indeed, the more that the media covered their relationship, the more his social media currency increased. And that currency also did something that Alejandro had never thought possible: it doubled almost overnight. After Kansas City, almost fifty million more people followed Viper on the different social media applications: YouTube, Vine, Instagram, Facebook, and Twitter. He was rapidly becoming the King of Social Media, and all because he had declared Amanda his queen.

The value her role added to his career was proved by the steady rise of those numbers. Fans began demanding more of Amanda, both onstage with their beloved Viper and with him at his interviews. Every public appearance request included Amanda. Unlike less secure celebrities, Alejandro was only happy to oblige.

Of course, all of that had been before the last little unexpected drama that played out in the media: the situation with his former manager, Mike, as well as Alejandro's former friend-with-benefits, Maria. She had always been Alejandro's go-to person to help him out of unwanted publicity, often posing as if she were his date so that he could keep the paparazzi away from his real love interests. Last December, at the Los Angeles after-party, Mike had set up Alejandro, making it appear as if he had broken his marriage vows with Maria. Neither Alejandro nor Amanda had had any prior knowledge of Mike's sinister plan, and they both had fallen victim to it. From the moment the story broke until well after the truth was revealed, they both had declined to discuss the alleged indiscretion with each other or with the media. As far as Amanda was concerned, there was no need to relive the unpleasant conspiracy Mike had planned to separate them. What was done was done, she reminded herself on the few occasions that her thoughts lingered on what could have happened: a tragedy resulting in two broken hearts, caused by one person's endless greed for money and fame.

Alejandro picked up his fork and speared a piece of fruit. "After breakfast, let me make a few phone calls, Princesa, and then we can leave." She heard his phone start to vibrate in his pocket, as if on cue. He groaned and rolled his eyes, but he reached into his pocket nonetheless, withdrawing and answering it in one fluid motion. *"¿Sí? Dígame."* He stood up and walked away from the table, his rapid-fire Spanish words rising and falling in a fast-paced rhythm, almost similar in tune to his songs.

Because his attention was diverted, and most likely for more than a few minutes, Amanda returned to her letter writing. Almost a month had passed since Christmas and so much had happened. She managed to write to her family once, if not twice, a week, but no letters had been waiting for her upon their return to Miami—a fact of which she was all too aware. She told herself that her family was busy; it was a lot of work taking care of the farm and her *daed*. And with Anna having recently returned from Ohio, she would be busy visiting people on the weekends to introduce her husband, Jonas. Traditionally, newly married Amish couples spent upward of three months visiting with friends and family on the weekends. It enabled them to get to know each other's family.

She tried not to worry. After all, the hired man, Harvey Alderfer, still helped Jonas with the chores. Both her mother and Jonas had spoken to Alejandro, telling him that he need not continue to pay for Harvey to help at the farm. While Alejandro had listened politely to their concerns regarding the expense of the workman's wage, he had responded, rather firmly, that he felt the contribution to the family was the least that he could do, given the fact that Amanda was no longer there to help.

"*¿Listo,* Princesa?"

Surprised, she looked up as he returned to the table. "So soon, then?"

He reached for her hand and helped pull her to her feet. Walking backward toward the door, still holding her hand, he acted nonchalant about her comment. "Did you think I would let a phone call interrupt our private time?" He raised an eyebrow and peered at her over the rim of his sunglasses. "Especially when I have a wonderful day planned for my beautiful wife?"

"A whole day? Whatever have I done to deserve such a treat?"

Her teasing evoked another eye roll from him. "Perhaps you haven't," he teased back. "Yet." He pulled her toward him and wrapped his arm around her neck, turning as he guided her to the front door that led to the elevator.

The Porsche was waiting for them at the curb, and he opened the door for her. "Princesa," he said, bowing gracefully before her.

She couldn't remember the last time he had driven her anywhere.

Once he was seated beside her, his foot tapping the gas pedal to rev up the engine, he pursed his lips and gave her a half-smile. "Listen to that purring engine." He tilted his head, as if that would help him hear better. "Beautiful!"

It sounded noisy to her, just another loud car. She much preferred the quiet of the hired cars that drove them from place to place. Even better was the sound of a horse and buggy trotting down the road. For a moment, she felt a sense of longing for Lancaster County. The emotion overcame her, and she fought the urge to say something. After all, it had only been four weeks since they had left her parents' farm after Christmas. Perhaps it was the lack of correspondence from them that had triggered her sudden ache for her family. Regardless, she remained silent, not wanting to spoil Alejandro's good mood or his surprise.

The valet was waiting for Alejandro when he pulled up to the marina. Amanda tried to contain her excitement. Only when they were walking down the dock, their fingers entwined together, did she finally lean against him and whisper, "I'm so excited!"

He didn't say anything, but she could tell that he was pleased with her reaction.

"Viper!"

The captain stood at attention on the dock beside Alejandro's boat. His white uniform was perfectly pressed, not one wrinkle anywhere. His attention to detail, particularly when it came to his personal grooming, was obvious, and Amanda suspected it was one of the things that endeared him to Alejandro. *"¡Buenos días,* Capitan*!"* Alejandro extended his hand to shake the captain's. "Everything is ready, no?"

"Absolutely." The captain gestured toward the boat. "Whenever you are ready."

"¡Buenísimo!"

Alejandro stepped aboard and turned back to help Amanda. Carefully, she stepped on board and waited to take her cue from him. He held her hand and led her inside the cabin. "Señora Perez packed a few things for you." His phone must have vibrated in his pocket because he reached in to get it, pausing to look at the screen. "Ah, Geoffrey," he said. "Let me take this while you get changed. The bag should be in the bedroom." Without waiting for her to respond, he swiped his finger across the screen and raised the phone to his ear. *"Dígame, hombre."*

By the time she'd descended the spiral staircase and found the bag on the bed, she could hear him talking rapidly and occasionally laughing at something Geoffrey had said. She could see the top of the water through the small round window over the bed. It was a clear day without much wind, but the boat was at the end of the pier and smaller boats created miniwaves as they passed. The soothing noise of the water hitting the boat reminded her of the rhythmic beat of a horse's hooves against the pavement. But unlike the pounding of hooves, the sound of the waves did not stop.

As she changed into a lightweight dress with thin straps and a flowing hemline that brushed against her knees, she heard the engine churn; the captain was preparing to leave the dock. Once they were away from the marina, Alejandro would be free from text messages, e-mails, and cell phone calls. Amanda found that she was anxious for the boat to leave.

Alejandro was off the phone when she returned to the main deck. He stood by the open sliding glass door, his back to her and a frosty bottle of beer in his hand. She approached him quietly, placing her hand on his shoulder as she neared him. He glanced at her and reached up, covering her hand with his own and sighing.

"*La vida loca,*" he said. There was a weariness in his voice that she had only heard on a few occasions. "We have a few long weeks ahead of us, Princesa. I wanted this day for us." He rubbed his hand up and down her bare arm. "Just us—for one day."

They spent the day on the yacht, which the captain kept directed northbound, along the coastline. Alejandro and Amanda relaxed on the back deck, watching the swell of the wake and waving to the occasional passing boat, upon which there was usually someone standing with a camera in hand, eager to see who the passengers on such a gorgeous yacht could possibly be.

A cook prepared their evening meal, which they ate while sitting inside in the dining area. The twinkling lights of the coastline moved from starboard to port side when they turned back south, toward Miami. As the sky grew black, Amanda sensed that the boat had slowed. Alejandro poured her a glass of champagne, then gazed at her over the rim of his own glass as he sipped it, watching and waiting for her to do the same.

"You like?" he asked.

She wasn't certain how to respond. The bubbles tickled her nose and made her eyes water as the liquid ran down her throat. She had not yet developed a fondness for alcohol, but she hated to disappoint him. "It's . . ." She hesitated, not wanting to lie, either. "It's bubbly."

He laughed. "It's a very nice champagne, Amanda. A Dom Perignon White Gold." He took another sip, then set down his glass and stood up, holding his hand out, palm up, for her to take. "You don't have to drink it if you don't like it. But you do have to dance with me. I insist."

Just for good measure, she took another sip, ignoring the way he smiled at her. He was not one to tell her this, but he had most likely spent a small fortune on the champagne. Not so long ago he had surprised her with a whole new wardrobe. When she'd looked at the price tags that someone had neglected to remove, she'd been not awed but actually appalled by how much money he had spent on her. Returning the champagne flute to the table, she placed her hand in his and stood. While she wasn't certain she would ever get over the idea that alcohol was a sin, she knew that dancing in the arms of her husband had long ago been removed from that category.

With one arm around her waist and the fingers of his left hand entwined with those of her right, he maneuvered her slowly throughout the large room, toward the sliding doors that led to the deck. The music was soft and the singer Spanish. Alejandro sang along with the song, alternating between looking over her shoulder, as if lost in his thoughts, and gazing down at her.

She pressed her left cheek against his shoulder and shut her eyes. The motion of the boat combined with the slow movement of his dance caused her to sigh. She felt lighter than air. Or mayhaps it was the few sips of champagne, she admitted to herself.

The pressure of his hand on the small of her back increased. "Why the sigh, Princesa?"

She lifted her head and looked up at him. "I'm content, Alejandro."

"Um," he said and slowed down. "Just . . . content?"

"Is that a bad thing?"

He shrugged. "I'd rather you be happy, no?" He took a step backward and lifted his arm, the motion indicating that she should turn. When she did, he grabbed her waist and dipped her backward, the gesture swift and surprising to her. "And I know what might make you happy."

With his hips still swaying, he leaned down and kissed her lips. She released her hands from his and let them run up his chest and over his shoulders, wrapping her arms around his neck. She felt her feet rise off the ground as he picked her up and slowly moved backward, heading toward the spiral staircase that led to the lower floor where the master bedroom suite was located.

When she awoke on Sunday morning to the noise of boat engines and cries of seagulls drifting through the open window, it took her a minute to realize where she was. Alejandro was already gone, his place beside her vacated. She touched the pillow where, hours before, he had slept, a slight indent left behind. The memory of the previous night caused her to smile to herself, and she pulled her knees to her chest, wrapping her arms around them as she shut her eyes and felt a warm glow spread throughout her body.

After dressing and fixing her hair, she padded barefoot up the stairs. She heard his voice before she saw him, dressed in white and seated near the sliding glass doors, a cup of steaming coffee in one hand and his other arm resting along the back of the brown leather sofa. Across from him were two men she did not recognize. They, too, seemed relaxed as they drank coffee and spoke in Spanish to Alejandro. There was always someone around Alejandro, it seemed.

He must have sensed her for he looked up and smiled, gesturing with his free hand. "Princesa! The day is half over! Come and meet Paolo and Eddie. You will see a lot of them over the next two months."

When she blushed and lowered her eyes, he chuckled.

"Ven aqui," he repeated as if coaxing a child and not his wife.

Obediently, she crossed the floor, and when he patted the seat next to him, she sat and crossed her ankles beneath her.

"Paolo will be overseeing the equipment setup and teardown," Alejandro explained, pointing to the older of the two men. He was a lean man with square shoulders and a small, pencil-thin, black mustache, something that Amanda immediately disliked. But his eyes were kind and he reached out his hand to shake hers.

"Good to meet you," he said, his thick accent making it hard for her to understand him.

Alejandro indicated the other man. "And Eddie, the tour manager. He will make certain everything runs smooth."

Eddie, too, leaned forward to shake her hand. Unlike Paolo's, Eddie's build reminded her of Alejandro's. His broad shoulders and dark skin made her wonder if they might be related. They could certainly pass as cousins, that was for sure and certain.

"Mucho gusto," he said, his accent resembling Alejandro's more than it did Paolo's.

"Are you related?" she asked.

Alejandro grinned. "I knew that you would see a resemblance," he said. "Everyone says that. But we are not related." He put his arm around her and pulled her toward his side, giving her a quick kiss atop her head.

For the next hour, she sat there, listening to their conversation but understanding very little of the details that were discussed. Just after ten o'clock, the two men left. Alejandro walked them both to the back of the boat, leaving her alone for a few minutes.

She looked around, amazed to see that the gathering room appeared as if no one had been there at all the previous evening. There were no dirty dishes or glasses on the table. The burnt candles had been replaced. During the twenty-four-hour jaunt, she had barely seen anyone on the boat, with the exception of the captain, who'd greeted them upon arrival the day before, and the steward, who brought them beverages and food. She wondered if there was a third person on board responsible for keeping it tidy.

What a strange life, she thought. And at what expense?

Walking back through the door, his dark sunglasses hiding his eyes and contrasting with the rest of his outfit—the white slacks, shirt, belt, and shoes—Alejandro clapped his hands twice and rubbed them together. *"¿Listo, Princesa?"*

"¿Listo?" She knew what he was asking her, but she had no idea what she was supposed to be ready for.

"Sí, mi querida. It is Sunday, no? I would like to escort you to a fine brunch before we head home. I have some work to do, and we have guests tonight."

Guests? Amanda didn't ask, but she did give him a look, silently inquiring about this announcement. Whoever it was, she wished that she had been told. After all, she didn't have time to prepare anything.

"Don't fret, Princesa," he said. "It's only Alecia."

"Your mother?" Immediately, Amanda felt a wave of panic. She knew what "only Alecia" meant. Alecia did not usually travel alone. "Only Alecia" traveled with her own entourage. "Oh, Alejandro," she said, giving him a look of despair. "Why didn't you tell me?"

He shrugged, glancing down at his phone. "I didn't want you to worry your pretty head. Besides, Señora Perez is preparing the meal so you do not have to do anything. Just show up."

Amanda frowned, but she didn't remark that, as his wife, it would be nice if she could cook once in a while. While she tried to help Señora Perez, more often than not she was chased from the kitchen.

Additionally, she wanted to do more than "just show up" for his mother. "Mayhaps we should go home straightaway, then? I'd like to see what I could do to help."

After only a moment's hesitation, Alejandro relented. *"Bueno,"* he said. "Then that gives me more time." He gave her a smile and held out his hand for her to take. "Come with me, Princesa. Your chariot awaits you."

She took a deep breath and stepped toward him, shaking off the irritation she had just felt and putting a smile on her face. After all that he had done for her the previous evening, she knew that she should feel more appreciative of his thoughtfulness. As she accepted his hand, she leaned forward and kissed his cheek. *"Danke,* Alejand*ro,"* she said. "I had a lovely time."

He squeezed her hand, his pleasure with her gesture of gratitude more than obvious.

Hand in hand, they walked down the dock to the sounds of the water lapping at the sides of the boats and the call of the seagulls resonating through the air. Amanda leaned her head on his shoulder, feeling remorse over her indignation just moments before. She said a silent prayer asking God to forgive her and to lend her the fortitude to remember what she'd known before marrying Alejandro: that being his wife would require adjustments on her part. She just needed God's strength to help her recognize those moments when she encountered them.

Chapter Three

Upon their return to the condominium from the marina, Alejandro excused himself right away and disappeared into his office. With the door shut, she knew that he was working on a new song and she wouldn't see him for hours. That was the way he came up with every new song: inspiration required isolation. And Alejandro's isolation meant that Amanda was left to assist Señora Perez, who happily prepared for the evening's guests, humming as she set a large table that had conveniently materialized from somewhere.

Amanda felt another wave of panic when she saw the long table and the number of place settings, which clearly indicated that her earlier suspicions about "only Alecia" had been correct. A quick count indicated that twelve people would be dining there that evening, although Amanda suspected that Señora Perez had a few other settings ready nearby in case Alecia arrived with additional people.

"Let me help," Amanda said as she hurried to assist the housekeeper. But Señora Perez merely shooed her away, saying something that Amanda couldn't understand since it was spoken in rapid-fire Spanish. However, Señora Perez's hand gestures made it clear enough: her help was not needed.

Even more upsetting was Amanda's observation that the white linen tablecloth was freshly pressed. Not one crease marred the plain but pretty coverings. There were beautiful flower centerpieces, three to be exact, that made the table look even more festive.

Exactly how long had Alejandro known that his mother and company were coming?

Before long, she got another surprise: his family started arriving.

She had been in the kitchen, trying to find something with which to busy herself. Standing around watching Señora Perez work had made the housekeeper so uncomfortable that she'd finally assigned Amanda small tasks, such as fetching something in another room or stirring something on the stove, most likely to keep her away from the other hired help, more than for any other reason. Still, feeling as though she was contributing to the preparations for the gathering improved Amanda's mood tremendously.

When she heard the front door open and the sound of at least two dozen pairs of feet on the marble floor, she looked up and sought out the clock. Two thirty? No sooner had she realized that Alejandro's family had arrived early than Alecia and her entourage simply marched into the kitchen. While the kitchen was large enough to accommodate them, given the big open space around the table that she and Alejandro hardly ever used, it seemed overcrowded with everyone standing behind Alecia and watching Amanda.

"Oh help!" Amanda muttered, more to herself than to anyone else.

She hadn't expected them for another hour or more. Immediately, she reached a hand to her hair, worried that it was mussed. She hadn't even changed her dress, which was soiled from helping Señora Perez. Even the menial task of dishing food onto serving platters had resulted in splatters of sauce staining the front of her dress.

Wiping her hands on a dish towel, Amanda turned toward the guests, her cheeks pinking up as she realized that they were waiting for her to say something. But no words came to her. She had never been a hostess before and, feeling shy among the strangers she knew were Alejandro's family, words escaped her. Without Alejandro by her side, her insecurities about maneuvering in his world quickly boiled to the surface.

To her relief, Alecia didn't waste any time. "Amanda!" She held out her arms, and when Amanda approached her, Alecia pulled her toward her bosom and embraced her. "How is your father? Improving, *sí*?"

"He's improving. *Danke* for asking." Amanda felt awkward in front of these people, all but two of whom were strangers to her. While she appreciated Alecia taking the lead with the introductions, telling her names that she knew she'd most likely not remember because they were strange names to her, she found herself saying a quick prayer for Alejandro to join them soon.

Alone with his family, she couldn't begin to think of what to say or how to behave. At home on her parents' farm, people knew what to do. The men would retreat outside to sit in the breeze and catch up on their plans for the upcoming planting season while the women, without being directed, would bustle about the kitchen, busying themselves with the final preparations for serving the meal.

She suspected that such assistance would seem unusual to Alecia and her entourage. When they came to Alejandro's for a gathering, they were used to being served, and for a moment, Amanda worried that they might think less of her for having worked alongside the hired help.

Besides, Alecia's presence in the kitchen seemed overwhelming to Amanda. It simply filled the room. Despite the simple and quaint appearance of her plain floral dress and flat cream-colored sandals, Alecia evoked an aura of a woman who was dignified and staid, with little tolerance for social blunders. Unfortunately, Amanda never knew whether she was making any.

Speaking in Spanish to the others, Alecia motioned with her head toward the open glass doors. The people wasted no time dispersing to the outdoors, leaving Alecia alone with her daughter-in-law.

Amanda wasn't certain which was worse: being with the entire group or facing Alecia one-on-one.

The older woman's eyes scanned Amanda from head to foot and then back up again, giving serious scrutiny to her midsection. "You've lost weight, *sí*?" Alecia met Amanda's eyes. "You are well?"

"I . . ."

The hesitation must have said it all, for Alecia shook her head disapprovingly. "Eat! You must eat, Amanda."

"Oh . . ." Words completely escaped her, and she stared at Alecia, stunned into silence. What was there to say? No one had ever spoken to her in such a blunt manner. All of her life she had been taught to respect her parents. The problem was that Amanda didn't feel as if Alecia was her parent. But she had also been taught that there were times to keep quiet, even if she didn't agree with someone. She suspected now was one of those occasions.

"If you are to give me grandchildren," Alecia continued, "you need some fat on those bones, *mi hija*!"

"Mamita!"

Amanda exhaled, relieved to hear Alejandro approach from behind her as he walked into the kitchen. He touched her arm as he passed her, a gesture of encouragement, and embraced his mother. Amanda noticed that Alecia gave him a quick perusal, as well. Apparently, he didn't pass muster either. She clicked her tongue, reminding Amanda of the noise Amish women make when they disapprove of something, and shook her head.

"Look at you, Alejandro! You work too much," she said sharply. "You look tired."

Amanda raised her eyebrows, surprised at Alecia's candor. From where she stood, Alejandro looked perfectly handsome. And while she agreed with the former statement, she certainly disagreed with the latter. At some point he had managed to change into white slacks and a black shirt, the perfect image of a host for a Sunday gathering. And she knew he was well rested.

"¡Ay, Mami!" He rolled his head to the side, lifting his eyes toward the ceiling. "Not today. I beg of you. Just for once, let's not start."

Ignoring him, Alecia gestured toward Amanda. "And don't you feed your wife? She should be gaining weight, not losing it."

He groaned, lifted his hand, and rubbed the bridge of his nose.

"Look at her! *¡Muy flaca!*" The look on Alecia's face showed her disappointment. Given her previous comment, Amanda could only assume that she had expected to see her daughter-in-law showing signs of pregnancy. Since she had only one son, it was understandable that she hoped for a grandchild right away.

This time, Alejandro openly rolled his eyes as he came to Amanda's defense. "She's not too thin." The exasperation in his voice and the way he leaned against the counter, his arms crossed over his chest, surprised Amanda. Her confident Alejandro always demonstrated such self-control, yet in the company of his mother, he deconstructed almost immediately. "Why do you have to be like that, Mami? It's a beautiful day, and we have just returned home. Can't we at least pretend to like each other for one day?"

"Don't get fresh with your *mama*!" Alecia snapped. After sending him a searing look, she stepped away from him and, to Amanda's surprise, walked toward her. *"Ven conmiga, mi hija,"* Alecia said, taking hold of Amanda's arm. "Let's find you some food before you blow away in the breeze." She clicked her tongue once again and mumbled under her breath about how a happy wife had much more to her than just bones and muscle.

Over her shoulder, Amanda caught Alejandro's eye as she was escorted out of the room, her arm tucked into the crook of Alecia's. Gazing at the ocean, she took a deep breath. The sun lingering over the horizon and the drained feeling in her body told her she hadn't gotten enough sleep.

Outside, the younger guests had already made themselves comfortable on the terrace. Alejandro greeted them, the men receiving warm hugs while each of the women was welcomed with a kiss on the right cheek. The older women sat around the table, watching the others as they talked to one another while standing near the cabana house. Amanda quickly learned that the two women she recognized were Alejandro's aunts. Their English was not as strong as Alecia's, so they spoke in Spanish, occasionally directing a question toward her for Alecia to translate.

For the first time, Amanda didn't mind when Alejandro's guests spoke in Spanish, engaging themselves in private conversations that excluded her. She much preferred that to having to speak with them, for they made her nervous with their inquisitive stares and intrusive questions about her and Alejandro.

But Alecia stayed by her side, insisting that Amanda sit next to her. When the food was brought out by a woman hired to help Señora Perez, Alecia instructed her to bring a plate of food to her daughter-in-law. The attention embarrassed Amanda, and she sank lower in her seat when she realized that Alecia was making her the center of attention.

"Cuban men like healthy woman, *sí*?" Alecia said, poking at Amanda's waist and backside. "You must have been working too hard, *sí*? Helping with farmwork." She shook her head, clearly disapproving. "I told *mi hijo* that he should have gone with you. If you were to help your father with the work, then he should have postponed his concerts and trips to California. While work always comes first with him, it's often his work and not anyone else's, no?"

Amanda didn't know how to respond, so she took a bite of the pulled pork. The gesture pleased her mother-in-law, who reached over and patted her arm. "I taught Señora Perez my own recipe for that one. See if you like it, Amanda."

Indeed, it was delicious and she said as much.

Leaning over, Alecia whispered, "The secret is to boil it for three hours before you put it in the oven for the same amount of time. I season with beef stock and Goya seasoning. But the other ingredient that I use . . ." She glanced around to ensure no one else could overhear. "A rub mix with Indian coffee grounds and smoked cinnamon."

"Oh my! I've never heard of such a combination!"

"*¡Mira,* Alejandro*!*" Alecia said, pointing to Amanda as her son walked over with his cousins to join them. "That's what we need. A good appetite means a healthy *mamacita.*"

"Mami!" He gave Alecia a pleading look and pulled out the chair next to Amanda, pausing as he sat to whisper "I'm sorry" into her ear. For some reason, listening to Alejandro stand up to his mother's belittling and faultfinding made her want to smile, but she managed to bite her lip and focus on her plate. The last thing she wanted was to destroy any advantage she had with Alecia, because it was clear that her mother-in-law favored her over her own son.

"Alejandro," one of the other women called out. "Tell us about the new tour."

"Just about five weeks in South America, starting with Colombia," he said.

One of his cousins leaned forward as he asked, "Hitting Brazil? I'm happy to fly down to do security detail."

Alejandro laughed. "I know what kind of bodies you want to guard. Not on my tour, *mi amigo.*"

The rest of the group laughed along with him, and his cousin threw his napkin across the table at Alejandro.

"Amanda," Alecia said. "You must be excited, no? I imagine you have never gone to another country, never mind a different hemisphere."

"*Nee,* I have not."

She glanced around at the people who had quieted down and were now staring at her. Her new family seemed as curious about her as she was about them. Many of them had come from Cuba seeking a new life in the United States. A few of the younger ones, cousins who were in their early twenties, had been born in Miami but still grew up with the Cuban culture at the core of their upbringing. She realized that in many ways they were just like her, having grown up among the Englische but not truly being a part of their world.

Only Alejandro had broken through and made such a success out of straddling the two cultures.

"This is a big trip, *sí?*" one of the aunts said.

Amanda nodded. "Growing up, the farthest I ever traveled was the neighboring church district. But last year, my parents sent my sister and me to Ohio." She paused, remembering how she hadn't wanted to go on the trip. She had wanted to stay home, to help her father. But her father had insisted, claiming that leaving Lancaster for a while would help her sister overcome her depression. "That was a big trip for me then."

"What is in Ohio?"

Amanda glanced down the table at the cousin who'd asked the question. "Oh, we have family there. They have such beautiful farms, tucked into the countryside with rolling hills. And where we stayed, there weren't so many tourists to invade our privacy. My sister didn't want to leave, it was so different from Pennsylvania."

"And you?" Alecia asked.

"Oh, it was pleasant enough," Amanda admitted. "But I liked being home with my parents. My sister, Anna, stayed behind and I left on my own to come home." She looked over at Alejandro and saw that he was listening to her, a bemused expression on his face. "Why, if I hadn't returned home when I did or if my sister hadn't stayed in Ohio when I left, I wouldn't have met Alejandro."

Amanda glanced around the table, realizing how silent it had become. Alejandro's family listened to her with a mixture of reverence and curiosity. Underneath the table, she felt Alejandro reach for her hand and gently squeeze it. "To think that my brother's death was the catalyst for all this."

"How so, *mi hija*?" Alecia asked.

"So many sad things occurred as a result of my younger brother's death," Amanda said, choosing her words carefully. "But each one brought me one step closer to following God's chosen path for me. In the book of Proverbs, it says *There are many devices in a man's heart; nevertheless the counsel of the Lord, that shall stand.* No matter what my heart had planned for my future, a future that most definitely did not include either leaving my family in Lancaster or traveling to foreign countries, God had a different plan for me."

Several heads nodded, and despite feeling self-conscious under the attention, Amanda took that as encouragement to continue. *"When I was a child, I spake as a child, I understood as a child, I thought as a child."* She gave a soft smile to Alejandro as she quoted the Scripture. "I suppose we are all children in the eyes of the Lord. But when God points us in the direction of his plan and we accept it, we morph and transform like the caterpillar emerging after living so long in its cocoon. No matter what that butterfly does, it cannot return to the cocoon nor can it go back to being a caterpillar." She felt Alejandro squeeze her hand under the table. "I believe that when we follow God's will without question, that is the day when we truly become an adult in his eyes and, at that point, there is no turning back."

Alecia remained silent for a long-drawn-out moment. Amanda couldn't help but wonder if she had said something to offend her. But then Alecia reached out and lifted up her wineglass: "To Amanda. To *mi hija*," she said, her loud voice booming across the table. "A true butterfly if ever I saw one."

The rest of the table cheered and lifted their glasses in the air. The embarrassment of being the center of attention brought color to her cheeks, but from under the table, Amanda felt Alejandro caressing her skin with his thumb. She glanced at him and saw the pride glowing in his eyes.

Pride, she pondered. Why is it such a sin? Whether or not it truly was, she knew that she relished the expression of gratification that Alejandro now wore. She sensed that he did not often have such moments in the presence of his mother. For whatever reason, a rift had formed, and Amanda understood that for it to be healed, she would need to serve as the bridge between mother and son. She tried to avoid feeling honored at being chosen by Alejandro—or, rather, she tried to let God take the lead in creating that connection between the two of them. But when she turned back to scan the faces at the table that looked at her, Amanda couldn't deny that she did feel that way.

If this is God's plan, she thought, I am happy to follow as he desires. She had been but a child in New York City on the day when she crossed that street, so eager to see and understand the ways of the world. She knew now that God had placed her on that street corner, where she'd been so unfamiliar with traffic lights, and guided her into the path of Alejandro's car. It was as if God had whispered in her ear: "Time to become a woman."

When she'd awakened in the hospital and Alejandro had entered her room, she had slowly started to fulfill God's plan. Despite the physical pain, the spiritual questioning, and, ultimately, the emotional stress—all of which had left Amanda reflecting on her faith and his will—she finally felt comfortable with the decisions she had made. God wanted her in Alejandro's life for reasons perhaps still unknown. But there was one thing of which Amanda was quite certain: she was where God wanted her to be.

Chapter Four

The reflection from the sun against the pool blinded Amanda as she stretched out on the chaise longue, halfway in the shade of the cabana. The air wasn't hot, just warm enough for her to enjoy the sunshine. An occasional cooler breeze that carried the salty scent of the ocean provided additional relief from the sun. With her eyes closed and one arm tossed over her head, both arms resting on the lounge chair's cushion, Amanda soaked up the warmth as she listened to the soft music streaming through the outdoor speakers hidden in the landscaping.

She pondered relaxation. An odd concept for a woman who grew up on an Amish farm tucked into the back roads of Lancaster County. Farm life did not lend itself to solitary moments of *relaxation* spent enjoying the sun, music, and inner reflection.

But she definitely needed this after the previous evening.

The impact of her comments at the table had shifted the energy for the rest of the night. Not only had Alecia been listening, and really *hearing* what was said, her bullish attitude toward Alejandro had also quickly dissipated, Amanda's words having sparked in her a new appreciation for her son. Amanda knew that Alejandro was pleased; for he, too, seemed more relaxed in the presence of his mother. Amanda's words that spoke of godly love had transformed the atmosphere of the gathering. The rest of the family members had looked at her with a new kind of respect, and she suspected that they no longer viewed her as just another one of Viper's women but as Alejandro's true wife. She could stand on her own two feet and speak in a manner that showed respect for God and an understanding of his plan.

It certainly had given the people something to think about, that was for sure and certain.

The tension had eased and the rest of the evening had progressed smoothly. There had been no more separation of the younger cousins from the older women. Instead, everyone remained at the table, talking and laughing. Alejandro, however, surprised her the most. He seemed to unwind and loosen up, telling stories from the recent trips that he and Amanda had taken. When he spoke, the rest of the people at the table listened, enthralled with his tales of fans and interviews, video shoots, and music recordings.

There hadn't been much time for Amanda to reflect further on what she had said about Aaron. Now, alone by the pool, she had only her thoughts to keep her company. And those centered on the realization that one event, the tragic death of her younger brother almost four years before, spoke of God's love for his children.

At the time, Amanda had thought Aaron's death would ruin her family. Instead, his death had actually saved them.

She sighed and shut her eyes, letting the sun warm her skin as she wondered when she had last thought of Aaron before the previous evening. She used to think about him on a daily basis, the guilt of his death still hanging over her head, for she knew she never should have left him unattended while he cared for that horse. There had also been her sister Anna's depression, which had ruined Anna's chances of marrying Menno. Amanda tried not to tear up as she remembered all of the sorrow and hardship that Aaron's death had caused her family.

Yet, what no one had realized at the time was that his death was part of God's greater plan, a plan that Amanda certainly could not have predicted. It made her wonder what God had planned for her own future, especially as it related to Alejandro's upcoming tour in South America and then in Europe. While she felt nervous about so much travel, she knew that, as long as she was with Alejandro, she was doing what God wanted. A husband needed the support of his wife, and she was only too happy to give it.

"Ah, there's my Princesa," Alejandro exclaimed happily as he strolled outside, a mug of hot coffee in his hand. Amanda took in the sight of his black shirt and cream linen pants, a perfect crease down the front of each leg; Alejandro was clearly dressed for the day.

She greeted him with a smile, her heart overcome with love at the sight of him. Since Christmas, she'd enjoyed every minute of his affection and attention, and the two of them had more than made up for time and trust lost to the emotional upheaval that his former manager, Mike, had caused.

"*Gut mariye!*" she said, her voice playfully exaggerating her Pennsylvania Dutch accent.

Alejandro laughed as he leaned down to kiss her. As his lips lingered above hers, she smelled the mesmerizing scent of coffee mixed with his cologne. He gently stroked her cheek and whispered, "*Buenos días, mi querida.*"

She caught her breath again, as she had when she'd thought of Aaron earlier, but this time for quite a different reason.

A slight hint of a smile touched Alejandro's lips as he slowly pulled away and sat down on the edge of the chaise longue beside her. After putting down his coffee mug, he removed his sunglasses and studied her. His concentration made Amanda blush, which made his blue eyes sparkle with delight.

"I see you are drinking in the sun," he said at last. "You are wearing your sunblock?"

She nodded and pointed to the pink bottle on the table next to her chair.

"Ah, good." He put the sunglasses back on and glanced up at the blue sky. "Perfect weather. You like Miami, no?"

"I like wherever I am," she replied truthfully, "as long as I am with you."

He reached over and took her hand in his, lifting it to his lips and kissing the back of her fingers. *"Ay,* Princesa,*"* he exhaled. "You fill the gaping hole in my heart, the one that exists when we are apart and can only heal when you are with me." He pressed his cheek to Amanda's hand and stared at her with an intensity that made her feel light-headed. "After what we have been through, we have learned a valuable lesson, no?"

Before she could respond, he gently placed her hand back on her lap and reached for his coffee mug. She sensed the shift in Alejandro as he switched into business mode. His ability to profess his profound love for her in one breath and then, seconds later, focus on something else always caught her off guard.

"Now, we must talk, Amanda," he said, the tone of his voice more serious.

She swung her legs over the side of the chaise and sat up, facing him. "Is there something wrong?"

"Not at all," he reassured her. "But we have to discuss preparations for South America."

Ah, she thought. The upcoming five-week tour in South America. There had been so much discussion about this tour, and it had always been in the future. Yet, she knew all along that it was approaching rapidly, and now the future was suddenly upon them. While she was excited about traveling with him to countries that a year ago she hadn't even known existed, she felt apprehensive, too. Different cultures, different languages, different countries.

She didn't respond, but simply waited for him to speak.

"We must prepare for the tour," he said. "I am booked with appointments, *mi querida*, for the next few weeks. Mornings working on video productions and afternoons overseeing choreography. Geoffrey also has scheduled some interviews and meetings with sponsors."

She felt deflated. His new manager certainly hadn't wasted any time in overbooking Alejandro. Gone were the days of being alone with her husband. She had always known that she had to share him with the rest of the world. Knowing something and welcoming it, however, were two very different things.

"Shall I get ready to go, then?" she asked.

When he shook his head, she felt a moment of panic. He drummed his fingers on the side of the table as he said, "Dali will be here shortly to review your schedule."

Dali? Schedule? Now Amanda was confused. "I'm . . . I'm going with you, *ja*?"

He shook his head, still serious as he spoke. "Not today, Amanda. You must prepare for the tour."

"Prepare?" This was news, indeed. What on earth did she need to prepare for?

"*Sí*, prepare," he affirmed. "Let's start with your clothing. You will have appointments with our new stylist, Jeremy. He will organize your outfits."

Outfits? she thought. "I have a closetful of clothing."

He chuckled, amused at her statement. "Amanda, you are going on tour. You cannot wear the same clothing you have worn before."

"Why ever not?" She frowned. More clothing? It seemed so wasteful to her. "You do."

He laughed and said something in Spanish before switching back to English. "You still haven't realized that the fans and the media will be watching you as well as me. They will scrutinize your outfits. And while I am happy to step aside for the photographers to focus on you, I am certainly not going to have you critiqued at every stop." He reached for his coffee mug and closed his eyes as he drank. "Jeremy will take care of everything. He has our itinerary and will organize your wardrobe."

"Oh." The word came out like a soft puff of air. She wanted to ask why this was so important; it hadn't been when she traveled with him before. And as far as being scrutinized by anyone, that was of little importance to her. Yet clearly it was to Alejandro. "I see," she said, her voice barely audible.

"And there is more, Amanda."

Whenever he called her Amanda in that tone, eyes leveled at her and his face betraying no emotion, she knew that he was getting ready to talk seriously about something that she most likely would not care for. Undoubtedly, it was business related. Patiently, she waited for him to continue speaking.

"You'll be taking dance lessons so that you can work with the choreographer."

"The . . . what?" This time, she almost choked on her words. Her voice was high-pitched, almost a squeak. She leaned forward and stared at him with wide eyes. Was he serious or was he teasing her? She knew what a choreographer was from their previous travels. The backup dancers were constantly working with Alejandro's choreographer, incorporating new moves into the show performances. But Amanda had no idea why *she* would need to work with him. After all, she wasn't a dancer and had no intentions of becoming one! "Whatever for, Alejandro?"

He rubbed his hands together, an indication that he was hesitant to answer her question. She hadn't seen him nervous very often, so she knew that, whatever it was that he needed to tell her, he anticipated her reaction would not be a positive one. "The tour, Princesa," he responded, his voice smooth and soft. "You will come onto the stage for a song . . . your song."

Her mouth dropped as she stared at him. Surprising him during his opening performance in Kansas was one thing, but now he wanted her to actually become a part of his show? "I . . . I am speechless," she managed to say.

Placing his elbows on his knees, he leaned over and took her hands in his. His thumbs caressed her skin as he stared into her face, studying her reaction. If he noticed that she tried to avoid eye contact, he made no indication of it. Instead, he gave her that half-smile: the one that always made her pulse quicken.

"You are so beautiful when you are speechless!" He lifted her hands and pressed them to his lips. "I like it when you are speechless."

She felt the color rise to her cheeks and looked away.

"And that silence," he said, gesturing with a great flourish, "will be important when you work with Stedman. You will need to listen to him and work hard. We don't have much time."

Amanda tried to compose herself even as she felt aware that he still held her hands, the warmth of his skin setting hers on fire. The way that he looked at her, with those blue eyes so intense and powerful, unnerved her. Whatever he asked of her, she would do. Even if that meant dancing onstage.

"Who is Stedman?" she asked, trying to focus on the discussion and not the energy that she felt radiating from him.

"Stedman is your new dance instructor." He glanced at his phone, and she knew that he was checking the time. *"¡Ay, mi madre!"* He stood up, distracted from their conversation. "Dali will tell you more when she arrives. In the meantime, *mi* Princesa, I have an appointment and must leave you." He shoved the phone into his front pocket and gazed down at her, sitting on the lounge chair. "With all regrets, Amanda. I would like nothing more than to stay here with you." His gaze roamed down her body, the approving glow in his eyes causing her to blush for a second time that morning. "Remember your sunblock," he added with a light touch to her shoulders. "I'd prefer to return home this evening and enjoy your golden skin, not a little red lobster, *sí?*"

Without waiting for an answer, he leaned down, brushed his lips against hers, and touched her arm before he turned back toward the house.

She watched him as he walked away and realized that she had been holding her breath. Since their return to Miami, he had been catching up on his sleep and withholding his affections. Now, with the feel of his touch lingering on her skin, she realized how much she missed his tender and soft kisses in the privacy of their room at night. She shut her eyes, too aware that her love for him was equally matched by his power over her. He overwhelmed her with his sensual gestures, his glances, and, most of all, his self-control.

Yet now that he had left, a different emotion invaded her. Loneliness. It felt as if each second apart from Alejandro left her feeling increasingly hollow inside. Now that he was gone for the rest of the day, she was, once again, surrounded by quiet. Growing up, she'd found quiet moments to be few and far between. If it wasn't the noise of the cows or horses, it was something else; there was always a horse and buggy passing by or a person stopping at the farm for a visit. Besides, despite theirs being an unusually small Amish family, someone was always at home, whether it was Anna or Aaron, her *mamm* or her *daed*.

Amanda was becoming increasingly aware that living in Alejandro's world included an element of isolation—often lengthy. While she didn't know anyone else in Miami, based on what she had seen the few times she had accompanied Alejandro into the city center at night, Amanda wasn't certain she *wanted* to make friends in this city. Everywhere they had visited was full of fast-speaking men and faster-acting women. Miami was a far cry from Lititz, Pennsylvania, and in moments like these, when she was left alone with nothing to do, Amanda missed her family more than ever.

Determined to make the best of things in her husband's absence, she stood up and collected her belongings before walking across the patio toward the open doors. Even with Señora Perez and Rodriego in the condo, it still felt empty. Amanda and Alejandro had been together for so many weeks that knowing he was gone created an empty feeling inside her that she couldn't ignore. But she knew that sitting around and feeling sorry for herself wouldn't make her feel any better.

Since Alejandro had mentioned that Dali would be stopping by to review a schedule, Amanda hurried up the stairs toward their room. She wanted to be showered and dressed when her assistant arrived. Perhaps she could even persuade Dali to stay for lunch. Her company would be a welcome diversion in what Amanda envisioned would be a long day spent waiting for Alejandro's return.

An hour later, Amanda sat at the kitchen table writing a letter to her sister. She preferred to sit in the kitchen so that she could hear Señora Perez as she went about her duties. No matter what task the older woman undertook, she always seemed to be passing through the kitchen. With Alejandro and Amanda back in Miami, there was certainly more work for her to do.

"Amanda!"

She started at the sound. Turning around, Amanda saw Dali standing in the doorway behind her, her dark hair pulled back and her youthful face staring at her. She always seemed so organized and calm, quietly managing everything in Amanda's new life. Today, however, Dali did not look pleased. There was a tense look around her dark eyes.

Amanda gave a nervous laugh and put her hand over her heart. "Oh help, Dali! You gave me quite a fright!"

Even more frightening was the look of irritation on Dali's face. "You aren't ready to leave?"

Amanda set down her pen. "Ready to leave? For what?"

Dali pressed her lips together and reached into her attaché case for her black leather planner. "Your day is packed, my dear. We're meeting with Jeremy to discuss your wardrobe for the tour, we have an appointment with an interview coach . . . and not a day too soon!" She looked up at Amanda. "You know you have two interviews next week, yes?"

"No."

Another look of irritation crossed Dali's face, and she shook her head. "And did he tell you about the dancing lessons?"

"That he did tell me, *ja*." Amanda nodded and tried to swallow her feelings of annoyance about this news. Interview coach? Interviews? Alejandro knew that she had little to no desire to speak to the press or meet with reporters. "What type of interviews, Dali? And who set them up?"

Dali peered over the rim of her glasses at Amanda. "Why, I did," she responded. "That's what my job is . . . organizing your schedule. And with the tour starting in just a few weeks, we haven't much time, Amanda. So let's get going, my dear." She shut her planner and glanced at the time display on her phone. "We only have until three o'clock to spend with Jeremy. And the interview coach was difficult to book on such short notice. We dare not be late."

Amanda understood none of this. There was an unnecessary sense of urgency to Dali's clipped words and anxious behavior. Whatever was going on, Amanda knew that it was something that she'd have to address with Alejandro. As his wife, she had agreed to travel with him on tour, but she had never agreed to be an integral part of the tour. Between the fashion designer, interview coach, and dance instructor, it was clear that Alejandro had different expectations than she did regarding her role in his professional life.

Chapter Five

"Come on, Amanda," Stedman said, clapping his hands. He took a deep breath as he walked around her, and the way he watched her with his dark eyes was not unlike the gaze of a hawk staring at its upcoming dinner. With his dark skin that glistened with sweat and his black clothing, he reminded Amanda of a bird of prey. Even his black hair, slicked back as if still wet, contributed to that image.

If she suspected it when she first met him the previous week, now she knew for certain she didn't care for him, especially when he scowled and added, "Let's get this right! Slow, slow, quick, quick, slow. And keep your head looking away from him."

"There is no him!" she responded.

He rolled his eyes. "Just pretend, Amanda."

The problem was, Amanda didn't understand most of what Stedman wanted from her. When he barked a command, she didn't know what to do. He used words that meant nothing to her: chassé, glissade, promenade. It was as if he expected her to know how to do these things and understand his commands.

But she didn't and when she asked questions, he merely gave her a look that showed a mixture of impatience and irritation at her ignorance.

Today, Stedman wanted her to dance as if she was with Alejandro, but he wasn't there. Instead, she faced a mirror, her arms held up in "position," whatever that meant. That was part of the problem: Stedman repeatedly insisted that she look at her own reflection, pointing out that her feet were not pointed in the line of direction or that she wasn't stepping toe to heel.

She had no idea what he meant and also couldn't stare at herself in the mirror. Seeing her reflection with her arms lifted or pushing her knees forward as he tried to teach her the mambo moves made her want to cry, but she had always been taught that crying was for *kinner*. Adults didn't cry over silly things such as feeling overwhelmed, anxious, or self-conscious.

Amanda had been taught to turn to God, pray for strength, and trust in his decisions for her life. Still, she found it hard to believe that his decisions for her included dancing lessons with Stedman.

"I can't do this," she said, dropping her arms and turning away from the mirror.

"Can't or won't?"

His dark hair, usually slicked back, hung over his eyes, thick curls that hid any sort of emotion on his face when he was displeased with someone's performance. But when he was pleased, he would smile, his face lighting up as he reached to brush back those curls so that he could watch his partner without anything blocking his vision.

Unfortunately, smiling was not something he had done often during the past five days.

Five days and far too many hours, she thought.

"I don't *want* to," Amanda replied, dropping her hands to her sides and facing him straight on. "I am very uncomfortable with this, Stedman."

"I see that."

From the start, she'd hated the dance lessons. Even more so, she didn't care for Stedman's flippant attitude, constant interruptions, and invasive hands that kept repositioning her hips and shoulders. He wanted her to look up at the mirror-lined walls while he was constantly pointing out what she was doing wrong, and never what she did right. Just the manner in which he talked to her made Amanda want to run from the room and never return.

"Amanda," he said, making an effort to sound patient. "You have to learn these basic moves." He walked over and stood before her, his arms crossed over his chest. His dark eyes studied her face. He was taller than her, but lean of build, and he always wore black slacks and a white button-down shirt with no collar. If there was something nice she could say about Stedman, it was that he had a real passion for dance. "This is a tour. A megamillion-dollar investment. Viper hired me to teach you to dance."

She looked down at her feet, ashamed of her reaction. This was for Alejandro, after all. The upcoming tour meant a lot to him and not just for financial reasons. "I know that."

"Good!" Stedman clapped his hands and smiled. "Then let's get your body moving a bit more, shall we? And remember, Amanda, that when you are onstage, everything needs to be bigger than you think." He demonstrated by extending his left arm to the side, a slow and deliberate movement. "Reach to the sides, but don't let your shoulders lift. Keep them down and back. Proper posture is essential . . ."

"I don't even understand what that means," she mumbled.

He rolled his eyes and reached out, placing his hands on her shoulders. He pressed down. "Relax," he snapped. "It's all about the lines, Amanda. Keep your shoulders down and create a clean line here." As if to demonstrate his point, he ran his hand up her back. "Pretend an imaginary thread is running up your spine to your neck and out the top of your head. It's a line."

She pressed her lips together, hating his hands on her body.

"Much better!"

"I don't even know what I did," she said, annoyed at his forced praise.

He ignored her. "Muscle memory, Amanda. That's what will happen when you do this enough times."

Her eyes flickered toward the clock. When would Dali walk through the door to save her?

"I saw that," he said, reaching out and grabbing her hand. "You still have another thirty minutes. Let's go."

When the door finally opened and Dali slipped inside, Amanda wanted to run to her. But she couldn't have, even if she'd tried. Her legs ached from trying to keep up with Stedman.

"Practice over the weekend," he told her. "Remember that the music, the lyrics, and the actual dance are only part of a performance. It's your presence that they want to see. We're just completing the package."

Ignoring him, Amanda hurried off the dance floor.

"And work on your posture!" he called after her. "Elongate your spine! And keep those shoulders down!"

Amanda gave him a look that said exactly what she was feeling. She sat down and removed the special dance shoes that he'd made her wear for her lesson.

When he made a disapproving noise, Amanda shoved the dance shoes into their black drawstring bag and grabbed her sandals. She couldn't leave fast enough, and she made a mental note to speak to Alejandro about the situation over the weekend. If she had anything to say about it, she would *not* be returning, that was for sure and certain.

"Please, I want to go home," she said to Dali as she followed her assistant toward the door. "I simply cannot stand all of these appointments!"

Abruptly, Dali stopped and turned around, pausing to smooth back Amanda's hair and hand her a pair of sunglasses.

"What's this?" Amanda asked, staring at the glasses.

"There are people outside."

Dali said this as if she was answering a question about the weather or something else that couldn't be any less important. Amanda frowned. "People?"

Dali glanced at her phone, checking the time. "Media." That one word needed no further explanation. In fact, Amanda had been pleased that no one had discovered where she was during the previous week. The respite from the fans and paparazzi had been refreshing. Apparently, that was over. "Just keep moving, smile, and keep your eyes on my back. Chin up. You photograph better that way."

Without another word, Dali pushed through the first set of doors, pausing just long enough for a stunned Amanda to catch up with her. As Dali plowed through the second set of doors, a bright light blinded Amanda for a second, and she struggled to slide on the sunglasses. When she realized that it wasn't sunlight but the bright lights of reporters' camera flashes, their brilliance reflected off the white umbrellas stationed outside, Amanda forgot Dali's advice and stopped walking.

"Amanda! Amanda!"

Voices called to her from both sides. Amanda looked to her right and saw a tall young man with red curly hair and freckles on his nose, waving his arms in her direction.

"One photo. Please!" he begged, standing on the balls of his feet and shifting his weight eagerly from one to the other as he tried to capture her attention.

The look of desperation on his face, the longing for just one photo with her, tore at her heart. She had seen that look before in the eyes of the women at the Meet and Greets before Alejandro's concerts. It was the same look worn by the even younger women who lined up outside of buildings and hotels, hoping that, just maybe, they could catch a glimpse of Viper as he walked from the car to the entrance.

Amanda glanced toward the car where Dali stood with her lips pressed tight together, visibly irritated that she had not listened to her. For a moment, Amanda hesitated. But then, as if she'd heard Alejandro's voice inside her head, Amanda knew what to do. She smiled and walked over to the lanky boy who didn't look to be much older than she was. She let him hug her, his lean body pressed against hers. When she pulled back, she was surprised to see that he was weeping.

He gave a nervous laugh, wiping at his eyes with the back of his hand. Words seemed to escape him.

To save him from further embarrassment, she smiled. "You wanted a photo, *ja*?"

"Oh yes!" He turned around, positioning himself so that he could take a photo of her standing beside him. With his cell phone held up in the air, he took the selfie, a big grin on his face. "I can't thank you enough," he gushed. "You just made my life."

She would have found the statement unusual, but she had heard it so many times at Alejandro's events that the words did not surprise her. However, she couldn't believe that he was saying such a thing to *her*. Before she could reply, several other people pushed their way through and began to take photos of her, two of the women crying and hugging her before taking a picture with her. Slowly, Amanda made her way through the crowd, pausing to meet with fans and smiling for the professional photographers.

"What was *that*, Amanda?" Dali snapped when Amanda finally made her way into the car. "I was most specific in my instructions to you!"

Dali's voice had an edge to it that startled Amanda. No one had ever spoken so sharply to her. "I . . . I'm sorry."

"You should be! What on earth were you thinking?"

Amanda didn't respond right away. She sank down in the seat of the car, wishing that it could just swallow her up so that she could disappear. What had she been thinking? The crowd had surprised her. All week she had been at the dance studio and no one had made a fuss over her. Usually, the fans waited for Alejandro . . . their Viper. Amanda was just his wife, and as far as she knew, they wanted photos with her only because she was in a relationship with him.

"It's what Alejandro would have done."

"I suppose I don't have to point out that you're not Alejandro!" Dali dug through her attaché case, until she finally found her phone. Shaking her head, she began typing something on it. Her cheeks blazed red, whether from anger or agitation, Amanda didn't know. "I don't think you understand it yet. You are a brand, Amanda. And there is a price associated with your brand image. Don't cheapen your brand image in such a way," she snapped, "because if you do, you cheapen his!"

"A brand?" The word sounded cold and unfeeling, but she had no idea what it meant. The only brand that she could think of was what some farmers did to their livestock. Amanda frowned. "I have no idea what you are talking about."

"Really?" Dali scoffed at her. "Well, *I'm* not going to be the one to explain it to you. Clearly, you aren't about to listen to me."

"Dali . . ."

Her own cell phone vibrated, and Amanda pulled it out of her bag. She glanced down and was only slightly surprised to see that Alejandro was calling her. Turning her shoulder so that her back faced Dali, Amanda answered the phone. *"Ja?"*

"Amanda."

She'd already known who it was. The stern tone of his voice, however, dismayed her. "I don't understand," she whispered. "What was so wrong?"

There was a pause on the other end of the line. When he spoke again, the edge was gone from his voice. "I know, *mi querida*. But it's not safe to mingle with the crowds if I am not there."

"You make the fans happy." She fought the urge to cry. "That's what you always do, and it was what I wanted to do. For you."

"*Sí, sí,*" he replied. "You must be careful, though. And posing with people on the street . . ."

"I've seen *you* do it!" She felt like a child, being scolded by her parents.

When he laughed, she knew that she couldn't stop the tears. With the back of her hand, she wiped them away.

"I do, *sí,*" he said softly. "But there is always a reason. A strategic reason, Princesa. There is a price for such a photo, and today no one made any money but the media. You'll learn more on our trip, *sí*? Just listen to Dali when she tells you to do something."

"I thought I was being kind," she whispered, part of her wanting to turn off the phone and the other part to justify herself.

He lowered his voice so that, presumably, whoever was near him could not hear. "And you are, Princesa. You have a large and caring heart. I love that large and caring heart. Don't change. But be safe about it."

After he'd said good-bye, Amanda held the phone in her hand for a few minutes. She stared out the window of the car, embarrassed that she had been reprimanded, both by Dali and Alejandro, as if she were a schoolgirl. Her cheeks burned from the humiliation of having cried in Dali's presence, so she refused to turn around and apologize to the woman. Instead, as soon as the car pulled up to their building, Amanda grabbed her things and darted out of the door that the doorman opened for her, barely pausing to thank him.

All she wanted was to spend time with Alejandro. But his time seemed to be an increasingly rare commodity these days. His days were spent with his team in endless meetings about the tour, and his nights kept him in the music studio. When he finally returned home, she was often already asleep. He'd quietly undress, leaving his clothes over the back of a chair, before sliding under the sheets and tucking his arm around her waist as he gently pulled her toward him. That was usually when she awoke: the exact moment that her back pressed against his chest and she felt his warm breath on the nape of her neck.

He'd sleep and she'd lie there, listening to the sounds of his breathing and feeling the strength of his arm holding her tightly against his chest. Sometimes she'd stroke his arm, tracing her fingers along the outline of his tattoo. He would awaken, just for a moment, and kiss her shoulder before falling back into a deep slumber.

Now, as she exited the elevator and proceeded toward the main entrance to their condominium, she felt the tears begin to fall. Once inside, she ran up the stairs and headed for the bedroom, ashamed by her reaction to all that had happened. She flung herself across the bed, knowing that she needed to let it out and just cry. No one was home besides Señora Perez and maybe Rodriego. They wouldn't disturb her even if they overheard her sobs.

She must have fallen asleep because she awoke to the noise of the light switch clicking in the bathroom. As her eyes fluttered open, she realized that the sun had already set. She sat up and rubbed at her eyes, feeling groggy and fuzzy headed. "Alejandro?" she called out. She knew it must be him for she heard the water running in the sink. She slid off the bed and quietly tiptoed across the carpet to the bathroom. The door was slightly ajar. "Alejandro?" she asked again as she pressed her fingers against the door handle.

He stood at the sink, splashing water on his face. When he saw her in the reflection of the mirror, he turned off the water and grabbed a towel. "Princesa," he said, his eyes watching her as he dried his face. "You were asleep. Did I wake you?"

She shook her head, sections of hair coming loose from her bun. She must have lost her pins while she slept, for strands of her hair hung down her shoulders and brushed against her face. Pushing it back from her cheeks, she let her hand linger on the back of her neck. "I'm sorry," she whispered.

"For what, Princesa?" He dropped the towel into the sink and turned to face her, leaning his hip against the edge of the marble vanity. The corner of his mouth lifted into a smile as he reached out his hand for hers. When she took it, he pulled her into the room and against his chest. "Ah, Princesa," he sighed, burrowing his face into her hair. "I have missed you these past few days."

His confession almost made her cry once again, but she didn't think she had any tears left.

He kissed the side of her head, still holding her tight in his arms. "Such a life for you, no? There is much to learn."

She wanted to learn, but she did not know what understanding she was missing. She still didn't see why she shouldn't have taken photos with the fans. Nor did she understand what Dali had meant about her being a *brand*. Even Alejandro had said that there was a price for photos. Price? What price? And for . . . a photo? She didn't understand what they were talking about, and the confusion weighed heavily on her. She wanted to do the right thing. But if she didn't know what the right thing was, how was it possible for her to do it? She wanted to ask him for an explanation, some clarification that would help her avoid making inadvertent mistakes that would upset others. But navigating his world was becoming increasingly difficult, especially now that they had returned to Miami.

And that was one more thing that bothered her. Miami was supposed to be their home. She wanted to create a routine for Alejandro, but every day presented nothing but irregular schedules. The only constant thing in their lives was change.

As if reading her mind, he pulled away and held her at arm's length, keeping his hands on her shoulders and massaging them gently. "How was the rest of the day? Good?"

Amanda stood there, mute, staring at him. How could she possibly tell him the truth? That she abhorred Jeremy's dresses with their mesh fabric sides and low-cut necklines and how Stedman was trying to make her do things that she simply didn't want to do? The thought of telling Alejandro what she truly felt caused her to do the one thing she didn't want to do: burst into tears. Horrified, she covered her face with her hands and sobbed.

With his hands still on her shoulders, he leaned down and peered into her face. "What is this, Princesa? Tears? Not from *my* Amanda," he said in a soothing voice. She thought she heard him chuckle, not unkindly but in a bemused sort of way. "Such emotions, Princesa," he whispered. "Are you feeling all right?"

And there it was. The truth.

Did he know her so well, she wondered, that he sensed what was really bothering her? Burrowing her head against his shoulder, she continued sobbing, not caring whether her tears stained his shirt. She clung to him. "Yes . . . no . . . oh, I don't know anymore," she said.

He let her cry, rubbing her back and soothing her with a soft "Shh." When she finally calmed down, he released his hold on her and leaned over to pull a tissue from the container on the vanity. Leaning down again, he dabbed at her eyes. "Your emotions, Princesa," he said slowly. "Do you think . . . ?"

When he didn't finish the sentence, she blinked at him. "Think what, Alejandro?"

He smiled at her and gave a last dab at a final tear. "Perhaps something is bothering you? Perhaps there's a chance . . . ?"

A chance of what? she wondered. And then, all of a sudden, it dawned on her. Was he insinuating that she might be pregnant? Were her emotions caused by changes in her body? "I . . . I don't know," she answered. She hadn't considered such a possibility. "It *has* been a while." She felt herself blush when she said that and averted her eyes.

"Hmm." The way that he said it, a mischievous undertone to that single sound, made her dip her head and hide it against his arm as he embraced her again. He laughed and gently rocked her from side to side. "We'll have to find out, *sí*?"

A baby? Was it possible? She tried to remember when she'd last had her monthly course. And her emotions had seemed all over the place lately, especially since they had returned to Miami. A warm glow spread throughout her body at the thought that, mayhaps, she was carrying Alejandro's baby. Oh, she thought, how *wunderbar* that would be! To give him such a gift, and to share the miracle of life together! She laughed with him, suddenly feeling as if the weight of the day's emotional burdens had lifted from her shoulders.

Chapter Six

Wearing black slacks and a high-collared white shirt with black onyx cuff links at the wrists, Alejandro stood in the doorway, watching Amanda. She was leaning slightly over the bathroom counter and peering into the mirror, putting on the final touches of her makeup. She could feel the heat of his stare, and as she applied a clear lip gloss, she looked at his reflection beside hers.

"You're staring," she said, her eyes holding his gaze in the mirror.

"*Sí.*" His eyes never moved, and the corner of his mouth lifted, just a touch, as if he was trying to repress a smile. "*Sí*, Amanda, I am staring." His voice was soft, almost like a gentle purr. "I am staring at the most beautiful woman in my world."

His compliment caused her a moment of discomfort, and she looked away. Growing up, beauty was something to be seen in God's gifts to the world: nature, not people. Personal beauty was not something that was discussed among family, friends, or community. Doing so was a sign of one of the worst sins: vanity. Even though Alejandro knew this, he often made flattering remarks about her. She wasn't certain that she would ever get used to them.

As always, he chuckled at her reaction and she felt the heat rise to her cheeks.

She didn't know if she would ever get used to his compliments or the look in his eyes when he watched her with a mixture of mild curiosity and barely veiled longing. There were moments when she caught him staring and wondered how long she had been unaware of his silent observation. But always he wore that look, the same one he wore now as he watched her getting ready for an evening out in Miami.

"Is that a new dress, Princesa?" He crossed the room, the thick heels of his glossy black shoes clicking on the marble tile. "Did Jeremy pick that out?"

Amanda turned so that her back faced the mirror and playfully held out her arms as if she were a dancer. Unlike Lucinda, the horrible woman who'd picked out her clothing in Philadelphia and insulted her by calling her prayer *kapp* a hat, Jeremy not only understood Amanda's style but also embraced it in most of her day-to-day outfits. Still, her new wardrobe was not perfect. This dress, dark navy with a high neckline, was proof. Jeremy had added the rhinestones around her neck and the low-cut back, which Amanda had complained profusely about. And, of course, he disagreed with her over the style of her dresses for the tour. In fact, several of the new dresses were a bit risqué for her taste. But in dealing with Jeremy, she had clearly met her match: her protests were ignored, the dress with the low back now adorned her body, and she knew that her stage dresses would be suggestive, to say the least.

"You like, *ja*?"

"I like, *ja*," he teased, reaching for her extended hand and gently pulling her toward him. With his other hand, he held her, the small of her back fitting comfortably against his palm. The warmth of his skin gave her a shiver, and she shut her eyes, enjoying his attention.

The past two weeks had been long and busy. She chastised herself now for having envisioned that their return to Miami would be followed by them living a normal life as newlyweds, something they had yet to experience. After all, she reasoned with herself, what about Alejandro was truly "normal"? Certainly not his lifestyle, that was for sure and certain.

Now, her days were filled with so many appointments, she barely realized that she hardly saw her husband until the evenings when he returned to their condominium—sometimes with an entourage, occasionally by himself. Always she made certain to be ready for his arrival so that when he walked in the front door and called out for her, she was just in the other room, waiting.

Always waiting.

If he was alone, she didn't mind that he would sweep her into his arms, sometimes lifting her off the floor as he carried her into the living room, her weak protests mere pretense, for she wanted nothing more than to stay in his arms. Instead of putting her down, he'd spin her around, nuzzle at her neck, and warm her lips with a kiss before setting her back on her feet. Leaving his embrace always made her heart ache. It hadn't taken long for her to figure out the routine, a routine she accepted despite it being far removed from the one she'd envisioned for their life in Miami.

Most nights Alejandro appeared around seven o'clock; he would pour himself a drink and offer her a glass of champagne or wine. Usually she would simply shake her head and instead accept the sparkling water with a twist of lemon that Señora Perez had waiting for her, as if by magic. At that point, Alejandro would then join her on the sofa, stretching out his large frame as he leaned his head back and sighed. He would remain silent for a few minutes as he unwound from a long day of meetings and interviews. After he'd had a few minutes to relax, he'd ask her about her day, which had been filled with just as much activity as his.

After an hour, sometimes less, his phone would vibrate and he'd glance down at the intrusive device. Not once was it a call or text that didn't require his immediate attention.

And then there were the evenings when he would arrive home with his entourage. Amanda thought they were as intrusive as Alejandro's cell phone. She knew what to expect when Alejandro called for her on those evenings: the same embrace, the same lifting off the ground, the same nuzzling at her neck. Yet she felt uncomfortable with his affection for her being displayed in front of those men, some of them looking like hoodlums from the street in their T-shirts and caps.

Alejandro appeared oblivious to her uneasiness in their presence. He delighted in showing off his wife and made certain to compliment her appearance or tease her about something that would bring that all-too-familiar flush to her cheeks. Then he would excuse himself and escape with the men to his recording room or take them outside to sit around the pool, where they'd drink and discuss business. Occasionally, more people might arrive—his friends, cousins, other entertainers— and the music would start. On other nights, Alejandro might work on writing new songs until well after midnight. Either way, she retired to bed alone, waking early in the morning with Alejandro beside her, sometimes with his arm draped around her waist, but always in a deep sleep.

Tonight, however, he was taking her out.

He traced her cheekbone with his thumb, and she opened her eyes, eager to have his undivided attention for one whole evening. She didn't even mind that their dinner reservations were for nine o'clock, the time of night when she was usually washing her face and changing into a nightgown so that she could settle into bed after her evening prayers. She'd read the Bible for a while until her eyes drooped, and then she would drift off to sleep, sometimes with the light still on.

"Let's cancel those reservations," he murmured as he leaned down and brushed his lips across hers, his thumb still on her cheek. "I'm no longer hungry . . ."

She felt light-headed and realized she was holding her breath. It seemed impossible to breathe in his presence. The less time they spent together, the more strongly she felt the need to be near him.

As if reading her mind, he pulled away from her, letting his thumb slowly fall from her cheek. He half smiled in his mischievous way as he whispered, "Later, *sí*?"

He took a step backward and glanced in the mirror, taking a moment to straighten the sleeves of his shirt and brush a piece of lint from his pants. She watched as he assessed himself, straightening his shoulders and lifting his chin. Like a beautiful rooster preening, she thought, and felt an immediate longing for the simplicity of what she feared she would always secretly consider her home: Lancaster. Wherever Alejandro went, he was prepared for paparazzi. Not once did he leave the house in anything less than what Amanda would consider equivalent to his Sunday best. Tonight was no exception.

The doorman nodded to them as he opened the door and stepped aside. Amanda smiled and greeted him with a soft hello. She had attempted numerous times to engage him in conversation until Dali finally informed her that she was not to fraternize with such people, by which Amanda quickly realized she meant hired help. Amanda hadn't responded to Dali, but the comment had stayed with her, tasting foul in her memory each time she remembered it.

"Ah, here she is!" Alejandro said as the valet emerged with his Porsche from the underground garage. He gestured toward the car with a great flourish and smiled at her. "Your chariot, Princesa."

"And the occasion is . . . ?"

"Do I need an occasion?" He opened the car door and gave an exaggerated bow. "Perhaps *you* are the occasion."

With one foot inside the car, she pivoted on her other to look at him. "I am?"

"*Sí*, Princesa." He reached out to take hold of her elbow so that he could guide her into the passenger seat. "I have been so busy. I fear I have been neglectful of my most precious jewel."

"I wouldn't go so far as to say neglectful . . ." she teased gently.

Alejandro rolled his eyes and placed his hand over his chest. "Ouch."

She laughed, enjoying his playful mood.

The week had been long. It had taken her time to get used to the fact that the pregnancy test she took on Saturday had come back negative. At first, she hadn't wanted to tell Alejandro, hoping and praying that the test might be wrong. But on Wednesday, a second pregnancy test displayed the same negative sign on the plastic stick, and she recognized the truth: there was no baby—not now anyway. The realization felt overwhelming; she had been ever so certain that she carried his baby. While he was working, she had crawled into bed, curled into a fetal position, and wept silently for the baby she had conjured in her mind.

With it being February now, she knew that enough time had passed for her to have conceived a baby. Even considering the time she and Alejandro had spent apart before Christmas, there was no reason for her not to have become pregnant. The disappointment was devastating; she felt like a failure. There were very few Amish couples who didn't have a baby by their one-year anniversary. And when that was the case, it was usually because there was a problem.

She hadn't wanted to tell Alejandro in person, so when her tears had dried up and she'd gathered her strength, she did the cowardly act of sending him a text message by phone:

```
I'm sorry. Not this month.
A.
```

Barely five minutes had passed before her phone dinged, announcing a new incoming message. She'd hesitated, feeling worried about what his response would be. She waited to look at it, fearing that his disappointment would increase her feelings of inadequacy. When she finally found the strength to retrieve his message, she covered her mouth with her hand and stifled a tearful laugh of relief:

Why sorry? Trying is the best part,
Princesa.
V.

That night he'd brought home two dozen white roses and, without even giving her a chance to ooh and ahh over them, had swept her off her feet and up the staircase. She didn't have time to feel sorry about her lack of immediate conception. Alejandro made good on his promise to keep trying.

Now, as he drove her to the restaurant, singing along with the radio as he did, she leaned back and enjoyed the pleasure of just being with him. Not once had he seemed disappointed or upset that she wasn't yet pregnant. Instead, he treated her with tender care, acting like he normally did and without making any mention of what could have been.

His support certainly helped her overcome her erratic swing of emotions. It will happen when it happens, she told herself. When God wanted her to have a baby, that would be the moment when she would conceive.

The music faded away, and it took her a moment to realize that he had turned down the radio.

"Did you say something, then?" she asked him.

"I did not. But if I had," he replied with a sideways glance, "it would have been to comment that you seem relaxed tonight."

And she was.

"Where are we going, if I may ask?"

Alejandro lifted an eyebrow and pursed his lips, one corner raised just enough to show that he was in one of his playful moods. "You may ask," he said, flicking on his turn signal. "But I am not going to answer, Princesa."

"Ah." She knew better than to press him. When he wanted to do something special for her, he would not be convinced to divulge any information. "I see." She tried not to smile back at him. "It's a right *gut* thing that patience is a virtue, then, *ja*?"

Five minutes later, Alejandro pulled up to the restaurant and stopped the car under a burgundy canopy so that the valet attendant could take it away. The driver's side door was opened by the attendant, but before Alejandro exited the car, he turned toward her. "Tonight is going to be very special, Amanda."

Her curiosity was piqued as she wondered what he had up his sleeve. His secrecy was one thing; the use of her name was another. Usually when he called her Amanda, something serious was about to be discussed. But he didn't seem to be in a serious mood. No, he looked fresh and happy, his face glowing with pride as he walked around the car, bent his arm, and waited for her to take it so that he could escort her inside.

The restaurant was dark, illuminated only by sconces that clung to each panel of the rich red walls, the light creating a seductive effect and adding to the dramatic atmosphere. From somewhere inside came the sound of music, a dull, muffled noise that seemed to come from far away. Blue lights glowed from the underside of the bar in the cocktail lounge at the back of the restaurant. The people at the bar were all dressed in fancy clothes: the men in stylish slacks and silky shirts, and the women in form-fitting dresses and high heels that made Amanda feel unbalanced just by looking at them.

"Ah, Mr. Diaz," a woman said as she approached them. "Your table is ready."

She led them through the lounge, and several people looked up as they passed. Amanda saw the subtle movements of people leaning forward and whispering to each other. Alejandro, however, acted as if he didn't notice although she knew that he noticed everything. If he acted aloof and preoccupied, however, he wouldn't have to stop and pose for photos; neither would he be obligated to talk to anyone. This seemed reasonable to Amanda. After all, she rationalized, this was his time, not time he owed the fans.

As she thought these things, something dawned on her: Alejandro orchestrated every move that he made. The realization struck her hard, and she stopped walking just long enough for him to pause and turn around.

"Are you coming, Princesa?"

She stared at him, remembering that first weekend in Philadelphia when he had taken her hand and asked her to dance. It hadn't been their first dance together; he had danced with her back on the farm in the *grossdaadihaus*. But that second dance had taken place as several dozen people stared at them, watching the international superstar dance with the fresh-faced, straight-off-the-farm Amish girl. She had felt awkward and shy, but he had said something to her that she hadn't thought to question at the time: *They need to see this. Remember the goal.*

While she stood there, digesting this realization, she watched as Alejandro took a few steps toward her and stretched out his hand. The gesture broke her trance, and she saw that people were watching them. *Remember the goal.* And she understood: reality was the fantasy that the public saw. From the corner of her eyes, she had seen several people take their photo. And she remembered that every photo had a price. Fans would circulate them on social media while the paparazzi would sell them to the news media. Regardless, she knew that every photo had the potential to either add to or detract from Viper's success.

She smiled at him, tipped her head demurely, and took his hand. Trying to maintain a straight posture, something about which Stedman constantly criticized her, she caught up to Alejandro and let him lead her to the private alcove in the back of the restaurant.

"Well done, Amanda," he said under his breath as they settled into their seats. "Now, may I ask what that was about?"

"You may ask," she said as the server set the linen napkin across her lap. "But I am not going to answer."

It took him a second to digest what she had said, her voice so serious that it had caught him unprepared. Then, when the words sank in, he tossed his head back and laughed. "Touché, *mi querida*. Touché."

She pursed her lips and batted her eyes at him, trying to act coquettish, which only made him laugh again. He reached across the table and took her hand in his. She squeezed his hand, enjoying the way that he looked at her, as if he was appreciative of her humor as well as happy to be in her company.

"Danke, Alejandro,*"* she said in a soft voice.

He tilted his head and arched one eyebrow, waiting for her to continue. When she didn't, he finally asked, "For?"

"For being patient with me," she answered. "I needed your support this week."

Alejandro released her hand and glanced at the server who was approaching the table, a bottle of chilled champagne resting against his arm. Alejandro glanced at the label and nodded before returning his attention to Amanda. "I know you are disappointed," he said. The flat tone of his voice surprised her. He might as well have stated that the sun was shining or the sea was calm. "Aren't you?"

He took a deep breath, looking as if he was trying to choose his words carefully. The hesitation was enough to let Amanda realize that he had a different opinion on the situation than she did. "We have a busy few months, Amanda," he started. "The South American tour is going to be followed by Europe. And when we return from that, we will play more venues in the States." He lifted the flute of champagne to his lips, hesitating before he sipped it. The tiny bubbles traveled from the bottom of the glass to the top. "Try your champagne, *mi querida*. It's a night to celebrate."

"I . . . I'd like to hear more about what you were just saying." She couldn't just brush aside his comments. She needed to truly understand what he meant.

"About the tour?" He twirled the stem of the champagne flute between his thumb and fingers, thoughtfully watching the rising bubbles in the glass. "It's a busy time, Amanda. Days and nights merge into one on a tour like this. It's different from touring in the US. More difficult. And during the downtime, what little there is of that, I'll be recording new songs."

"From where?" This was news to her. She had figured that while he was on the road, his focus would be strictly on promotions and performances.

"In hotel rooms, if I must. The EP is scheduled to release in time for summer with the remaining songs releasing in time for the Christmas tours." He sighed, meeting her gaze with a look of sorrow in his eyes. "My joy, Amanda, comes from your joy. Would I have been happy if you were pregnant? *¡Sí, claro!* I know how happy that would make you and that, in turn, would make me happy. But there is so much going on right now, and I know there is time for family later. For now"—he lifted the glass and tipped it toward her, a silent toast—"I am enjoying a wonderful evening with my beautiful wife."

Reluctantly, she lifted her glass and touched its rim to his. But she did not drink the champagne. Instead, she set the glass back down on the table and tried to understand what he had just told her. She paid no attention as Alejandro spoke to the server in Spanish, gesturing toward her and then toward himself. The server must have said something that struck Alejandro as funny for he laughed out loud and reached out to touch the man's arm.

Give them what they want. Remember the goal.

Amanda wondered if he used that same philosophy with her, giving her what she wanted in exchange for the end goal. But she couldn't imagine what that end goal could possibly be. Alejandro loved her; that, she never once questioned. Her greatest concern was his constant need to orchestrate situations, all conveniently and impeccably timed to either tease or reward the fans.

So what is this mysterious goal? she wondered.

And just as she had experienced the beginnings of an epiphany earlier, she now had another thought: the price of the photos was a metaphor for the concept of a brand. Alejandro wanted whatever photos were taken of her to work either to build the image created by his marketing team or to provide the paparazzi with nothing. If the photos didn't help sell the image his team wanted to create, then she should simply walk away. To stop and greet the fans was a great photo opportunity if the paparazzi were taking photographs. But to allow random selfie photos to be taken with her and posted on social media was a different matter, especially if the photos did not match the image that was being built of her.

Clearly, the image of her earlier that week—one in which she was leaving a dance studio after three hours of practice with her cheeks flushed as a result of Stedman's constant criticisms regarding her performance—was not the image of Amanda that Alejandro wanted circulated.

"I hate dancing," she blurted out.

"Excuse me?" For once, he appeared truly taken aback.

"I hate dancing," she said, forcing herself to continue with her confession. "And I am not particularly fond of Stedman."

"I see."

"Please don't make me continue, Alejandro."

He seemed to consider her request. "Stedman is working on the choreography for the show. You know that, *sí*?"

"He's unkind," she said sharply. "And I don't want to be treated in an unkind manner. He gets angry that I have an improper sidestep on the line of dance and that my hips don't open during the three-eighths turns in the waltz. He keeps telling me to listen to the music, to feel the rhythm, but I just don't understand what he means." She lifted her chin and took a big breath, trying to muster the courage to say what she really felt. "Dancing is just not something I am comfortable with."

For a long second, Alejandro merely stared at her, a blank expression on his face. He took a moment to sip at his champagne while he studied her. She couldn't tell if he was irritated or amused. When he set down the champagne, he slid out from the alcove and extended his hand, palm up, in her direction.

She looked at it, confused. "What is this?"

"Come, Princesa," he commanded. "Take my hand and let's go."

"We're leaving?" She placed her hand in his as panic welled up inside of her. "Is it what I just said?"

With a slight shake of his head and a soft clicking of his tongue, he indicated that she should not continue speaking as he led her back through the restaurant's lounge and to a doorway that she hadn't noticed previously. A stairwell curved down to another floor of the building, and as they descended, Amanda could hear music coming from wherever they were headed. The closer they got to the bottom of the stairs, the louder the music grew.

A man nodded at Alejandro and opened a door for them, the music suddenly filling the air. Alejandro led Amanda through the door and onto a small dance floor that was already crowded with people.

"Oh help!" she muttered, knowing that he could not hear her.

Once they were out on the floor, he spun around and faced her. One eyebrow raised and the corner of his mouth lifted as he started to sway to the Cuban beat. Immediately, he began to dance, his feet moving in perfect rhythm to the music. Feeling lost, she watched him for a minute and then recognized the dance as the cha-cha. I know this, she thought. He reached for her hand and began to guide her with the simple dance steps: forward, back, cha cha cha. As her comfort level increased, he began to smile and proceeded to guide her through even more advanced steps. He did not speak—for it would have been impossible to hear him over the loud, pulsating music. Instead, he used pressure points: his hand on her back, his fingers on her palms, his thigh pressed gently against hers.

As Amanda became more comfortable with the rhythm, she relaxed and just followed his lead. She even laughed when he spun her around and pulled her into his arms, her back pressed against his chest and her face near his shoulder. Alejandro tilted his head down and peered at her. The music stopped, and she looked up into his sparkling blue eyes.

"Ah, there you are," he teased softly. "My Princesa."

Yes, she thought. Here I am, in your arms . . . the only place I want to be.

"I think Stedman must be doing a good job, no? You danced quite well." He released her by spinning her away from him, although he still held her hand. "Now you just need to integrate some of those moves into a pattern for the stage. You'll do quite nicely, Amanda." He bowed to her and kissed the back of her hand. "Another dance before we return to our table, *sí*?" As if on cue, the music began again, but this time, the DJ was playing one of Viper's songs.

The other people cleared the floor and cheered, clapping their hands and moving their hips in time to the music. Alejandro laughed and waved at the DJ.

"Let's go!" He swung Amanda around again and began moving his hips and feet in one fluid motion that reminded her more of poetry than of dancing. Amanda watched him for a few long seconds, mesmerized by his ability to not just dance by himself but to visibly enjoy it. When he turned and grabbed her by the waist, pulling her to him so that they were pressed against each other, she had no recourse but to mirror his movements. Before she knew it, they were dancing the mambo. While her own moves felt stilted and forced, Alejandro moved as if the dance was second nature to him.

At first he'd pull her into a closed position and then fling her out into an open position, his feet never once stopping their perfectly timed rhythmic movement. The crowd cheered when Alejandro broke into a dance solo, his feet moving so fast that Amanda couldn't keep up. She found herself laughing and taking two steps backward so that she didn't get in his way.

When the song finally ended, several people approached him, the men clapping him on the back and a few women enjoying a warm, sweaty hug. Amanda watched all of this, trying to understand exactly what the point of bringing her downstairs to the dance floor had been. It was when Alejandro posed with several women—his smile lighting up his face and his expression the same one he wore in all of the photos for which she'd seen him pose—that she realized this, too, had been orchestrated.

They returned to the table. Alejandro was barely out of breath from his dance, although sweat glistened on his forehead. Once they were seated, he used his napkin to dab at it. "Fun, *sí*?"

"I get it," Amanda admitted.

He looked up in surprise. "*¿Sí?*"

How could she not? He hadn't told her what was important; he had shown her. Viper, the international sensation, could not put his wife onstage, where thousands of cameras would be taking videos and photographs of her, if she was just going to stand there with no idea of how to enhance his entertainment value. The fans wanted to see Amanda, but they were there for Alejandro. By learning how to dance and entertain his fans, she increased his brand image and that was the name of the game.

"*Ja,*" she replied, sounding more confident than she felt. "I'll keep working with Stedman."

"Good girl." From his reaction, she could tell that Alejandro had never once doubted that she would give in to his wish. However, he had opted not only to count on her submission but also to show her how important it was for her to honor his request and work with Stedman. Amanda now saw that if she wanted to truly be helpful and supportive of Alejandro's career, she needed to develop skills for dealing with the fans and presenting herself onstage. It was all part of the package.

"But," she added, lifting her water glass and taking a small sip, "that doesn't mean I'll like it!"

He laughed at her sassy remark and leaned over to plant a kiss on her cheek. "I'd imagine it no other way," he whispered.

Unaware that he was interrupting an important moment, the server approached the table and carefully set two plates in front of them. "Compliments of the house," he said. "The chef prepared a special appetizer for you: *foie gras au torchon*, prepared using the old French recipe."

"Wonderful!" Alejandro dipped his head as if bowing. "My regards to the chef."

The served nodded and backed away from the table, leaving them alone once again.

"How very special!" he said as he placed a portion of the sliced foie gras onto a piece of toast. She watched him as he tasted it. No sooner did he bite into the toast than he shut his eyes and gave a soft moan. *"¡Ay, mi madre!"*

"It's good, then?"

He nodded his head and opened his eyes, a look of ecstasy on his face. "A little taste of heaven. Try it, *sí?*"

Hesitantly, she touched it with her fork. "What is it again?"

"Foie gras au torchon."

While the arrangement of the food on the plate presented a pretty picture, the fact that she couldn't pronounce the name was a clue that this was something she normally would not eat. Copying Alejandro, she cut the foie gras with the side of her fork and placed some on a small piece of toast. "And what is it, exactly?" she asked as she lifted the food to her mouth and took a bite. "What an odd texture," she commented.

"You like?" He didn't wait for her to answer as he spread some more on his own piece of bread. "I'm surprised. Most people do not care for raw duck liver."

She stared at him, the rest of the toast with foie gras still in her hand. "Did you say 'raw duck liver'?"

"They soak it in milk for a day before deveining it. An absolute delicacy, no?"

Horrified, Amanda dropped the toast from her hand and shoved the plate away from her, causing her water glass to topple over. The sound of glass clinking against the plate caused several heads to turn. "Alejandro!" she exclaimed. "How could you?"

Alejandro remained motionless, his mouth agape as he stared at her.

Raw duck liver? She could think of nothing more disgusting. If he hadn't reacted with such ecstasy to the dish, she would have thought he'd just played a trick on her. The taste in her mouth repulsed her so that she reached across his plate and grabbed his water glass, drinking as much from it as she could.

When she looked up, she saw that he still hadn't moved. People at the tables closest to them, the ones without an obstructed view of the alcove, stared at her, too. The din of the room faded, and she suddenly realized that it was because of her.

She looked around the room without moving her head, her eyes wide and her cheeks warm. "Oh help," she mumbled.

To her surprise, Alejandro tossed his head back and burst into laughter, the sound resonating throughout the quiet of the room. The people seated nearby began to titter along with him and offer her benevolent smiles; one of them gave her a thumbs-up. Clearly, they had watched the entire scene unfold and, like Alejandro, found her reaction amusing.

Despite her embarrassment, Amanda composed herself and reached for her champagne glass. Casually, as if nothing had happened, she lifted it toward Alejandro and gave him a soft smile.

Alejandro shook his head, still chuckling as he reached for his glass, an amused expression on his face as he tilted his glass toward hers. "Here is to your brand image," he quipped. "I knew you had it in you, *mi amor.*"

Chapter Seven

The bright lights shone down on Amanda, and she felt the intense heat of the high-wattage bulbs on her face. It felt as if her skin were baking under the intense blaze of illumination, especially with the light bouncing off the reflector umbrellas set up to keep her completely shadow-free in front of the white cloth backdrop.

As if the heat wasn't bad enough, a small crowd of people also stared at her. Amanda felt more than self-conscious; she felt downright nervous and uncomfortable. She didn't know who most of the people were or what purpose their presence served. In Viper's world, every activity involved dozens of people, most of whom stood around and soaked in the energy of stardom without contributing, while just a few worked excessively, immune to the atmosphere of celebrity fame.

In the background, music blasted—every song one of Viper's. She could barely concentrate on her own thoughts. The music was so loud, she could almost feel the floors shake in time with the bass. Some of the workers moved in rhythm to the music, their hips swaying and feet lifting as they danced in place. Others talked to each other, their voices raised and heads tipped close together so that they could hear each other over the blasting sound. And then there was the photographer who was now walking around Amanda, his knees bent and legs spread in a crab-like fashion as he snapped photos of her in a long, fast sequence.

"Come on, Amanda," he said. There was an edge to his voice. "Let's work this a bit more."

If the photographer expected her to dance to the music, Amanda's stiff posture and expressionless face told him otherwise. After three weeks of dance lessons, her body ached, and she didn't really understand why she was there or what they wanted from her.

Just the previous evening, Alejandro had informed her about the photo shoot.

His announcement had taken her by surprise. "Whatever is it for?" she had asked, setting down her book. She had been lying in bed, reading a devotional book, when he arrived home around nine o'clock. He hadn't looked tired, and she'd wondered if he was going out again. But when he changed into a pair of lightweight sweatpants and a sleeveless white undershirt, she realized that he was home for the night.

He'd crawled over the top of the bedding before throwing himself down beside her. Leaning his head on her shoulder, he peered at the book. "What is that?"

"A devotional," she responded. "You didn't answer my question."

He reached out and took the book from her. That was the one thing she never saw him do: read for recreation. Business documents, e-mails, even articles on his tablet, but never books. And certainly not the Bible. Despite his profession of the Catholic faith in which he'd been raised, he showed little signs of living a life of spiritual devotion.

"You like this?" He handed the book back to her before raising his head and leaning his cheek on his palm, his elbow pressed against the mattress. With his other hand, he traced an imaginary line down her shoulder to her wrist. "I would think you'd prefer a nice romance novel."

Amanda had shrugged. She had never been much of a reader. Alejandro had introduced her to that practice, which made his own lack of reading now even more curious. "Mayhaps the classics," she admitted. "But it's *gut* to focus on inspirational books and Scripture, too."

He nodded as if thinking about something she'd said. After a few long moments, he had taken a deep breath. "I'm going downstairs to my office for a while," he said. "Watch some television and relax." Sliding toward the side of the bed, he'd sat up and stretched as he stood.

"Maybe there is a *fútbol* game on."

"You still didn't answer my question," she'd said.

"*Qué* question?"

"About the photo shoot."

He'd smiled in that mischievous way that was unique to Alejandro. And she'd known that, whatever the photo shoot was for, it was about business. "Because you are so beautiful, Princesa," he had said as a simple explanation. "I want to share Mrs. Viper with the world . . . but only in photos."

She had watched him leave, knowing that he had something planned for the photographs that would come out of this session. Perhaps she would find out the reason one day, but she had quickly realized that that would not happen anytime soon. Only when he wanted her to learn about the photo shoot's purpose would he tell her, and not a minute sooner.

"Focus, Amanda!" The photographer interrupted her thoughts. "Lift your hair off your shoulder." He crouched before her, his black camera aimed in her direction. He was constantly telling her things to do, ways to move, where to focus. She hated it. But she complied, placing her hand under her loose hair and sliding it upward so that the one side of her hair lifted away from her face. "Good girl."

For hours, she had let them do everything they wanted to do: fix her hair, apply her makeup, and dress her in different outfits. Some of the clothing was familiar to her; she had already tried it on. Jeremy had designed the outfits for her to wear on tour. Other clothing, she did not recognize. But everything was well coordinated: each outfit had matching shoes and accessories.

Now, however, her patience was at an end, especially since she'd learned that they wanted her to pose for another two hours. All she wanted was to get away from these people and their false compliments. Whenever the photographer asked her to do something, to move a certain way, Amanda had tried to comply—at least in the beginning. But her willingness to participate had dwindled with each outfit change and hour that had passed.

Off to the side of the white backdrop and just beyond the glare of the bright lights, Dali stood watching. In her hands, she held a planner that Amanda knew contained a schedule, *her* schedule of events and appointments, for every day between now and when the Viper Tour left the United States and headed to South America. Earlier, during a coffee break—for everyone here lived off coffee, and not food, she had observed—Amanda had reviewed the schedule. To her dismay, every day was crammed with lists of places where she needed to make an appearance. And not one day included time with Alejandro. *That* realization had done little to improve her mood.

"This cannot be right," Amanda had said, handing the schedule back to her personal assistant. She was disappointed with what she'd seen: a visit to a local Latino community school to read stories to children, a luncheon for foster children, interviews with four women's magazines, a ribbon cutting at a new shopping center. The schedule was filled with an endless stream of appointments of that nature. The only thing that was missing was the one thing she longed for. "Not *any* time with Alejandro?"

Dali hadn't even blinked.

"Dali, please." Amanda hated that she sounded as if she were pleading with her assistant. "Tell me this is wrong."

But Dali responded only with silence.

"And who are these people? Why would they want to see me?" She pointed at the list. "What's a ribbon cutting?"

"A grand opening. You stand there and cut a ribbon while they take photos," Dali explained drily. "And they want you in order to get to Viper."

That had sounded ridiculous to Amanda. She understood what the marketing machine behind Viper was doing: making her the unspoken ambassador of the Latinos in Miami on behalf of her husband, Viper. Attending functions that helped those who were downtrodden or in need of assistance was not in itself a distasteful idea to Amanda. In fact, she remembered fondly her visit with Alejandro to the children's cancer hospital after a concert in Kansas City. The experience had moved Amanda. She'd hated seeing those sick children, lying in cold hospital beds during their treatment for cancer. When Alejandro had visited the cancer ward, Amanda had been touched by the children's reactions. So she didn't mind standing in for him at some of these types of events, thus freeing up his time to continue recording, practicing, and meeting with his team.

She was, however, mindful of the need to schedule time with her husband.

Dali crossed the room and motioned to someone. Because of the glaring lights, Amanda couldn't see who it was.

"Turn to the left, Amanda," the photographer shouted, still snapping photos.

Obediently, she did as instructed, despite her discomfort level, which was increasing by the minute.

Jeremy had picked out her outfits for the photo shoot, and, as usual, the dresses and evening gowns, all of which covered her legs, still revealed too much for Amanda's taste. She hated the feeling of exposed skin on her shoulders and, even worse, the way that Jeremy designed her more formal clothing so that the backs draped down. Still, Alejandro had explained the purpose of this photo shoot: marketing. Since he had asked, she would not say no.

But to *smile and pose*? That was something Amanda simply could not do. Throughout her Amish childhood, she had been raised to believe that exposing herself to picture taking was an expression of vanity, something that was totally in opposition to the values of subservience to God and community—values anchored deep in her faith. Allowing someone to take her picture as a means of providing support to her husband, the man she had been taught to consider the head of her household, was already hard enough on her. But to smile and strike different poses while doing so? That was definitely crossing the line.

The song changed, and as a new one began to play, a couple of younger women shimmied their hips as they danced to the beat. One glance in their direction told Amanda that she didn't care for either woman: their shirts exposed their stomachs and far too much cleavage while their skirts barely covered their backsides. She knew exactly what she was looking at: women who would do anything to spend one night with someone like her husband. Their morals were in the same category as those of a barn cat, Amanda thought, and she knew that they didn't care whether he was married.

"Take five, everyone!" someone called out.

Amanda relaxed a little, lifting her hand to wipe the moisture from her forehead. She hated the lights. She hated the attention. She hated the intrusion into her privacy. Without being told, she knew what the word "marketing" meant. The white backdrop could easily be replaced with other backgrounds using computer graphic programs so that Alejandro's marketing team could use the photographs any way they wanted, to promote any aspect of Viper or his tour. And she had no control over what the graphic designers put in those new backdrops.

"*¡Ay, Princesa!*"

Startled out of her thoughts, Amanda turned in the direction of Alejandro's voice. Immediately, she smiled and started to walk toward him, but before she could take more than a few steps, he stood with her in the center of the backdrop. "Alejandro!" She didn't care if people lurked in the shadows behind the bright lights. Just seeing him made her feel better, and she flung her arms around his neck. "Oh, I am ever so glad you are here," she whispered into his ear.

"*¿Sí?*" He gave a little laugh, wrapping his arms around her waist. "And why is that?"

"I hate this."

At this statement, so direct and clearly truthful, he tossed his head back and laughed, this time loudly. Several people glanced in their direction to see what had entertained Viper so much. Even Amanda had to smile at his reaction.

"Oh, Princesa," he said. He pulled back and stared down into her face. "Why am I not surprised, eh?" He glanced around at the cameras, nodding when he recognized one particular photographer standing off to the side of the room. "It's a lot for you to take in."

"*Ja*, it is," she admitted. Having grown up in a culture that frowned upon vanity—and along with that, photography—she found that being the center of attention was not something she could easily embrace.

He returned his attention to her and, bending his knees just a little, looked straight into her eyes. "Then you will love my surprise for you!"

Alejandro and his surprises! These were his way of letting her know that even if he was not with her or was busy with his work, he was always thinking of her. "I think you being here is surprise enough!" Still, she smiled. "What are you doing here, anyway?"

He brushed off her question, focusing instead on his news. "I know these past few weeks have been busy, *sí*? I requested that Dali clear your schedule for a few days." He hesitated and lifted an eyebrow. "And mine."

Oh! If she were a typically demonstrative Englischer, she would have hugged him, showing him how delightful this news was. Clearing the schedule meant time together! Try as she might, she couldn't contain her pleasure with the unexpected news. Still, she had seen the schedule earlier that day. "When did you speak to her?" Amanda asked, concerned that Dali might have misunderstood Alejandro. After all, it was only an hour or so since Dali had shown her the schedule.

"Just now." He motioned with his head toward where Dali stood, her cell phone to her ear. She was likely shuffling around Amanda's appointments now. "There's more, Princesa," he said softly. "Before the tour, I am taking you back to Lancaster. Just for a few days. I think you need a break from all of this." He gestured toward the photographers and the lights. "Besides, I know you miss your family."

She gasped. Lancaster? To see her family? She jumped into his arms and clung to him, loving the sound of his laughter as he swung her around, her skirt wrapping around his legs. With her head on his shoulder and a smile on her lips, Amanda could do no more than just hold him, fighting back tears of joy at his thoughtfulness.

To return to Lancaster and spend time visiting with her parents and her sister? She couldn't even begin to express her gratitude. How had he known that she longed for routine days spent doing simple barn chores and evenings spent quietly, whatever the outside temperature at her Pennsylvania home? The idea alone rejuvenated her spirit. Good home-cooked meals, fresh-baked bread, and time spent with people she loved was exactly what she needed. And then a thought occurred to her.

"You are coming too, *ja*?" she asked.

He squeezed her and whispered a soft "But of course!" in her ear, his breath warm on her skin.

She shut her eyes and enjoyed his affection. Since their night out the previous week, she hadn't seen much of Alejandro. She felt as if they were on two completely different time clocks. On more than one occasion, she had forced herself to stay in bed, despite having woken up early, just so she could enjoy the pressure of his chest against her back. And when he awoke and pulled her tightly against him, his hand slowly caressing her bare arm, she felt the all-too-familiar wave of flutters in her stomach and the light-headedness that always preceded his private tenderness.

Now was no different. She forced herself to ignore the fact that other people were near and, undoubtedly, watching. Receiving an unexpected five minutes of his time and attention was worth the cost of the public display of affection that she would have previously shunned. She reveled in his arms holding her, his words caressing her ears, and his heart beating against hers for those few minutes.

When he finally pulled away, he held her at arm's length and stared at her, his glance darting over her shoulder for just a second, as some-one must have distracted him. "I must get back to work, Princesa," he said in a low voice. He then pulled her back to him, pressed his fore-head against hers, and whispered, "I will see you later this evening, *sí?*"

"*Sí,*" she whispered, her eyes shut. She savored the moment as if she were a starving person who was eating a last meal that was about to be taken from her. That was how she felt around Alejandro: starv-ing. While she had known that he would be busy in Miami, the few moments they had together made her long for more. Now, knowing that she would have him all to herself for a few days in Lancaster, she began to count down the days until her fast was over.

"I must get back to my meeting." He gently disentangled himself from her.

She walked beside him as he slowly headed toward the door, pausing to shake hands and give a few people bear hugs along the way. When they finally stood before the doorway, she turned to him. "You never did answer me, Alejandro. Why are you here?"

He laughed. "I own the building, *mi querida*. My offices and a small recording studio are on the top floor."

Amanda's mouth dropped open. The building was located on Biscayne Boulevard along a strip of commercial buildings. And while it wasn't the largest one in the small industrial zone, it was far enough from downtown Miami that tourists didn't know it existed . . . just as Amanda hadn't known. "What else haven't you told me?" she asked.

Laughing, he leaned forward and kissed her forehead. "Finish up here, Princesa, and maybe I will tell you more surprises later tonight."

More? Amanda stared after him as he left the room, the door slowly shutting behind him. For a moment, she didn't move. While she didn't know much about real estate or property values, she certainly knew enough to suspect that the building was expensive. Her Amish upbringing had taught her that money was not important; in fact, people could often begin to idolize not just money itself but also the act of acquiring it. While she didn't care about money, she was beginning to wonder how much of it Alejandro truly had. She knew that he was a businessman and that he considered every opportunity to be a business opportunity. But she was beginning to wonder if he knew when enough would be enough.

Life was meant to be lived. That was God's ultimate plan for everyone: live life and give thanks to the Lord. Too many Englische people sacrificed their health—physical, psychological, and spiritual—to chase after material things. But at the end of the day, whatever had been acquired seemed insignificant in light of their desires for more. The last thing that she wanted was for Alejandro to face God one day realizing that, despite being alive, he had never truly *lived*.

That thought lingered with her long after his departure.

Chapter Eight

"Amanda!"

No sooner had the driver stopped the car in the driveway of the Beilers' house than the front door opened and Anna ran outside, a big smile on her face and her head covered by a navy-blue knit scarf. She wore no coat, despite the weather being cold. When Amanda saw Anna's dark-blue dress and black apron were covered with flour, she knew that when they walked into the house, the familiar scent of fresh-baked bread would greet them. It was a smell that she had missed.

Amanda stood by the car, Alejandro at her side, as her sister embraced her. "It's so *gut* to see you," Amanda said, returning the warm hug. "I've missed you so!"

Pulling back but leaving her hands on Amanda's shoulders, Anna stared at her and shook her head, the smile still on her lips. "Look at you now! So Englische and worldly!"

Instinctively, Amanda glanced over her shoulder at Alejandro. He stood by the open car door in his black slacks and white shirt, his dark leather jacket unzipped, his hands behind his back, as he observed Anna's greeting, a pleased look upon his face. He didn't appear offended by her comment about the Englische.

"Oh, I'm not so certain about the worldly part," Amanda said, returning her attention to her sister. While she knew that her appearance was different—for certainly she no longer appeared plain—she also knew that she was anything but Englische.

And that was the main problem.

In Alejandro's world, she straddled the fence between plain and worldly. There were some things she refused to change, such as how she wore her hair or avoiding slacks. She had tried once but hated the feeling of the fabric against her legs. And even though Alejandro loved to see her with her long brown hair at nighttime, during the day she always wore it pulled back and in a tight bun at the nape of her neck. After all, Amish decorum dictated that only a woman's husband should ever see her hair loose.

She knew that since her dancing lessons had begun, she had lost weight, something that concerned her, especially after Jeremy began to take in the clothes that he had purchased for her. Her face was gaunt, with more defined cheekbones, and her chin jutted out after hours of Stedman yelling at her about her posture.

But Amanda knew that she would never truly relinquish the part of her that was plain. Just standing in her parents' driveway, the pungent odor of the dairy mixing with the fresh breeze that blew from the north, reminded Amanda that there was more to life than Miami and Los Angeles. As she glanced toward the porch and saw her mother at the door, Amanda fought back the urge to release her emotions.

Four days had seemed like such a gift. Now, four days seemed nowhere near enough, like one bottle of water in a desert; the joy of drinking it was almost ruined by the anticipation of the inevitable dry spell that would follow.

"*Kum, kum,*" Anna said, tugging at Amanda's arm. She walked backward toward the house as she pulled her younger sister with her. "We've much catching up to do, *ja*? And just enough time to do it before supper."

Inside, Amanda greeted her mother with a shy embrace. "Missed you, Mamm," she said. "*Danke* for your letters."

Her mother gave her a quick once-over and clicked her tongue. "You've lost weight, Amanda! You aren't eating enough, I reckon!"

Amanda gave a little laugh. "Oh, Mamm, I'm eating just fine." Still, when her eyes fell on Anna and her stout waistline, Amanda felt disappointment all over again. Without being told, Amanda knew that her sister was pregnant. And while she was happy for Anna, she felt a deep longing to bear her own child.

Her father sat in his wheelchair by the sofa, his eyes following her and the right side of his mouth lifting into a smile. Amanda hurried over to him and gave him a quick hug, letting her hand linger atop his. She glanced around the room, comforted by its familiarity, despite the realization that her memory of the house and kitchen must have changed; for now, as she stood there and looked around, everything seemed smaller than she remembered. How long have I been gone, anyway? she wondered. And why didn't I feel this way when I returned home to help care for my father after his stroke?

"Everyone is doing well, *ja*?" The question sounded as awkward as she felt. Amanda simply did not know how to break through the layer of nervousness that lingered in the room.

Anna motioned toward the sofa. "Sit, Amanda," she said. "You must be awful tired after such a long travel day."

"Oh, it wasn't so long." Amanda didn't want to sound prideful, so she neglected to mention that they'd flown into Philadelphia on a private jet.

Of course, the truth was that she hadn't slept the previous night and she *was* tired. Alejandro had returned late after wrapping up some last-minute business, and she had been far too excited to fall asleep. When he walked into their bedroom, tugging at his black tie with one hand and carrying his jacket with the other, he had looked surprised to see Amanda waiting up for him. With her legs tucked underneath her body, she had curled up in one of the chairs by the bedroom window overlooking the pool. She'd held a book in her hands but wasn't reading. Instead, she'd been staring out the window, watching the ripples in the water and thinking.

Dropping his jacket on the edge of the bed, he walked toward her. "You can't sleep, Princesa?" he had asked.

"Nee." As he had approached her, she lifted her hand and reached for one end of his tie that now hung against his white shirt. She tugged at it, and when he responded with a slight smile, she pulled it free. "I don't know what I'm more excited for," she said, unfolding her legs and sitting up straight. "Spending time with you or seeing my family."

He knelt before her and rested his head in her lap, one arm wrapped around her waist. "Be excited for your family, Princesa, for I will always be with you, no?"

For several long minutes, they had remained like that, Amanda stroking his hair and Alejandro holding her waist. For Amanda, it had been one of those moments that she hoped she'd never forget. Her heart simply could not love Alejandro any more than at that moment.

Now, as Amanda sat on the sofa and tried to figure out how to fit back into the life of her family, she realized that Alejandro was not in the house. Immediately, she sat up straight and looked around the room, a moment of panic overtaking her. "Hasn't Alejandro come in, then?"

"Nee, Amanda," her mother said, leaning forward to glance out the kitchen window. "Appears he's on his phone by the barn."

Amanda noticed the way her mother emphasized the word *phone,* as if it left a bad taste on her tongue. Understanding her mother's contempt for the intrusive device was easy. Amanda remembered that when she had first met Alejandro, she, too, had questioned his constant use of his cell phone. Eight months later, while she still disliked the endless interruptions, she recognized the importance of his accessibility. Although he had planned this trip to Lancaster so that she could visit with her family, that didn't mean there weren't things that required his attention. With the South American leg of the tour just two weeks away, the demands on Alejandro's time would only increase with each passing day. And while she would have preferred that he sit by her side, helping her transition from Viper's wife to Amish daughter, she knew whatever phone call had temporarily separated them must have been important.

"So tell me," Amanda said, shifting her attention back to her sister. Just seeing Anna hurry to the rocking chair and sit down, her eyes glowing as she leaned forward and stared intently at her sister, made Amanda feel better. It seemed like years had passed since they had last visited, especially since her previous trip home had not been under ideal circumstances. "I want to hear everything I have missed since Christmas!"

Anna wasted no time filling her in on the details from the past two months. Even the poor winter weather couldn't stop the Amish grapevine from spreading. It didn't take long for Amanda to learn that her friend, Katie Miller, had slipped on some ice during the winter and broken her arm; that Jeremiah Smucker, the butcher, had accidentally cut off the tip of his finger, and that their neighbors, the Zooks, had lost one of their draft horses to colic.

"Oh help!" Amanda shook her head at the news. "Hasn't anything good happened since I left?"

Lizzie clicked her tongue. "Sure does seem that bad news accompanies winter," she said.

Anna glanced over her shoulder. "Well now, that ain't entirely so," she said, contradicting her mother. "Daed's been doing better."

Amanda brightened at this news. "That is right *gut* news, indeed! Tell me more, Anna!"

Anna began updating her about their father's condition. As Anna spoke, Amanda glanced at her father and reached out to touch his knee. She learned that while his speech was still poor, he was now able to move his arms and, with the help of the physical therapist he saw three times a week, had managed to walk a few steps.

"Why, that's just *wunderbar!*" Amanda gushed, turning to her father. "I'm so glad that you are feeling better, Daed!"

He gave a slight shrug of his shoulders and tried to motion with his hand. "Better . . ." he said slowly. "What is better?"

Anna laughed, and there was a lightness about her as she playfully said, "Oh, Daed! You know the deal. Keep working hard with your therapist, and Jonas will get you outside to help with the fieldwork." She looked at Amanda and lowered her voice a little, although they both knew Elias could still hear her. "He says he'll only be better when he can farm again."

The two women enjoyed the moment, teasing their father as they had so long ago, when their younger brother, Aaron, was still alive. For the first time since his death, Amanda felt an aura of happiness about the house. Had it been almost four years since Aaron's untimely death? Had it truly taken that long for life to regain some semblance of normalcy?

The squeaking of the mudroom door, followed by the sound of heavy footsteps, caused Amanda to look up. Jonas walked through the doorway on the other side of the room near the kitchen area, his brown work pants dirty after a day spent in the dairy barn. Behind him came Alejandro, a sharp contrast to the Amish man. When she saw the two together, Amanda fought the urge to catch her breath. Her husband was much taller than her brother-in-law, and his presence emanated a sophistication that she couldn't help but notice. Would the others see it, too? she wondered.

In typical Amish fashion, Jonas greeted her with a simple wave of his hand and an impish smile. Shyness around newcomers was not a behavior that was limited to the children.

Alejandro, however, wasted no time in approaching Amanda's mother; he greeted her with a warm embrace that was not necessarily returned. He either didn't mind or didn't notice for as soon as he had greeted her, he crossed the floor to do the same to Anna. Finally, he stood respectfully before Elias and extended his hand. To Amanda's surprise, her father slowly lifted his arm. Alejandro waited patiently while Elias struggled to find the strength to shake his hand.

When he sat beside her at last, he took a moment to pinch the crease of his slacks so that they wouldn't wrinkle. Amanda turned to him. "Is everything all right?"

"*Sí, sí*. Just fine, Princesa."

She suspected the call had been from his new manager, Geoffrey. Unlike Alejandro's previous manager, Mike, Geoffrey was of Hispanic descent and, given his extensive background in music and marketing, was able to connect better with Alejandro. The few times that Amanda had met Geoffrey, she'd found him to be much more respectful and well mannered toward her than Mike had been. Not to mention his reverence for God and his Catholic faith. She had liked him immediately.

"You have some big travels ahead of you, *ja?*" Anna asked. "Sounds exciting."

Alejandro winked at Amanda. "You must ask Amanda afterward if she found it exciting," he said. "So many countries in such a short period of time is tiring. I look forward to having a few days to relax in Argentina, to reenergize our batteries."

Anna caught her breath when he mentioned Argentina. "Oh my! That's clear on the bottom of the world!"

"That it is," Alejandro agreed. "When it is winter here, it is summer there. So to spend a few days at the beach will be a perfect respite, no?"

"Oh, I wouldn't know about those things," Anna responded lightly. She looked over her shoulder at Jonas. "Have you been to the beach, Jonas?"

He shook his head. "*Nee,* can't say that I have." Then, after a short pause, he added, "Now hold on there. That's not quite true."

Amanda loved his accent: a different type of singsong manner of speaking than that practiced by the Amish in Lititz. She had forgotten that the Ohio Amish emphasized their words differently and elongated their vowels.

"I did go to a *lake beach* one time," he continued, crossing his feet at the ankles, his once-white socks now gray from too many wearings and washings, as he leaned against the counter. "Was for a youth gathering one year." His eyes found Anna's. "Summer before last, I recall. Water sure was cold. I remember that much."

Alejandro laughed.

"Jonas," Anna said as she turned around. "You still going to that horse auction with Edwards tomorrow?"

"*Ja,* I sure am."

Amanda frowned. "Edwards?"

"Jake Edwards," Anna said. She looked at Alejandro. "You met him last summer, ain't so? His *fraa,* Sylvia, talked about meeting you."

To Amanda's surprise, Alejandro responded with an eager "*¡Sí, sí!* I remember Jake. He has a good sense of humor, as I recall. Elias took me there to see his horses. Magnificent creatures."

Considering all of the people who Alejandro met on a daily basis— the fans and the media representatives, as well as the other celebrities and management people—Amanda could hardly believe that he remembered not only meeting Jake Edwards but also the circumstances surrounding their encounter. Since the Edwards family lived in another church district, they were not people with whom Amanda had frequently interacted, especially since Jake had joined the Amish church only after marrying his wife.

"You should go with Jonas," Anna said to Alejandro and then, as if an afterthought, she quickly looked at her husband for approval. "What say you, Jonas?"

Before Alejandro could respond, Jonas nodded. "Oh *ja*, sure! Why that would be right *gut*! Jake's to sell three of his horses, and I told him I'd help. An extra pair of hands would be appreciated, I'm sure." Amanda waited, wondering what Alejandro would say. She knew how busy he was. The fact that he'd arranged for this short visit had truly taken her by surprise. She suspected he would need to spend the majority of his time making phone calls, answering e-mails, and resting before they left for South America.

Once again, he surprised her.

"Unless Amanda has other plans for me," he said, "I'd find that most interesting, Jonas."

"*Vell* all right, then!" Jonas seemed genuinely pleased that he would have Alejandro's company. "The driver's picking me up after morning chores. Won't be too early for you?"

Alejandro laughed. "I'll manage," he said, taking the bait. "I've been known to awaken before dawn. Right, Princesa?"

Amanda was stunned by the instant camaraderie between the two men, who seemed the most unlikely of brothers-in-law. She knew that Alejandro was a master at making other people feel ten feet tall. But he seemed genuinely comfortable as he sat on the sofa and talked with Jonas, Anna, and Elias—for he was always considerate enough to include Elias in the conversation. Lizzie's lack of contributions to the conversation did not surprise Amanda, but Alejandro seemed unfazed by his mother-in-law's obvious disapproval regarding Amanda's choice of a husband. He continued conversing with the others and occasionally asked Lizzie a question. Whenever she gave a one- or two-word answer, he accepted that and moved on to another topic.

At four o'clock, Jonas excused himself to start on evening chores. Alejandro stood up and, without even changing his clothes, followed Jonas outside. Amanda could hardly believe her eyes. She felt impressed by his ability to adapt to whatever situation presented itself. Whether in this case that came out of his love for her or his true love for people, she did not know. She only knew that he was a special man and that God had blessed her when he put her in the path of Alejandro's limo that day in New York City, a day that seemed to have happened a lifetime ago.

After the sound of the two men's footsteps on the porch faded, Anna looked at Amanda. "Seems like things are going right *gut* with you and Alejandro."

Amanda nodded her head and gave a soft smile. "Life with Alejandro is different, I must admit."

Anna clicked her tongue. "Such travel!"

"*Ja*, the travel is different," Amanda admitted. "He works so hard with so many demands from every which way!" There was no way that Amanda could explain all of the different people who pulled at Alejandro: singers, producers, sponsors, endorsers, promoters . . . the list was endless. And she knew better than to mention how the paparazzi and fans followed her. Her mother, especially, would not approve. "But we are together and I wouldn't change anything for the world."

Lizzie sighed, her mouth downturned at the corners. Even without Amanda telling the whole story, her mother still disapproved. "There's just no questioning God's plan, even when it's something that on the surface doesn't seem to make sense."

Amanda glanced at her sister, and Anna gave her a reassuring look.

While Amanda knew that her decisions to leave the Amish way of life and forgo joining the church were unpopular with her parents and the community, her decision to leave with and then marry Alejandro was equally as upsetting. The holiday scandal had not helped, either. Even the bishop had learned of Alejandro's public "indiscretion" through the ever-present media and their love of spreading bad news. Even though his former manager, Mike, had admitted that the leaked photographs of Alejandro in another woman's arms were invented, Amanda suspected that ultimately Lizzie's willingness to forgive was stronger than her ability to forget.

"And Harvey?" Amanda asked, changing the subject so that they headed down a less arduous and more conversational path.

Anna inhaled sharply. "Oh, Amanda," she said. "What would we do without Harvey? Why, Jonas and Harvey are such a *gut* team. God sure was blessing us when Alejandro hired him. No matter the weather, he is here each day. If it gets too awful outside for him to go home, he just stays in one of the spare rooms."

"Sleeps on the sofa, most oft as naught," Lizzie said. "Not much of a bother, that one."

"And Daed!" Anna's face lit up. "*Vell*, let me tell you that Harvey sure does take *wunderbar* care of Daed. Ain't so, Daed?" She waited for her father to respond. When he didn't, she leaned over and peered at him. "Is he napping, then?" Without waiting for an answer, Anna hurried over to Elias. Seeing that his head was tucked down, his chin resting on his chest and his long beard covering the front of his shirt, she put her finger to her lips. "I'll put him in the bedroom," she whispered.

Lizzie dried her hands on a dish towel and tossed it on the counter. "Let me help."

Left alone in the kitchen, Amanda stood up and walked around, listening to the sounds of Lizzie and Anna pushing the wheelchair over the threshold of the bedroom and getting Elias out of it and into bed so that he could nap properly. It amazed Amanda to see how in control Anna was of the situation. She had truly blossomed since returning home with Jonas to tend to her parents' farm. Or rather, Amanda thought, her and Jonas's farm. Certainly it would be passed down to them, and rightfully so. How fortunate, Amanda thought. She gazed out the window at the dark fields, where a light cover of melting snow contrasted white against the plowed rows. If nothing else, certainly Elias took comfort in knowing that, after all of his years of hard labor and love, the family farm would be passed down to the next generation, even if it went from father to daughter instead of from father to son.

"Oh, how he likes his afternoon nap," Anna said cheerfully, shutting the door to the bedroom behind her. "Ain't so, Mamm?"

Lizzie didn't return to the sink but instead sat down in the sitting area that was off to the side of the kitchen. She sighed and rubbed the back of her neck. "That he does, Dochder."

Amanda left her spot at the window and sat down next to her mother. "How is Daed, then? Really, though. Is he improving any?"

Her mother's response startled her. "*Nee,* not much, Amanda." When she saw Amanda's expression, she quickly added, "Not in the area of will, I reckon. His spirit is broken, and he doesn't try like he might. That's what the physical therapist says, anyway."

That was not good news. Without the will to try or the spirit to believe, recovery would not improve, that was for sure and certain. "I'm sorry to hear that," Amanda said softly. "I had thought things were looking up, Mamm."

Lizzie patted her knee. "Nothing for you to worry about, Amanda."

"But I do worry."

Lizzie shook her head. "I rather think that you are enjoying your life as a newly married woman," she said. "Even if you are married to an Englischer."

"He's Cuban. Not quite the same thing."

"Not quite the same thing in a better or worse way?" Lizzie asked this in a light tone, as if teasing, but Amanda suspected that her mother's question wasn't an idle one.

"Aw, Mamm!" She shook her head. "In a much better way!"

Anna laughed and even Lizzie chuckled.

"Oh, Amanda." Anna joined them, sitting down in the rocking chair for a few more minutes of respite before it was time for her to help their mother prepare the meal. "Spoken like a true woman in love, *ja*?"

The color flooded to Amanda's cheeks, and she couldn't help wishing that, for once, she could manage to mask her emotions. Yes: she was a woman in love. She just wasn't certain she wanted her sister to know just how much she loved Alejandro. And how she fed off his emotions for her. Anyone who saw Alejandro or listened to him talk would be able to understand that he filled up the empty places in her with a love so strong that it almost hurt. A painfully good love, she thought, for she often realized that her heart ached for him in a way that she knew—simply, irrevocably knew!—no one else had ever experienced. No other woman had a love like the love she shared with Alejandro.

Lifting her eyes, she looked at her sister and smiled a soft and knowing smile. "Aren't we both lucky, Anna?" she said. "And isn't love just a *wunderbar gut* thing?"

Chapter Nine

Anna and Amanda sat at the kitchen table in the *grossdaadihaus*, drinking coffee and nibbling on sugar cookies, a favorite of theirs. Lizzie had baked a few batches earlier that morning. Since Alejandro was more than willing to help Jonas with the farm chores, something that secretly pleased Amanda, the two sisters found themselves with an opportunity to visit privately.

"So tell me, when is the *boppli* due?" Amanda dunked her sugar cookie into her coffee.

Anna made a face. "That's so disgusting. How can you eat the cookie like that?"

Amanda laughed. "You always said that to me. It just tastes *gut* to me. And makes the coffee sweeter." As if to prove her point, she bit the damp edge of the cookie.

Anna shuddered and made another face, which caused Amanda to laugh again. It felt like old times: the two sisters sitting at the table and sharing a snack while they talked. Over the years, many a secret had been shared between them over cookies and a hot drink. When they were younger, however, the drink had usually been tea or hot chocolate. They'd shared stories about what they really thought of the Sunday sermons or about how they heard that one of the older girls in their *g'may* had ridden home from a singing in a buggy with a neighbor boy.

They'd also shared secrets about what they hoped for in life. And while they both had said the same thing—to live a godly life—they both had also aspired for more: home, husband, and children. While neither Amanda nor Anna would have suspected that their lives would change so dramatically after the tragic death of their baby brother, in the end, they seemed to have gotten everything that they'd wanted. Or, Amanda thought, at least one of them had.

"You didn't answer my question, Anna," she prodded.

"Oh *ja*, the *boppli*." Anna's voice was soft as her hand rested on her waist's slight bulge.

There was a look of pride in her eyes, a glow that conveyed how much she wanted this baby. Amanda remembered the moment not so long ago when Alejandro had suggested that she might be pregnant. While excitement about the unknown had been quickly followed by disappointment over the truth, Amanda harbored no resentment or envy toward her sister.

"I reckon July or so," Anna said. "Mayhaps late June; I'm not sure."

"You're not sure?" Amanda stared at her sister. "You haven't seen a doctor yet, then?"

A nervous laugh escaped Anna's lips and the color rose to her cheeks. "Oh, now you sound just like an Englische person, Amanda! Running off to the doctor right quick!"

The way that Anna said *Englische*, as if she'd spoken of a disease, struck Amanda. *Assimilation into the world is not contagious,* Amanda wanted to tell her. It was a choice: one that she had made because of her love for Alejandro. "You say that as if it's such a bad thing, Anna," Amanda said with caution in her voice. "I'm sure there are plenty of Amish women who rush to midwives or even doctors."

"*Ja vell*, Jonas and I talked, and we just feel like God will take care of us." Anna averted her eyes. "No need for fretting over what may or may not happen. What is the purpose of going to a doctor, anyway? To tell me what I already know?"

Stunned, Amanda worked hard to maintain her composure. "There's nothing ungodly about having a doctor look after you," Amanda said. "Or even a midwife so that you can plan better." Then, to soften her words, she added, "Why, I'd be at the doctor right quick if I suspected I was pregnant."

Anna smiled. "See? You've turned into an Englischer."

Amanda didn't respond. Instead, she took a long sip from her coffee cup. Had she really changed so much since she'd left the farm? Was the change so distasteful that it must create a divide between the two of them? The last thing she wanted was to exchange unkind words with her sister. It had been years since they had last quarreled, and after the past few years of hardship and sorrow, Amanda certainly didn't want to engage in an argument with her now. Like most Amish did, she merely shut down in the face of conflict and did not speak further on the subject.

Anna must have sensed that Amanda was finished with the previous topic, so she finally spoke, launching into a new conversation. "What about you, Amanda? It's been five months, *ja?*"

The reminder hurt. Five months of marriage to Alejandro, and she still wasn't pregnant. She had made up her mind that if she hadn't conceived by the time the concert tours were finished, she would see a doctor to make certain nothing was wrong. In her mind, obeying God's plan did not mean that she couldn't see a doctor. But she didn't say this to Anna. "Five months, *ja,*" she affirmed. Five long months, she added to herself. While she loved Alejandro and felt happy with their marriage, even if she knew it was not conventional, she felt a wave of remorse over her lack of conception.

"And . . . ?"

Amanda shook her head and swallowed the last bite of her sugar cookie. "Nothing." She sighed. Considering all of the weight that she had lost and the long days filled with appointments and interviews, Amanda hadn't been surprised when her cycle eventually arrived, just two weeks ago. Disappointed, yes. But, in hindsight, not surprised. "Maybe this month, *ja?*" She smiled at her sister.

"God willing," Anna said softly. "I'll keep you in my prayers, Schwester."

Amanda knew that the matter of becoming pregnant was in God's hands. She fought the urge to ask him why she wasn't pregnant yet. Oh, how she wanted a baby—Alejandro's baby! She wanted to share the love of a child with her husband, to see his eyes glow as he looked down into the face of their *boppli*. While she knew that, once they had a child, his schedule would not change, at least not much, she also knew that she didn't care about that. As long as she could hold their child in her arms and sing soft hymns while the baby nursed from her breast, Amanda would be happy. Besides, she had been raised in a culture where it was mostly the role of the women to care for the infants and always without complaint.

"*Danke,* Anna," Amanda whispered. "And I, you."

"My turn for a question," Anna said, changing both the tone and the subject of their conversation. "I read in your letter to Mamm that you are going to South America." Something sparkled in her sister's eyes. "Aren't you afraid, Amanda?"

"Of what?"

"Oh now! You sound surprised!" Anna leaned back in her seat and played with the edge of her napkin. "You must be a little frightened, *ja?*"

In that moment, she looked like the Anna from their childhood: young, fearful, reserved. Amanda felt a sudden epiphany as she realized that, while she had changed over the past year, her sister had not. The differences between their lives had created a gap between them. Amanda's world was so different now and her future so unclear that she found it difficult to explain to Anna what she truly felt.

"*Nee*, Anna," Amanda finally said. "I'm not frightened. It's not like you imagine. These places are just cities. Like Philadelphia or New York."

Anna shuddered.

"Well, maybe not exactly like those places," Amanda added, knowing that Anna's experiences with those cities did not extend beyond the train stations they'd passed through when their parents had sent them to Ohio the previous year. "And with Alejandro . . . oh, how can I explain it, Anna? It's not truly Englische life."

"It's certainly not Amish life." Anna lifted an eyebrow.

Amanda ignored this remark and sought the right words to help her sister understand. "His life is . . . different, Anna. As different from the Englische as we are from them. Wherever we travel, there are people who take care of us. His fans adore him, and there are very few places that we can go where people do not recognize him and crowd him. So it isn't as if we will travel to these places and see the sights very much. I've come to learn that travel with Alejandro is a lot of time spent on airplanes or in cars, being transported to new locations, and lots of appointments. It's pretty much the same, wherever we go."

"That doesn't sound like much of a life, Amanda."

On the surface, Amanda would have agreed. But Anna was forgetting one important element: Alejandro.

"I can't explain it," she sighed. "I wish that I could, but I can't."

Amanda knew that Anna loved Jonas. When she and Anna had been in Ohio and Amanda had wanted to return home, she had seen the glow on her sister's face. Like most Amish youth, Anna had remained quiet about the source of that glow. But Amanda hadn't needed to speculate too much. She had seen the way Jonas Wheeler had stared at Anna during the youth singings and gatherings to which their cousin had escorted them. And when Anna began to "disappear" instead of ride home with them afterward, Amanda had known that her sister was secretly being courted by Jonas.

But as it did for most Amish people, their courtship revolved primarily around God and community, not a romantic love. Amanda assumed that Anna and Jonas hadn't shared a passionate kiss in the buggy on the way home from getting ice cream or danced to provocative music as Amanda had with Alejandro. Certainly Anna had never awoken in Jonas's arms and traced the outline of tattoos on his chest while he slept. And there were no private jets, two-story penthouses, yachts, or paparazzi in the story of their marriage. There was no explanation of her life that Amanda could give that could possibly help her sister understand.

In the moment of silence during which Amanda realized this, it also dawned on her that Anna might very well be thinking the same thing. The choices that they'd made had changed their lives, and with those changes, the bond between them had also been altered. Still, that didn't mean that they were no longer sisters or, just as important, friends.

"*Ja vell,*" Anna finally said, breaking the silence. "I still think traveling to South America sounds very exotic, Amanda. I imagine jungles and colorful birds! Like in that book we both read as children."

"The *I Spy* book?" Amanda remembered it well. When the book was opened, each two-page spread showed a different scene with dozens of items hidden in the photo. Each time she and Anna had looked at the pages, they had spotted something new. The beach scene intrigued Amanda the most, for she had wanted very much to stand on the beach in real life—the end of the world as far as she was concerned—and stare out across the sea. Back then, she hadn't been able to imagine water that stretched far beyond the horizon. Sometimes she had pretended to be standing in that picture book, digging her toes into the sand, her shoulders bare to the sun. Yet when she had stared at that book during her childhood, she had never once even considered the possibility that she might actually get a chance to view both the beach and the horizon from the deck of a yacht.

Alejandro had ensured she could no longer claim such a thing. He had taken her to California and driven her to the ocean, then had actually taken her out on the ocean. He seemed to know every longing that she had, even the secret ones that she would never express.

"I am quite certain it's nothing like that book," Amanda said. "Colorful birds and spotted jaguars don't buy concert tickets."

They both laughed, the tension from their previous discussion slowly dissipating.

Amanda felt, rather than saw, Alejandro enter the room. As Anna's eyes flickered in the direction of the door, something changed in her expression. It wasn't disapproval that Amanda saw there; it was more like a wall surrounded Anna, as if she were guarding herself from outside influences. The familiarity of her reaction struck Amanda. Hadn't she, too, been that way around the Englische not so long ago? She remembered conjuring up a similar response upon meeting Alejandro for the first time after the accident in New York City. He and his warm smile had made an unforeseen entrance into her hospital room, and Amanda had immediately felt the same way as her sister seemed to now.

"Ladies," he said, by way of greeting. He stood in the doorway and cleared his throat.

"Back so soon, then?" Amanda stood up and hurried across the floor to meet her husband. "How was the horse auction?"

He let her kiss his cheek and nodded at Anna. "Horse auction was interesting." He reached down and let his fingers entwine with hers. "Beautiful creatures, those horses. Jake Edwards has raised some of the best. At least it looked that way, from the bidding that went on."

"Raised some *gut* money, then?" Anna asked and then continued talking before Alejandro could answer. "I'm not surprised. He tends to those animals like none other. Oh, I wish we could have gone!"

Amanda, however, was glad that she could spend a little time alone with her sister. Even though they were together over the holiday, they hadn't really been able to visit at the time. Not like today. And considering how busy Alejandro's tour schedule was for the next few months, Amanda didn't know when she would be able to return to Lancaster again.

Everything here was so comforting to her. And familiar. She wanted nothing more than to bottle up the feeling of everything she loved about being home with her family and take it with her. If only she could do that, she thought, life would be perfect.

"Amanda," Alejandro said when there was a break in the conversation. "Might I speak with you a moment?"

"Is everything all right?"

He had used her name. Not Princesa. Not *mi querida*, but her name. That always indicated something of a more serious nature.

"*Sí*, fine, but I need a moment."

Amanda gave Anna an apologetic look.

"I should be going anyway," Anna said in her quiet voice, the one that reminded Amanda of the barrier that stood between them. She stood up and pushed her chair back under the small table. "We'll visit more later, *ja*?" Without waiting for an answer, Anna walked toward the door, forcing a smile as she passed Alejandro.

He stood there waiting until Anna left.

"Alejandro," Amanda insisted. "What's wrong?"

Thrusting his hands into his pockets, he walked toward her. Even dressed in his jeans and boots, he still managed to look sophisticated and in complete control. The odor of the dairy barn lingered on his shirt and a piece of hay clung to the fabric. "I fear I have some bad news," he said, enunciating each word.

"I imagine so, from the expression on your face." She reached out to brush the hay from his shoulder, her fingers lingering there for just a moment. He remained so serious and disturbed that she felt panic set in. "What is it? It's nothing to do with your mother or the tour, is it?"

"The media."

Just those two words.

The media? The feeling of panic did not leave as Amanda worried that yet another story about them had been reported in the tabloids. What on earth could it be this time? she wondered. The last tabloid story had nearly destroyed their faith in their marriage. Luckily, they had learned an important lesson: question everything printed in the media. Amanda braced herself for whatever he was about to tell her.

"It's all right," she said. "We can get through it, Alejandro."

It seemed to take a few seconds for him to realize what she had meant. "No, that's not it," he reassured her. "When I say it's the media, I mean they are here."

She felt as if her heart hurt. Here? In Lancaster? Already? Why couldn't the reporters leave them alone, just for a few short days? This was her time to reconnect with her family, something that was proving to be much more difficult than she had expected. Now, if the paparazzi invaded the farm, it would only make things worse.

"Oh, I see."

He stood before her as if waiting for her to continue speaking, but she had nothing else to say.

To her surprise, he slipped his hand out of his pocket and extended it toward her, touching his fingers to the back of her neck while his thumb caressed her cheek. "You are so beautiful, Princesa," he murmured. She shut her eyes and let herself enjoy his uninterrupted attention. "What have I done to deserve someone as good as you?" He took one step forward and pulled her toward him so that her cheek was pressed against his chest. "You tolerate so much with never a complaint. You are a strong woman, no?"

"With you by my side?" She looked up at him. "*Ja*, I am strong."

He lowered his head and pressed his lips against hers, his arm tightening around her waist as he kissed her. "That is what I love about you, Amanda," he whispered.

"That's it?"

He gave a soft laugh. "One of many things."

"Much better," she teased.

"Now, we should go talk to your family, *sí?*" He took a step backward but still held her hand. "I imagine Jonas knows by now, but your mother will be out of sorts."

No doubt, Amanda thought. By now, Lizzie should be used to the attention. The paparazzi respected the law enough to not step onto their property. Granted, it was not pleasant knowing that people were lingering in the road and that a police officer was overseeing their behavior and making sure that they obeyed the law. But the paparazzi's presence didn't disrupt anyone's daily routine on the farm. At least, that was how Amanda viewed the situation.

"We aren't staying so long, Alejandro," Amanda commented as they walked through the dark room that connected the small *grossdaadihaus* with the main house. "I'm sure that a few days will be tolerable. Remember when I came home after Daed's stroke? Even the bishop was tolerant, *ja?*"

Alejandro pressed his lips together but didn't reply. She suspected that he was remembering how the bishop had come to the house with the tabloid magazine. Amanda tried to push away the memory of how embarrassed she had felt when her sister confessed that she'd seen at the main grocery store the magazine photos of Alejandro with that horrid Maria. Natural human curiosity led to a propensity for devouring gossip to which not even the Amish were immune. Still, Amanda had been surprised that such news had filtered through to Lititz, Pennsylvania. It wasn't as if the Amish communities or their neighbors cared much for the world of show business.

In the sitting area of the kitchen, Elias sat in his wheelchair, staring out the windows at the fields. Amanda noticed him as soon as she opened the door and entered the room with Alejandro behind her. Elias glanced up, and Amanda thought she saw him smile at her, a brief sign of joyful recognition. But just as quickly as it had shown up, the sparkle disappeared and he turned his head back to stare at the barren fields that he wouldn't be able to plow this year.

"Mamm, Anna." Amanda spoke softly, so as not to disturb her mother as she sat at the table, sorting through fabric that she wanted cut up into four-inch squares. Anna was at the stove, heating up water to make some instant coffee, the mugs and the jar of coffee already on the counter. "Alejandro noticed that the photographers are back," she said, sliding onto the bench at the table. She reached out and touched one of the squares. "Is this my old dress, Mamm?"

"*Ja*, it is." Lizzie snipped at the fabric and another square fluttered down to the table. "Why don't those horrid people just go away?"

Anna leaned her backside against the counter and crossed her arms over her chest, resting them on her expanding stomach. "They don't seem to come onto the property, so I don't quite see what's of interest to them." She gave a little laugh. "It isn't as if the view from the road is so beautiful, *ja*?"

Amanda appreciated her sister's comment.

Alejandro cleared his throat. "They will leave when we do, no doubt," he said.

"No doubt," Lizzie said through tight-pressed lips.

Without being asked, Amanda began to sort through the squares, putting like fabrics together in a neat pile. "They do go away, *ja*?"

It was Anna who responded with a chipper, "Oh *ja*, Amanda. They go away from the road—eventually. But they do seem to linger about the public areas."

This was news. Amanda hadn't been told this information. Out of all the letters she'd sent to the farm, only one had been answered, and the brevity of the message had been disappointing. Was this the reason why? Had they not wanted to burden her with the knowledge that the paparazzi never left Lititz? "I had no idea!" She turned to look at Alejandro. "Did you?"

A slight lifting of his shoulders answered her question.

"Why didn't anyone tell me?"

Anna busied herself with making the coffee. "I reckon a body can get used to anything," she said. Steaming water splashed against the sides of the mug in her hand. "Isn't like there's anything you can do about it, *ja*?" She put down the kettle. "Coffee for you two?"

Amanda ignored her sister's question and stared at her mother. "What has the bishop said about this?" She imagined that the bishop didn't need to see much more invasion of paparazzi within his church district in order to follow through on his threats to shun her parents.

"What's to be said, Amanda?" Lizzie answered. She set down the scissors and pushed away the fabric as she accepted the coffee mug that Anna handed her. "When you leave, they do, too. For the most part."

"It seems there's always someone somewhere eager to steal a photo or two. We send Harvey to the store now," Anna admitted. "He's not as bothered by them, and they don't seem as interested in him, anyway."

Harvey. Of course. That was how Alejandro kept in touch with her family, how they had known when the car service was arriving from the airport and how, undoubtedly, her husband had known that the paparazzi were still lingering in Lancaster County. Yet he had filtered this information, keeping it to himself and not sharing it with her. What else didn't he share with her? she wondered, feeling both hurt and angry at this deliberate exclusion on his part.

When she turned to look at him, she noticed that there was a distant look in his eyes as he met her gaze. He lifted an eyebrow, and she knew better than to ask him any further questions. Even if she asked him later, in the privacy of the *grossdaadihaus*, she doubted he would share with her the reasons he had chosen to keep that information to himself. She turned her head away and looked out the window, working hard to maintain her composure. Regardless of Anna's false bravado, Amanda knew that even though the bishop had demonstrated a more compassionate side during her last trip to Lancaster, he certainly had to be unhappy.

No wonder Alejandro had scheduled such a short visit.

Once again, she found herself confronted with feelings and emotions that she was desperately trying to sort out. It certainly didn't help that her mother was cutting one of her old Amish dresses into small squares. While Amanda knew that the squares would be used to make a quilt, it pained her to see how emotionless her mother appeared. To her mother, it was merely recycling an old dress. To Amanda, however, it felt like a symbolic gesture of her mother's acceptance that her daughter was no longer part of the community: not because of shunning, bitterness, or even a fight, but because her departure was accepted as God's will. Acceptance versus rejection, she wondered. Which one is worse?

She had been weaned away from her home of almost twenty-one years. She was not like Anna, who was all grown up, expecting her first *boppli,* and an integral part of the Beiler family. No. Amanda felt like an outsider.

Perhaps the worst part was that she felt as if she had not found a home of her own. The Englische often said that "home is where the heart is." And while her heart was with Alejandro and he loved her back—of that she was sure and certain—she still wondered: Where was *home?* Was it the private jet, the yacht? Was it the fancy condo or the hotel rooms? Was home found in the few hours carved out here and there when she could finally be alone with her husband, in the wee hours of the night? No, none of that was home. So where was *home?*

"Freshly baked sugar cookies, anyone?" Anna said cheerfully, bringing a tray of the fragrant treats and placing it on the table.

That was more like home, Amanda thought as she felt a deep sadness fill her as she realized that the vision of home she desired was one that she most likely would never have with Alejandro.

Chapter Ten

The Dorado International Airport in Bogotá, Colombia, was a small airport. But despite this, crowds of people waited in the main area, their bodies pressed against one another as they watched through the doors for the arrival of their loved ones. Some held signs written in Spanish, and a few had their children with them.

While they waited to be escorted through customs, Amanda looked through the glass doors and saw a crush of people, most of them young women with long black hair and smooth tanned skin. When they saw Viper walk with Amanda through the double doors, two escorts on either side of them, the women began to scream and more than a few began to cry. Security personnel lined the barricade, their backs to the passing couple as their eyes scanned the crowd, watching for anyone who might try to break through in order to reach him.

Alejandro wore his dark sunglasses, and his expression was hidden behind the black lenses. But he smiled and paused every few feet to let his fans take photos of him. Amanda stood behind him, uncomfortable with the scantily clad fans. After having left the penthouse at two o'clock in the morning for the airport, and following a three-hour flight, Amanda felt weary. Given that it was now only a little after four in the morning, she hadn't expected so many people to be waiting for Viper's arrival.

Clearly, she had been mistaken.

As she stood there, waiting patiently for her husband to slowly move along the line of waiting fans, she wondered at the power of this man. The idolatry his fans directed toward him never ceased to amaze her. Wherever he went, people gathered. Despite his shift in image, from globe-trotting bad boy to sophisticated married gentleman, his following had not decreased. If anything, the opposite was true.

Earlier, while en route to Colombia, Alejandro had met with his new manager. She had been too excited to sleep, so instead, Amanda had listened as Geoffrey and Alejandro reviewed his latest numbers, both in sales and social media. She could barely believe what she heard: he received $500,000 per show.

Most of the dates were sold out, which meant that overall revenue would be over $2 million per performance. After all of the expenses were paid and Alejandro received his cut of the merchandise, he would earn over $7 million in just five weeks.

She had been stunned to hear these figures—and to see a disappointed look on Alejandro's face.

"What is the latest on the US tour?" he asked Geoffrey.

After shuffling through some papers, Geoffrey had looked up and responded with a crisp, "Forty-one million."

"*¡Ay, mi madre!*"

Alejandro sounded irritated, but she couldn't understand why. "What's wrong?" she asked as she sat in the leather bucket seats of the private jet. "That's an awful lot of money, *ja?*"

He shook his head. "The average gross was one million per venue."

Geoffrey frowned. "If that," he added.

Amanda still didn't understand. "Oh? And that's not *gut?*"

Geoffrey suppressed a smile while Alejandro tried to explain. "No, Princesa. The South American leg will bring in less money because the venues are smaller. That means it will negatively impact the overall average profit per show." He pointed to one of the papers on the table. "See here?" He ran his finger down a column of figures and, at the end, tapped the total. "That is what we can expect from the next five weeks."

She peered at the numbers on the sheet, understanding little, if anything, of what she saw. "That's still an awful lot of money, *ja?*"

His shrug told her that he was not impressed. "We must make it up in Europe over the summer." This statement was directed to Geoffrey. "How are those dates holding up?"

"Sold out in the United Kingdom," Geoffrey said without referencing his notes. "Same with Switzerland and France. Germany is only at sixty-five percent, and Belgium at fifty percent."

"How many cities are on the European tour?" Amanda asked.

"Twenty." Geoffrey pushed another paper toward her. She glanced down at the list. Half of the places she had never heard of before.

When Alejandro mumbled something in Spanish then, shaking his head and looking out the window of the airplane, Amanda had suspected it was for the best that she couldn't understand what he said.

Now, in light of the throngs of people lined up throughout the airport and the noise being made by the screaming women, Amanda wondered if anyone in the country *wasn't* going to his concerts. Not even in Los Angeles and Miami had she seen so many fans at the airports.

As she waited for Alejandro to finish interacting with his fans, she felt someone grab at her arm. In the blink of an eye, a cell phone was shoved in front of Amanda's face as the young woman took a selfie with her. The woman screamed in delight and released Amanda, but other women then began to grab at her, too.

Immediately, Alejandro was at her side, quickly using force to extract Amanda from the overeager fans. He gave no outward sign of his emotions, and he did not scold the women, but the drained look on his face and the way that he held Amanda told her of his anger. There would be no more interactions with the fans, so he led her through the walkway, staring straight ahead instead of smiling at the crowds.

Once they were in the car, Alejandro turned to Geoffrey. "What was that?" he snapped at his manager. "What type of security is this? I will not tolerate Amanda being accosted! She could have been injured!"

The anger in his voice startled Amanda. She realized that she had never heard him raise his voice around her. With the exception of the time he'd confronted his former manager over the Maria incident, Amanda had never known Alejandro to demonstrate anything but complete self-control.

She reached out and touched his arm. "I'm not hurt," she said softly. The truth, however, was that she had a moment of fright when the first woman grabbed her.

He placed his hand over hers, his attention still on Geoffrey. "Get on the phone with Andres and find out how that happened. He is accountable for both Amanda's and my safety. Inexcusable!"

"*Sí*, Alejandro." Geoffrey's head was already bent as he typed furiously on his phone.

"Not a text! Call him!"

"Please, Alejandro," she pleaded. "Let's not make too much of this. Mayhaps I was standing too close, *ja*?"

He squeezed her hand, but shook his head. "I pay people to protect us, Amanda," he said. "That never should have happened."

Mindful not to contradict him, Amanda remained silent. She took a few deep breaths and stared out the window, tuning out the conversation between Geoffrey and Alejandro. When they started speaking Spanish and once Alejandro appeared to have calmed himself, she finally exhaled and relaxed.

They had a full day ahead of them: an interview at a radio station before meeting with an entertainment television reporter. Then they would go to the arena, Estadio el Campín, so that Alejandro could conduct a sound check. Since the majority of the equipment was being rented at each location, he wanted to leave nothing to chance. After sound check, he would shower and change before driving into the city to do a video shoot for a new sponsor: a Colombian energy drink manufacturer. Amanda felt more tired just thinking about all of these appointments, all of which were scheduled before late-afternoon meetings with more reporters prior to the VIP session and show.

She understood that he had to pack his days full of these meetings because they would leave Colombia immediately after the concert to fly to Quito, Ecuador. After a brief five hours in their next hotel, the schedule would start all over again. Just as Anna had said back when Amanda returned to Lancaster from Kansas City, it was a shame that the time spent in these amazing cities was too short for them to sightsee. However, Alejandro had promised her some free days between the concerts in Rio and Buenos Aires.

"You are sure you do not want the hotel?"

His question startled her, and she turned back from the window. *"Nee,* Alejandro," she responded. Unlike the times she had accompanied him to other concerts, this time she didn't want to leave his side. Instead, she wanted to experience everything that he did. "I'll be fine."

She hoped that she was right. She didn't feel fine, but she didn't want to retire to the hotel by herself while Alejandro, looking perfectly energized for the upcoming days, started the first day of the tour without her. From a media perspective, people would wonder where she was. From a personal perspective, she didn't want to appear weak, as if she couldn't handle the travel. She was here to support Alejandro, and that was exactly what she intended to do.

"Coffee," he announced. "Some good Colombian coffee!"

Oh, she thought, and lots of it. If only her eyes didn't burn from being so tired . . .

Their first two stops were radio stations. Amanda followed behind Alejandro, feeling immune to the voices around her. Naturally, everyone spoke Spanish, but unlike in Miami, no one here felt compelled to switch to English for her benefit. The lyrical melody of Colombian Spanish, however, was different from that of Alejandro's Cuban Spanish. For a while, as she listened to it, she wondered if Alejandro was experiencing any problems understanding people. But after he began laughing at something the DJ said to him, she realized that he understood just fine.

"Here," Geoffrey said, handing her something to drink.

"What is this?"

"An energy drink."

She eyed the canned beverage suspiciously. An energy drink? She wasn't so certain about accepting it. "I better not," she said and handed it back to him.

"It's going to be a long day and an even longer night" was all Geoffrey said.

Thinking twice, Amanda finally decided to try it. After all, they were headed to their third interview, and even after six cups of very strong coffee, she was still feeling as if she could sink into a bed and sleep for two days. The drink didn't taste bad, just like a carbonated juice. And as she stood in the waiting room behind the stage, watching on a small television monitor as Alejandro was interviewed for a popular talk show in front of a live television audience, she began to feel rejuvenated enough to face the afternoon.

Geoffrey looked at his watch. He remained silent but was clearly concerned about the time.

"What is it?" she asked.

"Sound check is in two hours. And then the Meet and Greet at seven."

She looked up at the screen again and was surprised to see that six scantily clad women had joined Alejandro on the set. They wore sleeveless dresses with three thick horizontal stripes of color: red, blue, and yellow. The pattern resembled the Colombian flag and might have been rather pretty, Amanda thought, if the dresses weren't skintight and the women's chests all but completely exposed.

The show cut to a break, and Alejandro walked off the stage. She could barely see him standing off to the side, the six women surrounding him and his arm around two women's waists. Behind him, the set was being changed so that he could perform one of his songs. He, however, was oblivious to all this activity as the women hung on him, smiling for the camera.

Amanda glanced over her shoulder at Geoffrey, but he was engrossed in reading a text message on his phone. She turned back to watch the screen and saw Alejandro kiss one of the women on the cheek. Her body pressed against his in a way that made Amanda more than uncomfortable.

The fans in the States also adored Alejandro, and on more than one occasion she had seen beautiful women try to throw themselves at him. But she had never before seen such an inappropriate public display of dress (or lack thereof!) and behavior as she did now. She could only assume that the women were dancers who would perform behind him while he sang for the audience. Somehow that only made Amanda feel worse about the way they clung to her husband.

Once the set was arranged, Alejandro moved back to the center of the stage and accepted a microphone from a sound engineer. He smiled over his shoulder at the dancers, who lined up behind him as the music started. Amanda watched as he began to sing. While she couldn't hear the words, she could tell that it was one of his older songs, one that had climbed the charts and hovered at the top for weeks on end. The women danced in sync behind him, their bodies moving in a way that Amanda couldn't ever have imagined. Their hips moved in a fluid motion while their legs, long and bronzed, all followed the same exact steps. Several times, Alejandro joined them, grabbing one and rubbing his hands up her torso.

Amanda looked away.

"They're a bit more demonstrative here," Geoffrey said.

Feeling embarrassed that he must have witnessed her reaction, she merely shrugged.

He directed his attention back at his phone. "Rio and Buenos Aires will be much worse, Amanda."

She couldn't imagine anything worse.

By the time the show finished and Alejandro was ready to leave, the six women had left. One of them had bumped into Amanda as she and Geoffrey waited in the corridor. Rather than excuse herself, the woman looked down her nose at Amanda, a look of disdain on her face as she whispered *"pobrecita"* under her breath.

"What does that mean?" Amanda asked Geoffrey when the women, laughing at the remark, disappeared around the corner.

"What does what mean?"

"Pobrecita."

He shoved his cell phone into his pocket. "Little poor one," he replied, "or just poor baby." His attention was not really on his answer, and Amanda realized that he didn't really explain what the women meant when they said that to her. Instead, Geoffrey was trying to catch Alejandro's eye. "Hey, Alejandro!" He pointed to his watch, and Alejandro nodded. As quickly as he could, he extracted himself from the Colombian fans who surrounded him on the edge of the stage to join his manager and wife backstage.

"Ah, Princesa!" he said, wrapping his arm around her neck. "You are still awake!"

They let security lead them through a set of double doors to an underground parking lot. A car waited for them, and as soon as they had shut its doors, it sped off toward the exit.

"What's next?" Alejandro clapped his hands together and reached into an ice bucket built into the side of the car, next to the facing seat. He grabbed an icy water and offered it to Amanda.

Geoffrey glanced down at some papers. "Sound check and then a short break before the Meet and Greet."

"*¡Perfecto!*" He looked over at Amanda. "Enough time for you to warm up with Stedman."

"Did you just say Stedman?" She knew that she had heard him correctly. She just couldn't hide her surprise at hearing her dance instructor's name. "Stedman the dance instructor?"

"No." Alejandro took a long, slow drink of the water and then, in an even tone, said, "Stedman the choreographer who worked with the girls and with you."

She stifled a groan.

Weeks ago, Alejandro had told her that new songs were being added to the tour and that the dancers had learned new routines. He had also explained to her that many of the dances needed to be adapted to accommodate the culture of South America, incorporating more salsa and tango elements than usually performed during concerts in the States.

She hadn't given any of this much thought.

The response to the concert in Kansas City, where Amanda had surprised him in the middle of a show, had been so overwhelmingly positive that that element had been made a part of the show. During the second-to-last song, she would walk down a tall stairway positioned in the middle of the set and dance with Viper during one song: her song. For weeks she had practiced with Stedman, working on foot placement, rhythm, and presentation. What looked so easy when it was done onstage by others was much harder to execute in reality than she'd expected.

But she hadn't considered that Stedman would be on tour with them.

Swarms of people were already waiting at the arena, and they screamed and yelled as the car pulled up to the security gate. Amanda startled when women began to pound at the darkened windows.

Neither Alejandro nor Geoffrey paid any attention to them. Knowing that the women could not see inside the car because the tinted windows provided privacy, Amanda slid over to the window and peered out. Just like in the States, the women here were crying and yelling, some of them holding signs that were written in Spanish: *"Nos encanta Viper y Amanda"*; *"Yo quiero a aguijón de Viper"*; and *"¡Te quiero, Viper!"* The women pushed and shoved at one another so that one woman fell and hit her head on the side of the car.

"¡Vamos!" Alejandro snapped over his shoulder at the driver.

He reached out for Amanda, gently pulling her across the seat and tucking her against his body.

"They are so . . ." She didn't have a word to use that could describe the women.

"*Sí*, I know," he mumbled. "These ones that wait out here are the worst. Dangerous, no?"

She could only imagine what the women would do if Alejandro actually stopped the car and got out. The thought caused her to shudder. How could they be so consumed by him, a man they only knew from the stage and would never meet? They didn't know him as a person, only as a presence. Yet if he was to get out and stand before them, she knew that the mob would crush them both.

Amanda turned her head from the window and rested it against his shoulder. No wonder idolization is a sin, she thought. It's an obsession that can destroy.

A security team met them at the underground entrance to the arena and led them through a series of corridors to their dressing rooms. Alejandro pressed a soft kiss against her forehead and left her at her door. He needed to meet with his team and check the equipment. Amanda watched him leave. A swarm of people surrounded him. Some she knew from the other concerts, while others had been hired just for the South American tour. When she couldn't see him anymore, she opened the door to her dressing room and slipped inside.

It was just a room. Nothing fancy: a dressing table, a rack of dresses, and a small sitting area. There was a linen-covered table along the back wall that held a tray of fruit and several bottles of water. On the dressing table stood a vase filled with white roses. She walked over to them, smelling their delicate scent even before she could lower her nose to inhale. A card poked out from the rear of the arrangement, and she reached for it.

```
Princesa,
The world awaits you.
V.
```

She smiled and leaned over once more to smell the flowers. His thoughtfulness warmed her heart.

"Amanda!"

Startled, she spun around as the door opened and Dali stormed into the room.

"You're late. What kept you?"

Amanda placed her hand over her heart. "You scared me half to death!"

Dali shut the door and hurried over to the rack of clothing. "As you did me! I expected you more than an hour ago! You have to change right now, Amanda. You have an interview with the newspaper. The reporter's been waiting for fifteen minutes."

Amanda watched as Dali pushed through the clothes until she found what she was looking for. "I had no idea, Dali." Amanda took the simple black dress that was thrust in her direction. "The show ran late, I reckon."

"Well, don't delay anymore!" Dali snapped, pointing to a screened-off section of the room. "Go on now. I'll fetch the makeup girl and have her fix up your face while you change."

Clutching the dress, Amanda watched as Dali stormed out of the room and called for someone in the hallway.

Interview? No one had mentioned that to her before. She still didn't understand why the media wanted to interview her at all. Especially here. Why would anyone in Colombia want to interview her? She didn't even speak the language.

Sighing, she turned around. "And so it begins . . ." she said out loud to herself. She walked over to the dressing area, saying a quick prayer to God that she would have the strength to survive the next five weeks.

Chapter Eleven

By the end of the first week, Amanda felt as if she didn't even know what country she was in—never mind which city!—and by the middle of the second, she was exhausted. The fast-paced schedule, so jam-packed with appointments, interviews, and travel, made the days and nights blur together. Often they flew into a city under the cloak of early-morning darkness and left again less than twenty-four hours later.

Arriving at such an early hour meant little time to sleep in the hotels. Amanda would crawl into bed, her burning and bloodshot eyes shutting even before she lay down, and immediately fall into a deep slumber. Alejandro, however, often went to an adjourning room to work on the EP songs before taking time to sleep. By the time she felt his hand on her shoulder, gently nudging her awake, he'd be showered and dressed, ready to down a hot cup of coffee and start the day.

She was amazed at Alejandro's ability to remain energetic and alert despite his lack of sleep. The less sleep he got, the less sleep he seemed to need. He changed his wardrobe at least three times a day and always looked refreshed, and he kept his mood upbeat and his smile sincere. Amanda tried to keep up with him, but this was a nearly impossible feat given the fact that she did not speak the language. Often, she found herself alone with just her thoughts while Alejandro was out conversing with the various people they had met. Wherever they went, a crowd of people met them and Alejandro would step into his role as Viper, smiling and greeting as many fans as he could, posing for selfies and shaking their hands.

South American countries were very different from US cities, that was for sure and certain. When the people here did something, they seemed to do it big. The bigger, the better. Even Viper was bigger and better here than he was in the States. His wardrobe changed; instead of the all-black slacks and shirts that he tended to wear in Miami and Los Angeles, he now wore more colors: bright blue or pink shirts with white slacks, and shoes that reflected the South American style. During the shows, he might go back to his black outfits, but he always wore them with the South American white jacket and white shoes.

And the fans adored him even more for his sense of style.

The women in South America stunned Amanda. Unlike in the States, women in these countries appeared more cosmopolitan, both in physique and in fashion. Now she understood why Jeremy had been so fastidious about her wardrobe. Wherever they went they saw tall, thin, and tanned women wearing tight dresses or short skirts with low-cut blouses and very high heels. It wasn't long before Amanda began to feel out of place and inadequate.

Not once did she complain, at least not out loud. She did her best to remain by Alejandro's side, following Jeremy's strict schedule of what to wear when and letting the tour's stylists fix her hair and makeup. When she was asked, she'd pose for the photographers, knowing exactly how to hold her head and how to smile after working with Stedman for all of those weeks. But inside, those feelings of inadequacy took root.

It didn't help, she realized, that she wasn't pregnant. While she had never been truly regular, she suspected that the constant travel and changes in her eating habits had negatively affected her periods.

"Amanda!" Someone banged at the dressing room door. "Let's go!" Stedman.

She groaned and rolled her eyes.

Stedman's role on the tour was to oversee the dancers' warm-ups, to critique each one's performance after the concert, and to give them tips and tricks to help them step up the dance routines and increase crowd response. Or, as Amanda saw it, to give them a lot of extra work based on what he viewed as being intensely flawed performances.

Amanda managed to escape much of the criticism since Alejandro whisked her away after the concerts. And, unlike the other dancers, she didn't have to attend all of the practices, a fact that irritated Stedman, who insisted on perfection from his dancers. She would accompany him to the arena to watch him during his sound check. Usually, from somewhere in the back of the arena she'd sit mesmerized, pretending for just a moment that she was not his wife but one of his adoring fans. It was a game that they played. He would sing a song to test the sound system. Then, when he realized that Amanda wasn't where he could see her, he would stop and look out into the mass of empty seats before him, his arm covering his eyes as he searched for her.

When he found her, he'd say her name into the microphone, calling out to her with a teasing, "Amanda! Come back to me, Amanda!" Usually someone working on the lighting equipment would make a comment in Spanish, something that made Alejandro and several other men laugh. She realized at those times that her inability to understand his native language was most likely a blessing.

"You are too far away, Princesa, and I want to sing you a song!"

She couldn't help herself. At these times, he triggered that addictive need within her, the one that caused her to eagerly make her way down the steps and onto the main floor, practically running to get to the stage. In just hours, these empty seats would be filled with screaming people, mostly women but also some men, and they would cheer for her husband as he sang. But first, she wanted to savor his attention and love and listen to him sing *her* a song. As he did so, she would lean against the barrier like a starstruck fangirl and gaze up at him, kneeling before her on the stage. Time stood still during these moments, and she forgot where they were.

Today, he had jumped off the stage and onto the main floor. She had laughed with delight, her hands clutched together as he placed the microphone down and grabbed her, pulling her by the waist into his arms, even though the security barrier still separated them. With the music still blaring, she could barely hear him as he nuzzled her neck and said something into her ear. When she didn't respond, Alejandro lifted his arm into the air, signaling for the music to stop.

Within seconds, someone had turned it off.

"Didn't you hear me?" he asked.

She shook her head.

"I asked if you'd be interested in coming backstage with me, little fangirl."

She looked over his shoulder and bit her lower lip. "Um, that might not be such a great idea. You see, I don't have a backstage pass," she said, keeping her expression serious. She blinked her eyes, feigning the innocence that she knew would feed his love of the game. "And those security guards . . . I'd hate to get thrown out before the show starts. I hear there's a wonderful performance tonight. Some Cuban singer named after a snake . . ."

"Hmm, I think I have some pull to get you back in," he mumbled. "Come with me, and let me introduce you to the band." He raised her arms so that they were around his neck. Then he lifted her up, slipping one hand under her legs so that he could carry her over the barrier and place her onstage. Quick as a flash, he jumped up beside her and reached down for her hand to help her to her feet. "See? No one will bother you, little fangirl."

He placed his arm around her waist and guided her off the stage, teasing her even more by pulling at the bobby pins in her bun so that she panicked when she realized her hair began to loosen. Laughing, he grabbed one more pin, and she gave up the fight, letting her brown hair fall down her back, still twisted together.

"You win," she said, lifting her eyes to gaze into his.

"Umm. I think we both win," he had whispered back, gently touching her hair and unwinding it as he walked backward, pulling her along with him toward his dressing room. "Let me show you . . ."

The banging at the door started again, interrupting the memory. Now, as she sat in her own dressing room, she felt irritated, especially since, of all people, it was Stedman who had interrupted her thoughts. How she wanted to stay in the memory of that afternoon and how Alejandro had pulled her into his dressing room so that, for just a few long minutes, he could escape into his own world, the one that he shared only with Amanda. With his hands clutching her hair, he had pushed her against the closed door and kissed her in a way that spoke of how much he needed her love. She had been only too happy to reciprocate, her hands slipping over his shoulders and wrapping around his neck.

But the show must go on, and a thump on the door spoke of Stedman's increasing frustration.

Reluctantly, Amanda stood up and glanced in the mirror. She wore a long black dress with sequins on the not-very-modest bodice. The top half fit her like a second skin, and the bottom half was slit to her hips on both sides. As she crossed the room, the skirt swished against her legs, and she knew without looking that her legs were exposed.

"What exactly were you waiting for?" Stedman snapped when she opened the door.

She stared at him.

"And I noticed that, once again, you missed practice."

His emphasis on the words *once again* did not go unnoticed. Instead of taking the bait, Amanda responded by changing the subject. "I hate this dress." She swirled around. "It's so long. I'm going to fall down those stairs."

Now it was his turn to roll his eyes. "You hate everything."

Her breath caught in her throat, and she made a noise of protest. "That's not true!"

Stedman crossed his arms, completely indifferent to her words. "It is true. And I don't care. Let's go."

He turned and started walking down the corridor. As she hurried after him, Amanda stepped on the bottom of the skirt and almost tripped. She gathered the fabric in her hands and ran after him. "Stedman! I don't hate everything!"

He didn't look back as he replied in a singsong voice that said how little he cared, one way or another. "Yes, you do."

She reached out and grabbed his arm, and when he finally stopped, she turned him around to face her. "Stedman!"

He pursed his lips and stared at her as if assessing her. "Look, Amanda, I know you hate the dancing, the dresses, the travel, and me. But you still must dance onstage, wear the dresses, travel on the tour, and deal with me. So get over it, and let's get you warmed up!" Without waiting for her to respond, he reached out and grabbed her by the arm. Without further warning, he placed his hand on her back and began to dance the cha-cha. She fell in step with him and did as he had taught her and as he continued to remind her to do, each night before the show: focusing on her posture and making sure that her gestures were big so that the audience could see them.

The music from the stage switched to another Viper song, this one with a fast Cuban beat.

"Merengue!" Stedman said and immediately began dancing in time with the music, his hips rolling as he moved his feet and knees at the same time. "Come on, Amanda. Swirl that skirt. Give it a shake, and let it catch the light so that it blinds every one of those front-row women dreaming about taking away your Viper!"

She laughed when he said that and stopped dancing.

Stedman danced over to where she had stopped and continued the smooth movements of his feet and hips. "*That's* funny? That makes you laugh?" He shook his head. "You're as crazy as he is," he mumbled, which only made her laugh harder.

Ten minutes later, Amanda stood at the top of the stairs, waiting for her cue. She knew it by heart: Viper would finish one song, and as he lifted his arm in the air, the lights would flash on him and then fall dark. Immediately, Amanda would step through a doorway at the top of the platform and stand in the darkness as she waited for the spotlight to find Viper, who had by then moved to a different spot on the stage. He usually took this time to address the crowd, thanking them for having attended the concert. The audience would then respond by screaming as loud as they could, and Viper would laugh.

Despite the repetitive nature of the performance—for that's what it truly was—Amanda smiled as she listened to his speech. Right after the screams of the fans, he would laugh. How he made it sound so natural truly mystified her. He was the master at making each laugh sound genuine and his interest in each fan seem sincere. In fact, it had taken Amanda a while to realize exactly what he was doing and why.

"They have to leave knowing that they matter," he had explained when she'd commented about his upbeat attitude and the scripted laughter. "People need to feel important in their lives. If I made them feel anything less, I fail to deliver on the promise, *sí?*"

At the time, Amanda hadn't fully understood what he meant by that. But as time went on, and especially during the past few concerts, she began to get a clearer picture of what he was saying. His job was not just to move people with his music but also to touch their souls with his performance, both on and off the stage.

His brand image, she thought wryly as she stood at the top of the stairs, waiting for the lights.

As the song ended and the crowd screamed in appreciation, the lights flashed and the stage went black. Amanda slipped through the opening and waited. The audience watched as the spotlight shone down, focusing just on Viper. He talked into the microphone, commenting about the amazing crowd and how he felt honored to perform in front of so many enthusiastic fans. She knew the speech by heart, even though he delivered it in Spanish.

Another roar from the crowd, a laugh into the microphone, and the music began once again.

She stood ready, waiting for the lights to flash on and illuminate the stage as the dancers rejoined Viper, their outfits changed since the last song. It would take a few seconds for the crowd to see her standing at the top of the staircase in the middle of the stage. Just as she had done in Kansas City, when she surprised Alejandro on tour, she would slowly descend until he turned around, pretending to have been unaware that she was onstage.

For a moment, the lights blinded her and Amanda paused to let her eyes adjust. With the lights on her, she walked down the staircase, knowing that Stedman was in the wings watching her. *Walk slow,* he always told her, *and don't be afraid to let them see those legs.* Just the thought of Stedman and his earlier comments made her start to laugh. She tried to find him in the wings, and when she caught his eye, she deliberately did as he instructed, exaggerating a slow, catlike prowl down the stairs.

The exaggerated movements were not lost on Stedman. Nor were they lost on Dali, who stood beside him watching. Dali frowned at this new, dramatic entrance by Amanda. When Amanda reached the bottom of the stairs, before Viper could approach her to take her hand, she spun so that her skirt flew out from both sides, the sequins catching the lights and reflecting them into the audience. When she stopped spinning, the skirt wrapped around her legs and Amanda snapped her head back as she quickly shifted her body into a promenade position directed toward Viper. She tried to glance over his shoulder at Stedman, who still stood in the wings, shaking his head and laughing while Dali glared at him.

Viper, however, appeared as amused as Stedman. He reached out, and rather than taking her hand to escort her to the front of the stage as usual, he grabbed her waist, yanking her toward him. With his one arm around her waist and his other arm free, he ran his hand down the length of her body as he began dancing merengue with her. The crowd screamed louder, delighted with the playful antics of Viper and his wife. When she let him pull her close and dip her, her knee raised to his hip, the noise from the audience reached a new level. Viper glanced into the stands, grinning mischievously before he leaned down and kissed her neck and then gently helped her back to her feet. She responded by leaning into him, brushing her hand across his cheek, their foreheads touching.

"¡Ay, Amanda!" he said, surprised by such a public display from her. The microphone amplified his words throughout the arena, and the volume of the crowd increased even more.

By the time he finished the song and their dance, she knew that he most definitely had enjoyed her over-the-top performance. He kept his arm around her waist, her hip pressed neatly against his as he yelled to the crowd to cheer for her. When they responded accordingly, he laughed and nodded to them, which only made the noise double. He leaned over and kissed her cheek.

"Such surprises, Princesa," he whispered into her ear.

He escorted her off the stage and handed her over to Stedman, who, to her surprise, pulled her into his arms and lifted her into the air. Viper raised an eyebrow and took a towel from Dali to dry the sweat from his neck and forehead. "Easy there, Stedman," he said. "I'm right here beside you, no?"

"You were wonderful!" Stedman said as he set her back onto the ground. "I knew you had it in you, Amanda!"

"See? I don't hate dancing," she teased. "Or you either, for that matter. The dress, however . . ."

He laughed. "Sass and vinegar, rising to the top!"

"Did I blind them?" she asked, looking over her shoulder at the stage. Viper was back in the center of it, his next song already begun. "Oh, I hope so!"

"Blind them? You dazzled them!"

Dali pried Amanda free from Stedman. "I'll tell you who else was 'dazzled.'" Dali turned her neck so that her head pointed toward Viper. "You both might want to go back to hating each other," she said. "Might be easier on one of your careers." She leveled her gaze at Stedman as she escorted Amanda back to her dressing room.

Inside the dressing room, Dali helped to unhook the straps to Amanda's dress. When Amanda disappeared behind the dressing screen to slip on her evening outfit, a black pencil skirt and sheer white top, she heard Dali grumbling.

"Now what is it, Dali?" Amanda peeked her head around the corner. "You always think he's going to be upset. He was laughing as much as Stedman was."

Dali pursed her lips together and gave her a look.

"What is it, then, Dali?"

"It's not my place to be giving you advice, Amanda."

She laughed as she emerged from behind the screen and sat down on the sofa to put on her high-heeled white sandals. "Look at these things," she said. "My word! I'll be six inches taller!" She stood up and tried to walk, laughing again as she wobbled and reached out for Dali's shoulder to steady herself. "I can't wear these! Why, I'd be taller than Alejandro." Quickly she kicked them off and hurried back to her dressing area to search for the flat sandals she'd worn earlier that day.

"When it comes to their women, those Cuban men are more concerned about other things than they are about height," Dali warned.

Amanda looked up. "What's that supposed to mean?"

"They don't share well," she said in a curt tone.

Having found her sandals, Amanda sat back down and slipped them onto her feet. She was annoyed by Dali's comment and knew full well that Alejandro would never suspect her of flirtatious behavior. Her difficult relationship with Stedman was public knowledge. "Neither do I," Amanda said as she stood up and straightened the bottom of her shirt. "So I suspect we are perfectly suited for each other."

Dali rolled her eyes and shook her head, looking away as Amanda opened the door. Wanting to hide her irritation, she tried not to slam it behind her.

What type of person did Dali think she was? Amanda wondered. Sharing? As if she was a toy? All because Stedman had picked her up in a moment of joy over her dancing? Ridiculous. She was Alejandro's wife, and the idea of anyone suspecting immoral behavior on her part infuriated her. Her job in life, not just on this tour, was to support the man she loved. Her vows to love and honor him had not been made lightly. There was no other person who Amanda could possibly love more than she loved Alejandro Diaz. Not now, not ever, she told herself as she stood in the wings of the stage, peering around the thick black curtain as he performed the last lines to his final song.

As he finished singing, the lights spun around and the stage fireworks exploded, both the noise and the fiery pyrotechnics the perfect finale. The audience cried out in surprise and delight, cheering even more loudly when they realized that the show was over.

Amanda anxiously watched as Alejandro waved to the fans, kissing his hands and waving them in the air as he took in the adoration and love from the thousands of people crammed into the arena. When he turned and glanced in her direction, she smiled and bounced just a little on the balls of her feet. He tossed a kiss in her direction before turning back for one last bow to his audience.

And when he left the stage and pulled her into his arms one more time, she knew that he would never doubt her status as his most adoring fan, the only one who loved him completely enough to heal that gaping hole of emotional need that dwelled so deeply within him.

Chapter Twelve

The old man stood just inside the doorway of the backstage greenroom. His black hat, tilted just a touch toward the back of his head, did not cover his deeply wrinkled forehead and receding gray hairline. His suit hung from his frame, despite the arms being just an inch too short, and the hems of the pants were frayed at the heel, but pride was etched into his eyes. Regardless of his appearance, he was clearly a man of dignity.

At his side stood a small child. The little girl was wearing a dress that, although perfectly ironed and clean, was two sizes too big. The scuff marks on her black shoes indicated that they, too, were hand-me-downs. Her skin, slightly olive in color, shone just above her cheekbones; she looked like she'd been scrubbed clean for her excursion with the older gentleman. Her dark hair was pulled back from her face into a single ponytail with a large pink bow attached at the base. But it was her eyes that caught Amanda's attention, for they were large and blue and stared in fright at everything around her.

Amanda was standing by Alejandro while he spoke with a reporter in Spanish. She put the cap on the bottle of water in her hand and watched the little girl for a while. She looked to be about four, maybe five, years old. People moved around the pair, ignoring their presence, a fact that piqued Amanda's curiosity. Most people who came to the greenroom before the shows were part of the tour or reporters with special press passes. Occasionally, other celebrities might also be there, visiting with Alejandro, but not tonight, at the second show in Rio de Janeiro.

When Alejandro finished conversing with the reporter, Geoffrey approached him and leaned over to whisper something in his ear. Alejandro's reaction was subtle, just a slight stiffening of his back and a muscle twitching in his neck. He nodded, just once, and took a deep breath before the next reporter approached, while a photographer took a few pictures.

The man and the child never moved from their spot.

Amanda remained at Alejandro's side, holding her shoulders back and stretched down to maintain good posture as Stedman had taught her. She tried to remain focused on the reporter as she had been instructed, but her eyes kept drifting toward the little girl. Once, Amanda thought she saw the child glance at her, just a quick flickering of her eyes to where Alejandro and Amanda stood.

Although Amanda smiled when the photographer aimed the camera in her direction, she could still sense Alejandro's change in demeanor. His normal pose—his arm around her waist, his fingers gently pressed against her dress as he held her—seemed tense.

"What's wrong, Alejandro?" she managed to ask when they had a moment alone.

"*Nada, mi querida,*" he replied with a forced smile on his face, sounding terse. "But you must excuse me. There is someone that I must see regarding some papers. Sit and relax. I should only be a few minutes." Unlike when he usually left her side, he did not kiss her cheek or touch her hand. He merely walked away with his assistant Carlos at his heels.

She watched him pass the old man and the child, never once glancing at them as he slipped through another doorway. Within seconds, the door had shut behind him. Whatever Carlos had told him must be important, she told herself and quickly prayed that nothing was wrong with either of their families back in the United States. Glancing at the clock on the wall, she saw that only an hour remained until showtime. A flat-screen monitor hung on the wall, and Amanda could see that the opening act—a band from Brazil that she had found not quite to her liking the previous evening—was still performing. After they finished, it would be time for Alejandro's Meet and Greet with the VIP ticket holders. During that time, the stage crew would tear down the equipment, remove it from the stage, and begin constructing the set for Viper. For the moment, however, there was nothing she could do but wait.

Moving over to the leather sofa, she sat down and leaned back, resting the side of her body against the arm. Across the hall was another greenroom for the fans with backstage passes. Most of them were Brazilian, and she couldn't understand what they said. She could, however, understand what they were doing: drinking, smoking, and hoping for a chance to meet Viper.

Instead of watching them, she directed her attention back to the monitor. She tried to listen to the band's songs, but couldn't understand a single word. While Portuguese sounded similar to Spanish, or at least to Alejandro's rapid-fire Cuban Spanish, it was definitely a different language.

"Amanda," a voice said from across the room.

As she looked up, Amanda noticed that the old man and the child were gone. Whoever they were, they definitely had been escorted somewhere else. And rightly so. Backstage at a Viper concert was no place for a child. Now, Dali stood there, shuffling papers in her hands before she walked over to Amanda. Dali's jaw was set tight, and she seemed paler than usual. The logistics of traveling was tough on everyone, Amanda observed.

"Are you all right, then?" she asked. "You look tired, Dali."

"No more than usual," Dali replied, a strain in her voice. As was typical, she got right down to business. "After the VIP session, you'll have to go change right away. Viper would like to switch up the set list so that your dance with him is in the first half of the show, not at the end."

That seemed a strange request. Alejandro had told her that the audience needed to have a buildup, their anticipation for the finale creating a vibrant energy in the arena. He never wanted to bring her out before the show's final number. His reasoning was that Amanda was part of the finale, and that seemed especially true here, given the Brazilian media and the fans' fascination with her.

"May I ask why?"

Dali bit her lower lip and averted her eyes. "Just more time to change, I suppose."

But she was hiding something. Amanda could tell. Dali wasn't someone who kept her thoughts out of her expressions. Yet it wasn't in Amanda's nature to probe. She hadn't been raised that way, and she knew that the source of the tension she felt in the air would be shared with her when, and if, she needed to know about it.

The level of activity in the room began to decrease as people hurried to prepare for the transformation of the stage. Alejandro reappeared through the doorway. With a look of determination on his face and his chin tilted slightly upward, he paused just long enough to straighten his cuff links and look in her direction.

His eyes. She noticed it right away. Something had changed in his eyes.

"Ready, Princesa?"

Quietly, she stood up and hurried to his side. He held out his hand, and when she took it, he smiled at her. Amanda reached up and, as gently as she could, touched his cheek. When he pressed his face against her palm and shut his eyes, she heard him exhale, a soft noise that, had she not been standing so close to him, she would not have heard.

"I love you," she whispered.

He turned his face so that his lips brushed her palm. Then, opening his eyes, he gazed at her for a long moment. She saw something soften in his blue eyes, and the look he gave her was one of relief. The corner of his mouth lifted into that mischievous smile that she adored so much. He squeezed her hand and pulled back from her, his eyes never leaving hers. *"Te amo,* Princesa.*"*

"Viper!" The voice called out again, sounding more urgent. *"¡Están esperando!"*

Amanda knew enough Spanish to know what that meant. People were waiting in the VIP Meet and Greet room, and the manager of that event was anxious for Viper to get started.

This time when Alejandro exhaled, he looked irritated. *"¡Sí, sí! ¡Un momento!"*

Giving him a soft smile, Amanda took a step toward the door. "We should go now, *ja?"*

With security guards accompanying them, they walked through the corridors that led behind the stage. Several people stared at them, but Amanda had grown used to that. It was no different from when tourists gawked at the Amish in Lancaster County. And while the hordes of people continually amazed Amanda, she took her cue from Alejandro, knowing that when she was in public, she needed to be "on" and project an image of tranquility and grace. She was finding this increasingly easy to do. While she was growing up on an Amish farm, she had been taught the importance of having peace in her life. Her version of peace seemed to mirror the Englische world's version of grace.

Over the past few weeks, the routine of the VIP Meet and Greet sessions had become one of her favorite parts of the concert. The fans, most of them women, glowed with happiness whenever Alejandro stepped into the room. He always opened the door and entered alone, standing there for just a moment so that the fans could admire him before he reached through the door for Amanda's hand, pulling her in to eventually join him. Tonight was no different.

A translator had been assigned to interpret for Alejandro, if needed. But many of the fans spoke either Spanish or English, at least enough so that he could understand what they said. Amanda always tried to stand off to the side, not wanting to impose herself on the fans' time with Viper. Getting that was, after all, the reason they'd paid the price of VIP admission. But they always seemed to be just as interested in her, and after they'd hugged Viper and posed for a photograph with him, they would ask her to join them.

If they spoke English, Amanda spent another few seconds with them, listening to them gush about their admiration for her. While the adoration of the fans bothered her from a spiritual perspective, the elation on their faces warmed her heart. She still could not understand why meeting another person could cause such an abundance of happiness, and she felt humbled that she was capable of bringing that emotion into the lives of strangers. Amanda could only pray that they also felt a stronger version of joy and peace that came from adoring God more than they adored a celebrity.

On their way back to the dressing rooms, Alejandro kept his hand protectively on the small of her back, guiding her through the path that opened up between people as they walked.

"Well done," he said, smiling at various people who greeted him along the way. "Again."

"You enjoy meeting the fans," she observed.

"¡Claro! They are the reason we are here!"

She already knew that and that he did, too, but she liked to remind him. Unlike other celebrities who seemed to get caught up in the world of fame, Alejandro seemed for the most part to be grounded in what was truly important—although Amanda wasn't certain that that had always been the case. From the way some of the women dressed, both in the audience and backstage, Amanda got the impression that they did not care whether Viper was married. In the past, those were the kinds of women who might accompany him to an after-party or a dance club in the city. His past reputation as a womanizer continued to haunt her, especially whenever she noticed him greet one of the scantily clad women with a warm hug, as if he knew her.

She reminded herself that it wasn't about the women for Alejandro, not anymore. Nor should it ever have been. The most important part of Viper's success was the fans: the average people who enjoyed his songs, the lyrics and music influencing their lives. Most of his fans would never meet him, a thought that saddened Amanda. And the ones who did were often the wealthier ones who could afford expensive VIP tickets. It didn't seem fair to Amanda, but she knew that life was not fair and to question it was to doubt God's plans.

As they stopped in front of her dressing room, Alejandro rapped twice on the door, signaling for her wardrobe assistants to open it. "You get changed now, *sí?*"

She nodded her head once.

"And you are wearing the black dress?"

"*Sí,*" she replied, loving how he tried unsuccessfully to suppress his smile.

There was no more time for talking. The stage manager grabbed his arm and began speaking rapidly in Spanish. Alejandro transformed back into Viper, smoothing out his black shirt and adjusting his sunglasses to shield his eyes from the bright lights that shone onstage. Amanda watched as he walked away, his broad shoulders the last thing she saw as he turned the corner.

"Come, Amanda," one of her assistants said from the doorway. Her Spanish accent was heavy. "We have not much time."

Sighing, Amanda turned around and followed the woman into the room where a small team of people waited to dress her, fix her hair, and touch up her makeup. This was, without a doubt, the part of her role in the tour that she disliked the most, especially the part when they sat her in a chair facing a mirror. Short of shutting her eyes, she had no way to avoid looking at herself, and that was something that she didn't think she'd ever get used to doing.

She could hear the music begin and knew that Viper was preparing to go onstage. In her mind, she saw him, standing beneath an opening in the stage. Above, the stage would fill with smoke, and when it dissipated, the audience would in one perfect moment see Viper standing there, having appeared as if from nowhere. His back would be turned to the audience with his hands folded before him; the platform, unseen by the audience, would slowly turn so that he was finally facing them. She could always tell the moment when he looked up; the noise of the audience often drowned out the music from the band.

"There!" The makeup artist stood back and admired her work. *"¡Qué linda!"*

Amanda lowered her eyes at the compliment.

Two quick raps at the door. It was time for Amanda to head to the stage. She wondered how the band had reacted to the change in the set list and hoped that the switch had not inconvenienced them. Over the past few weeks, one thing she had learned was that routine was one important way, if not the only way, to survive constant travel from one city to another. Inevitably, something always went wrong: the sound system didn't work properly, pieces of equipment did not arrive on time, or lighting failed. Such moments of temporary crisis were less stressful when the rest of the schedule remained intact.

Amanda stood in the shadows at the back of the stage, on top of the upper platform of his set, waiting for her signal to join her husband. No one seemed distressed by the change. Instead, the stagehands remained on point, their wireless headphones conveying directions to them from the stage manager while others in the crew hurried back and forth, doing their own jobs.

In her custom-made black dress, the crystals on its front and back sparkling under the overhead lights, she knew that she was dressed for the part. Unlike the scanty outfits of the dancers on the stage that showed off parts of their bodies in a way that still caused Amanda to look away, the color flooding to her cheeks, her dress mixed sophistication and class with plain simplicity. She smiled when she remembered the meeting with the fashion designer and how Alejandro had reacted to her requests, which had contrasted greatly with his and the designer's expectations.

As she heard Viper's song wind toward its end, she felt the familiar pounding of her heart and the nervousness that came over her in the moments just before she walked through the curtains. She always dreaded the walk down those stairs to reach Viper. The one thing she had gotten used to was the bright lights that blinded her, because they basically blocked her from seeing the thousands of eyes that stared up at her. She reminded herself, as always, to focus on one thing: Alejandro.

"And tonight I would like to introduce someone very dear to me . . ."

Alejandro's voice boomed over the microphone, quieting down the audience somewhat, although people were still screaming and yelling from their seats.

Shutting her eyes, Amanda said a quick prayer to God, something she always did in this moment. It was with his strength that she managed to do this. He had led her to Alejandro for a reason. She would not question his reasons or plans, but would merely abide by them, putting herself in his hands.

When she heard her name and the roar from the audience, she took a deep breath and waited for the curtain to be pulled back. After she'd stepped through the opening, she paused at the top of the platform and smiled at the deafening noise coming from the darkness just beyond the stage. She glanced from side to side, just the way she had been taught so that it looked like she was seeing the people. But the blinding lights hid most of the audience, and that minimized her fear of performing before them.

"Ah, *mi* Princesa!" Viper crossed the stage in three long strides and jogged up the stairs to meet her halfway. He reached for her hand, keeping his gesture slow and overreaching for dramatic effect, and helped her to complete the descent. She couldn't see his eyes behind his dark sunglasses, but she could tell from the way his mouth twitched that he was watching her. At the base of the stairs, he lifted her hand to his lips and gently kissed the back of it. Even though he had made this gesture so many times before on the tour, she still blushed and bit her lower lip as she averted her eyes.

In a genuine response of delight, he threw his head back and laughed, enjoying every moment of her discomfort with his affection.

The noise from the audience increased, the fans screaming and calling out for Amanda.

Still holding her hand, Viper walked carefully to the front of the stage and presented her to the audience. "Isn't she beautiful?" he said, looking out into the crowd and waiting for them to cheer even louder. "Do you think we can get her to dance for us?"

Amanda felt like a doll on display, especially when he lifted his arm and squeezed her hand, indicating that she should spin around as she had been taught. One full turn. Just enough for the bottom of her dress to fan out and sparkle, an effect caused by the crystals sewn into the hem. From the reaction of the fans, especially those closer to the stage, she could tell that the flow of the dress was an amazing sight, unexpected and beautiful, for sure and certain.

As she always did at that moment in the concert, she wondered about the people standing in the crowd. What was life like in Brazil for the average person? The cost of her dress alone was more than the average hardworking Brazilian made in one year. As they traveled from one city to the next, Alejandro spent most of his time on the phone or checking e-mails. She, however, spent her time staring out the tinted windows, observing the varied landscapes and fauna. Whenever they passed through villages or towns, she noticed the different types of housing. In the city she'd seen small houses built on narrow lots with little to no room for gardens. Yet as they had driven farther away from São Paulo on the Via Dutra highway, she noticed a change in the scenery. Farms lined the highway, mostly on the western side as they drove past the Paraíba Valley. Many of the farms were larger than the ones she remembered from Lancaster, yet she saw very few cattle grazing on the lush green land. She was told that the rich soil here lent itself to the growth of fruit crops, about which she knew nothing.

Viper spoke to the crowd in Spanish. As soon as he'd finished, the beat of the drums started up and he began moving his hips and feet in what Amanda knew was the samba. Behind them, the dancers emerged from the sides of the stage, dressed in skimpy costumes that were adorned with feathers and glitter. Their version of the samba was more pronounced, with engaging hip movements and exaggerated arm gestures that Amanda couldn't watch. Instead, she focused on what she had been taught to do: a simpler version of the samba, moving her feet as she slowly approached Viper while he sang a song in Spanish.

She didn't know the words, and given the way he danced toward her, she wasn't certain that she wanted to learn them. Still, she remembered Stedman's comment that the music, the lyrics, and the actual dance were only part of a performance. She and Alejandro were acting onstage to entertain the audience, and if Alejandro wanted her to be a part of the performance, Amanda knew that she would do whatever Viper requested.

Toward the end of the song, he grabbed her by the waist and pulled her close to him, wrapping one arm around her. She placed her hands on his shoulders and stared into the face of Viper, mesmerized by the energy that radiated from him. Despite the fact that the Viper the fans saw onstage was completely different from the Alejandro she had married, she knew that she loved them both.

With his free hand, he removed his sunglasses, a deliberately slow gesture that caused a stir among the fans. When he dipped her backward and leaned over to kiss the base of her throat before pulling her back to an upright position, the noise filling the arena deafened Amanda.

Once the song was over and Amanda's small role completed, Viper replaced his sunglasses before he gestured toward her one last time. The noise of screaming fans and the sea of posters that they waved demonstrated their adoration, not just for Viper but also for his wife. After a few drawn-out seconds, Viper reached for her hand and escorted her to the left wing of the stage. At the back of the stage, the dancers continued with their gyrations, only this time to a new song. He made sure that Amanda was delivered into the hands of a security guard who would accompany her to the dressing room before he jogged back onto the stage to finish the last few songs of the set.

Back in her dressing room, Amanda sank into a chair and sighed. The dressing rooms were plain and decorated simply, with only the basics. At each of the other venues, the rooms had been similar, only at this one there was a bouquet of flowers sitting on the vanity. "Oh my." She looked up at Dali. "Where did those come from?"

Dali glanced over her shoulder to see where Amanda was looking. "Ah, the flowers, *sí*. The *prefeito* sent them."

Amanda blinked. "I'm sorry. Who?"

"The mayor."

"Of Rio de Janeiro?" For a moment, she could not understand why the governing head of the second-largest city in Brazil would do such a thing. Such a kind gesture from a stranger truly touched her heart. But then she remembered last summer when Alejandro's limo had hit her on the streets of New York City. The mayor of that city had also sent her flowers. She hadn't understood it then, although she was beginning to comprehend that that kindness had more to do with publicity for the mayors than with her enjoyment of the flowers. Sharing the story of sending flowers to the media star of the week was a wonderful way to delight the constituents of his city. Important people sought allegiance with famous people in order to retain power. What better way to gain the favor of Viper than by showing respectful favor toward his wife? And an endorsement from Viper could be used during upcoming political campaigns for reelection.

"Alejandro asked to meet you back at the hotel." Dali paused before Amanda and gestured for her to stand up in order to change out of the dress.

"The hotel?" Amanda did as Dali indicated, yet couldn't help but express her surprise. "I . . . I usually wait for him and then we return together."

In the past, Alejandro had left Viper on the stage after the concert and retreated with her to the comfort of their suite at the hotel. Amanda knew that Geoffrey and Alejandro wanted the image of Viper as a club-hopping womanizer while on tour to be replaced by him embracing his new role as husband. Amanda wondered why, suddenly, Alejandro wanted to change this routine, especially without any advance discussion.

Dali didn't reply but merely continued reviewing some papers while Amanda stepped out of the dress and handed it to the fashion assistant before slipping back into her previous outfit: a simple long black skirt with a plain blouse. Once Amanda was dressed, Dali wasted no time before calling for the security guards to escort her to a waiting car. It happened so fast that Amanda could hardly digest the urgency with which the guards had whisked her back to the hotel and led her through the throng of fans who must have been standing outside the doors for hours. Stanchions, roping, and several large security guards kept them away from the entrance, but as Amanda walked down the sectioned-off walkway, she hesitated.

How long they had stood there, just in hopes that they might catch a glimpse of Viper returning from the concert! The smiles on their faces and the way they snapped photos of her made Amanda realize that she, too, had an effect on these people. Could some of them have been waiting for her?

"Just a moment," Amanda said before she stepped through the hotel's doors. She turned around and walked back to the fans. She smiled and let them hug her, a gesture that still felt uncomfortable to her when it came from a stranger. She posed for photos with a few of the fans before waving and retreating back inside the hotel.

"That was a breach of security," one of the guards said to her. "Viper won't like that."

She smiled her appreciation for his concern, but said nothing in response. She would deal with Alejandro's reaction later.

Upon reaching the suite, she thanked the security guard for escorting her and slipped into the room. With a sigh, she shut her eyes and leaned against the closed door, enjoying the moment of quiet. Her ears were still ringing from the loud music and noise of the screaming fans. She didn't know how Alejandro performed for so long under the intense heat of the lights and with the loud music battling to be heard over the fans.

Pushing away from the door, she kicked off her shoes and picked them up before she headed through the hotel suite's foyer and into the large sitting room. The crystal chandeliers and large flower arrangements on the tables enhanced the opulence of the room, which had floor-to-ceiling windows that overlooked the city. Never in her life could she have imagined such a world existed: a world of travel and champagne, fine dining and dancing. And while she felt uncomfortable with much of this, particularly the clash between her past world and the present, she knew that her heart belonged to Alejandro and that she would not complain about the drastic change in her life. After all, joining his world had been a choice. Her choice.

Amanda stood for a moment at the window, her hand pressed against the cool glass as she gazed out over the expanse of city lights that curved around the bay. In the distance, the lights of Sugarloaf

Mountain cast an orange glow upon the small island of rock that jutted out of the water. Alejandro had promised her that he would take her out there on the gondola during their break, the days they had off between concerts in São Paulo and Rio de Janeiro. But too many obligations had prevented that from happening. Again.

For once, she didn't mind. Seeing the city from this vantage point was more than enough for her. What she enjoyed even more than the view was the silence. Days filled to the brim with appointments and obligations were consistently followed by nights of screaming fans and loud music. The contrasting stillness calmed her. She stood there alone, staring into the distance, knowing that her husband was out there somewhere, performing. Once he was finished, the transformation from Viper back to Alejandro would take place and he'd come back to the hotel where he'd fall asleep in her arms.

Chapter Thirteen

When Amanda awakened, she noticed that she was alone. That was the first clue that something was wrong. Alejandro was not beside her. However, the tousled sheets and the wrinkles in the pillow indicated that he had come back to the room, probably long after she had fallen asleep, and had arisen before her.

She sat up and took a few deep breaths. In a few hours, they were to take a midday flight to Salvador for the last of his concerts in Brazil. Dali had already prepared Amanda for the day's schedule, which included four interviews before the show: one at a television station, one for a radio show, and two for popular magazines. It was going to be a long day. Then, right after the show, a private plane would take them to Buenos Aires, Argentina. There, they would be able to spend some time alone. From the tension she had felt the previous night, Amanda gathered that Alejandro needed a break, even if it was only for a few days.

Slipping out from beneath the sheets, she knelt by the side of the bed, clasped her hands before her, and bowed her head. *Dear Lord,* she prayed silently. *Into your hands I place this new day. Please protect us during our travels. Bless all of the people touched by Alejandro; I pray that they find their way to you, a wonderful God so full of grace and mercy. Bless me with your love and strength. Amen.*

The door opened, and Alejandro, already showered and dressed, walked into the room. He paused when he saw Amanda kneeling by the bedside. In silence, he stood with his hands behind his back and his head bowed, respecting her private time with God.

She smiled at him. "Alejandro! You are up so early!"

Amanda stood up and hurried over to him, expecting him to greet her with a warm hug. Instead, he stood before her, stoic and somber. The muscles along his jawline twitched, and there was a vacant expression in his eyes. Instead of warmth, they reflected a coldness that she had never seen before.

"What's wrong?"

He nodded toward the bathroom. "It's best that you dress and get ready, Amanda. We have something to discuss."

His somber mood set off her inner alarm. Immediately, she thought of her family. "What's happened? Is everything all right at home?"

"*Sí,*" he responded with no emotion in his voice. "Now go dress and meet me in the sitting room."

He waited at the door while she slowly crossed the room. She glanced back at him just once before she did as he instructed. Her heart beat rapidly, and she felt as though a weight pressed against her chest. Whatever was wrong, she knew it was serious. Yet he had indicated that everything was fine at home. Perhaps a show had been canceled? Had something he needed to discuss with her been leaked to the media? Were there more rumors about something that Viper had—or hadn't—done? Her mind filled with worry as she quickly donned a simple dress that buttoned up the front, its belt highlighting her small waist.

Before she finished, she took a moment to look into the mirror. With her hair pulled back and her cheeks not covered with makeup, she looked more like herself, or at least the self that she remembered from her life in Lancaster. She just hoped that she had the strength to deal with whatever troubling situation awaited her in the sitting room.

Bless me with your love and strength, she repeated silently. Taking a deep breath, she turned around and headed through the bedroom to the sitting area as Alejandro—or was it Viper?—had instructed her to do.

An older woman sat on the sofa. She wore a beige suit, and her dark hair was pulled back into a bun similar to Amanda's. Looking up as Amanda entered the room, she nodded her head once in acknowledgment. The files spread out on the table clearly indicated to Amanda that the woman was there on business. What kind of business, Amanda could not imagine.

Alejandro stood at the window, in almost the exact spot where she had stood the previous evening. His hands were clasped behind his back, and he did not turn around as Amanda approached.

She sat on the chair opposite the woman and smiled. "I'm Amanda," she said when no introduction was given. "And you are . . . ?"

The woman hesitated, and Amanda wondered whether she spoke English. But after a second or two, she responded with a simple, "Senhora Diaz, it is nice to meet you." Another pause. "Senhora Maria Fernanda de Sousa."

Uncertain of whether she should offer to shake hands with the woman, Amanda waited to see if the gesture would be made toward her first. When it wasn't, Amanda crossed her legs at her ankles and folded her hands, resting them on her lap. A heavy silence filled the room, and Amanda made no attempt to break it. She merely waited, willing her heart to stop beating so rapidly inside her chest.

Finally, after what felt like an eternity, Alejandro took a deep breath and turned around. He pursed his lips as if deep in thought before he called out something in Spanish, as if to someone in the next room.

"Amanda," he then said in a flat, emotionless voice. "There is someone I need for you to meet."

Amanda's eyes flickered in Maria Fernanda's direction. "You must have been deep in thought, Alejandro. We just introduced ourselves."

The noise of the door opening and several people entering the room distracted her. She turned her head and looked in the direction of the sound. Two people had stopped just inside the room: an older man and a child.

"I must introduce you to Isadora Daniela da Silva." Alejandro paused for just one moment before he added, "My daughter."

Amanda tried to remain poised as she stared at the two strangers. She recognized both of them right away: they had been backstage the previous night. Amanda felt the pressure in her chest increase. She slowly returned her gaze to Alejandro. "Excuse me?" was all that she could say. Words escaped her. She thought she had heard him introduce the little girl as his daughter. Surely she was mistaken.

"*Sí,* Amanda,*"* he affirmed. "Isadora is my daughter."

She pressed her lips together. *Isadora? Daughter?* Her mouth felt dry, and she could barely swallow. "I . . . I don't quite understand, Alejandro."

Across from her, Maria Fernanda began to speak. Her heavy accent made understanding her nearly impossible. Most of what she said went over Amanda's head; she was still fixated on the word "daughter" that had slipped through Alejandro's lips as casually as if he were introducing her to a new employee or a reporter. Maria Fernanda didn't seem to notice, or care, that Amanda wasn't following what she was saying. She continued to spill out an endless stream of words that blended into one another. However, what Amanda did understand were the words "death," "father," and "legal guardian."

As Maria Fernanda's voice faded into a blur of noise, Amanda turned her head slowly so that she could get a good look at the little girl. She wore the same dress as she had the previous night, although the bow in her hair was blue today. Her blue eyes seemed devoid of expression, and she stared at the floor in front of her feet.

Alejandro remained standing where he was, but his words were clear enough. "Her mother has died, and the grandfather is ill."

Amanda felt light-headed as she tried to understand what he was saying. Was he talking about the girl's mother? Was the old man standing there the grandfather? "I . . . I still do not understand what any of this means . . ."

Maria Fernanda shoved some papers at her. "You must sign here, Senhora Diaz."

"Sign? What am I signing?" As panic overtook her, Amanda stood up and crossed the room to stand before Alejandro. She placed her hand on his arm and stared into his face. "Please," she whispered. "What is happening, Alejandro? I . . . I don't understand any of this."

He didn't move when she touched him. "Isadora has no other family to care for her, and the government of Brazil will put her in an orphanage unless she is turned over to our care," he said, his eyes unwavering as he stared out the window.

And there it was.

Amanda glanced over her shoulder at the older man. She saw it now, the pallor of his skin and sunken shadows under his eyes. Most likely he had cancer and, from the looks of it, would not survive the year. Her gaze traveled back to the little girl. Isadora. She had a name, Amanda reminded herself, and was no longer a stranger: she was family.

There was no resemblance to Alejandro in Isadora's face. Except for the eyes. Clearly, the blue eyes that peeked at Amanda were Alejandro's: the color, the shape, the expression in them. Amanda chastised herself for not suspecting the truth the previous night. A blue-eyed Brazilian was as uncommon as a blue-eyed Cuban.

"When did her mother die?" Amanda asked, keeping her voice low.

"Almost a year ago."

"A year? How?" she demanded.

"Amanda . . ."

She turned to look at him, the sharpness of her sudden motion causing him to pause. "I want to know how the mother died. And did you know about this?"

He shook his head. "I did not know, no."

Amanda raised her eyebrows as she waited for the answer to her first question.

"The mother . . ." he started but stopped. Amanda wondered why it was difficult for him to speak of the child's mother, his former lover from a one-night stand during his wild days. There had been no discussion between Alejandro and Amanda about this child. He had made just one mention of her, and that had been done in such a casual manner, back when Amanda first met him, that, frankly, Amanda had forgotten about the existence of his illegitimate daughter.

"Tell me." She needed to know. The initial anger and hurt that she felt was countered only by her feelings of guilt. Why had she never inquired more about the child? How had she not known anything about that tryst? Why hadn't he prepared her for the fact that the mother and child lived in Brazil? At least then she wouldn't have been completely blindsided by this news.

"Drugs," he finally admitted.

Drugs. Amanda took a deep breath. "I see," she said, mustering the strength to remain calm. While what she imagined about the situation caused her considerable pain, she knew the truth was probably worse than anything she could envision.

Amanda shifted her body so that she faced the man and the child. Quickly, she assessed the situation, knowing that she could not question God's will and that there was no sense in arguing with Alejandro. The child existed and needed help. Amanda could never live with herself if she knew that she was the reason a child had been sent to live in an orphanage. She hadn't even thought that such places existed anymore, having never really considered that they were anything more than an unpleasant element of a fairy tale. Amish children always had relatives to care for them if anything tragic happened to a parent.

Love and strength, she repeated to herself.

Without another second's hesitation, Amanda walked across the room and stood before the man and the child. She stretched out her hand, which, apprehensively, the man shook. His grip was weak, and there was sorrow etched in his face. Amanda then knelt down before the child and looked into her face. She was a pretty little girl, and those blue eyes stared right back at her.

Amanda held out her hand and gave a slight smile. "It is nice to meet you, Isadora," she said softly.

The child startled at the sound of her name and looked up at her grandfather.

"She does not speak English," Maria Fernanda said.

Amanda kept the smile on her face and continued to look at Isadora as she processed this new information. No English? Reaching out her hand, Amanda touched the girl's shoulder and gently slid her hand down the length of her arm until her fingers touched Isadora's hand. The girl looked back at her, a frightened expression on her cherubic face. Amanda couldn't help but wonder what Isadora knew about the man who stood by the window, his back to the rest of the room.

Amanda walked back to the chair. She sat down and leaned forward, her attention on Maria Fernanda. "What is it that I must sign?" she asked. "And what should we know about Isadora?"

For the next thirty minutes, Amanda listened to Maria Fernanda, trying her best to comprehend what she was saying, despite the heavy accent and mispronounced words. The woman explained the different papers that granted legal guardianship under Brazilian law. When she finished, Maria Fernanda slid the papers across the coffee table in Amanda's direction for her to sign. Amanda noticed that Alejandro had already signed them; the date next to his name reflected that he had met with the woman the previous day. Most likely, Amanda thought, after the show.

She wasn't certain whether to be upset that Alejandro had not consulted her before signing. On the one hand, he accepted his responsibility. He could have never mentioned the situation to Amanda and merely sent Isadora to the orphanage. On the other hand, the fact that he had agreed to such a life-changing commitment without asking Amanda's opinion concerned her. What would have happened if she had refused to sign the papers? It dawned on her that, as the stepmother, she had no legal responsibility for Alejandro's daughter. If she hadn't signed, Isadora would still be his responsibility and turned over to his care.

Once Amanda finished signing the paperwork, all of which she could not read because it was written in Portuguese, she handed it back to Maria Fernanda, who shuffled the papers into a neat pile and slid it into her briefcase. She stood up and looked down at Amanda for a moment before she turned to Alejandro and said something in Spanish. He replied and nodded. Whatever had transpired between them, this was the end of Maria Fernanda's business with Isadora. She departed from the room, barely pausing to bid farewell to the grandfather and the child.

"Amanda . . ."

She shut her eyes and lifted her hand, a gesture that made him pause. She needed time to digest what had just occurred. And she certainly needed more time before she could speak to him with any trace of calmness in her voice. What she needed was time alone and time to pray. In just a matter of minutes, she had become a mother to a child who did not speak her language and was born out of a past love affair between her husband and a woman she did not know. Nor did he, she reminded herself.

"I need some coffee," she said and walked away from Alejandro.

In a room behind the sitting area was a kitchenette. A carafe of coffee and a tray of bread and fruit had been placed on the counter. Amanda did not ask Alejandro if he wanted anything. Instead, she poured herself a cup of coffee and, with her back turned toward him, tried to steady her nerves as she sipped it.

A child. A five-year-old child. How was she to mother another woman's daughter? The bittersweet irony that Amanda had hoped for her own baby was not lost on her. God had answered her desire for a child, but not in the way Amanda had expected. *For I know the thoughts that I think toward you, saith the Lord, thoughts of peace, and not of evil, to give you an expected end.* She finished her coffee and set the cup back on the counter. She thought of the future and hope. This was all part of God's plan, and she knew better than to question it.

She took a deep breath and exhaled. Despite the rapid-fire manner in which Maria Fernanda had presented the paperwork, Amanda had signed willingly, knowing that, like Alejandro, she was accepting responsibility for the little girl. And while she did not appreciate being ambushed by Alejandro, Amanda knew that it wasn't Isadora's fault.

Taking a white plate from the small stack on the counter, Amanda placed several pieces of fruit and bread on it. It was still early, and surely the little girl was in need of food. The universal language of hunger and satiation might begin the formation of a bond between them. She walked to the glass table and set the plate down before turning to look over at Isadora.

"Isadora," she said gently. When the girl looked up, Amanda smiled, gesturing with her hand. "Come."

Isadora made no attempt to move, although her eyes shifted to the plate of food.

Smiling, Amanda walked across the room and knelt down once again. *"Venga a comer,"* she said in Spanish. There were very few words and phrases that she knew in Alejandro's language, but she certainly had heard Señora Perez call them to eat enough times. She only hoped that the phrase was similar enough in Portuguese for the girl to understand her.

Isadora looked up at her grandfather and waited. He nodded his head, and hesitantly, Isadora stepped forward. Amanda grasped her hand and led her to the table. Gently, she helped the child into the chair and touched her shoulder.

"She doesn't speak Spanish," Alejandro said from where he still stood.

Amanda had already guessed that. She felt a tightness in her chest, realizing that she had just adopted a child with whom neither she nor Alejandro could communicate. On the inside, Amanda wanted to cry, but she managed to maintain her composure. All of her life, her mother had taught her and Anna that questioning God's will was the same thing as admitting a lack of faith in him. Whatever God had planned for her and Alejandro with the arrival of this child . . . well, Amanda knew that she needed to remain calm as she accepted Isadora with an open mind and heart.

Ignoring Alejandro, she continued to sooth Isadora in both Spanish and English. She hoped that the calm and reassuring sound of her voice might relax the child. After all, Amish children often did not speak English at home, learning it only when they started school at around the same age Isadora was now. And they often did not know the High German used by the preachers and bishop during worship service. It was the tone of voice, the comfort of sound that helped to instill the message of love and devotion, both in the home and at the worship service.

To her relief, her approach worked well enough for Isadora to reach out and take a piece of pineapple. While her small hands were clean, the dirt under her fingernails told a different story. Her grandfather had to the best of his ability prepared his granddaughter to be presented to her new parents: a reckless man who hadn't known the child's mother well and the man's young wife, who hadn't known her at all.

Amanda wondered if he spoke Spanish and, if so, what type of exchange he'd had with Alejandro.

The click of a door shutting caused Amanda to look back toward the front door. The grandfather was gone. A small suitcase was all that remained of Isadora da Silva's past in Brazil. Amanda felt her heart rate increase. How could he leave without even saying good-bye? Looking back at the little girl, Amanda fought the tightness in her chest. Fortunately, Isadora hadn't noticed her grandfather's departure. Nor did she realize that, most likely, in several years, she would forget most of her experiences living in Brazil. She might even lose the ability to speak Portuguese. The death of her mother would become a faint memory, something that just happened when she was a child. The imprint of her past would remain deeply embedded but not remembered.

With the departure of the grandfather who'd left only a dirty suitcase behind for the child, Amanda knew that Isadora's future had been changed forever.

She hadn't heard him approach her. But when she felt Alejandro's hand on her back, Amanda startled. Using every ounce of her strength to remain calm and respectful, she lifted her eyes and stared at him.

"I'm sorry," he said.

From the expression on his face, she knew that he meant it. *I'm sorry.* Two simple words that said so much. Oh, she could see that he felt forlorn. He didn't need to use any additional words. But she wasn't certain how to respond. After all, a year ago, she hadn't even known that this world existed. Now, she was fully immersed in it, standing in a foreign country with the man she loved and a stepchild she did not know. To say that she felt shocked by these events would have been putting it mildly.

Of course, she knew that this development had come as a shock to him, too. As she replayed the events from the previous night, she suspected that he might have learned about the unexpected arrival of the old man and five-year-old girl right before the show. Now she understood his request that she perform earlier and leave for the hotel right away, for he knew that he would have much to discuss with the social worker, the grandfather, and probably Geoffrey as well. The presence of a child on the tour and in their lives would affect everyone on both a personal and professional level.

I'm sorry.

These two words said a lot about how Alejandro was certainly feeling, but words could not erase his past mistakes. Amanda wished she could tell him that there was nothing to be sorry about, but the words would not form on her lips. She knew that his mother had raised him to respect God, but he had chosen a different path, one that was as far from godly and righteous as a path could be. The consequences of his actions, actions she chose not to hear discussed but could certainly imagine, could not be ignored.

"You must believe me when I say I had no idea." He looked at Isadora and shook his head. "No idea at all."

His daughter, Amanda thought as she watched him. With his reserved manners and stoic front, he might have been staring at a complete stranger and not his daughter. A daughter from a woman he never really knew, she reminded herself and immediately felt a chill in her heart. She remembered him telling her about this daughter, and how he'd said that he didn't know her but took care of her by sending money. A money transfer into a bank account was all that Isadora had been to him. Now, she sat at the table devouring the pineapple that Amanda had set before her.

Oh, Amanda knew that Alejandro was dealing with this unexpected development in the best manner possible. The way that he fought to maintain his aura of control hinted at the underlying stress that he undoubtedly felt. The situation was not ideal, Amanda thought, her gaze moving from Alejandro back to the little girl. But this was the way that God wanted it to be. There was a reason Alejandro had never learned of the mother's death and a reason he'd only learned about it while in Rio with his wife, in the midst of his tour. There simply was not enough time now to think about what to do or to consider different options. So while only he could take the blame for his past behavior, Amanda also realized that this unexpected situation was not his fault. And regardless of blame or guilt, there was only one outcome: together, they would have to deal with suddenly becoming a family of three.

"What do we do now?" Amanda kept her voice low even though she knew Isadora could not understand her words. She expected that he had a plan. He always had a plan; he was always in complete control. Now, more than ever, she needed to know what he thought and how they were supposed to proceed.

But, for the first time, he didn't offer a plan or advice on what needed to be done. The worn expression on his face as he lifted his hand and rubbed at his jaw told her without words what she did not want to hear: he, too, was at a loss. His lack of an immediate response indicated that, for the first time since she'd known him, he had no proposed solution to a problem.

"Alejandro!"

He backed away from her. "I am thinking, Amanda. I have been thinking all night."

"Ja vell!" she snapped. "That's a lot longer than I have had to process this!" Immediately, she hated the words and her tone. If she could take them back, she would. Not once while growing up had she heard her parents argue. She didn't want to be like the Englischers who spoke in such a disrespectful way to their spouses. "I'm sorry, Alejandro. I'm just . . . taken aback," she said, struggling to find words to express how she felt, "by the suddenness of this."

Alejandro took a deep breath, and after he'd exhaled, acknowledged her words by nodding. "I understand, Amanda."

When she realized that he was struggling to maintain his composure, her sense of compassion as well as her love for him overcame her. She took a step toward him and pulled him into her arms, a gesture he returned by pressing her against him. She could feel his heart pounding beneath his shirt, another indicator of how troubled he truly was. Oh, how she wished she could take away his pain.

Leaning back, she reached up and pressed her hands against his cheeks. As she studied his face, she noticed for the first time how tired he looked. She couldn't fathom what type of restless night he'd had. "We will get through this, Alejandro," she said. "Together, *ja*? And what does this change? Nothing, really." She smiled and glanced at the little girl. "There will just be three of us now."

"Three," he repeated, a hint of disbelief in his voice.

"And you said you wanted to start a family, *ja*?"

"*Ay, Princesa,*" he said, leaning forward to touch his forehead against hers. "No teasing. Not about this." But she could sense that he felt less stressed. Had his biggest fear been accepting the responsibility of a child he had fathered but did not know, or had it been her reaction? Her acceptance of the situation and willingness to work together seemed to calm him, if only a little.

The vibration of his cell phone interrupted them. He released his hold on her, but only after he kissed the top of her head, his lips lingering just long enough for the phone to vibrate a third time. With a sigh, he reached into his pocket and answered it as he withdrew from the room.

Alone with Isadora, Amanda wasn't certain what to do. She hesitated before she pulled out a chair and—slowly, so she didn't startle the little girl—sat down. The girl turned to look at her with those blue eyes, so familiar to Amanda but in a strange face. Isadora glanced over Amanda's shoulder toward the door. In an instant, a look of panic crossed her face and she jumped up. Her little legs ran toward the spot, now occupied by the suitcase, where her grandfather had stood.

Amanda quickly followed.

"*Onde está o meu avô?*" Isadora cried out, her voice sounding small. "Avô?"

From the way Isadora looked around, tears falling from her eyes as she repeated that word, Amanda suspected that she was calling out for her grandfather.

"Shh," Amanda whispered and knelt down. She reached up one hand to press against the door so that Isadora could not open it. She felt her heart breaking as the child began to sob, her shoulders heaving as she realized that Avô was gone and she was to stay with these strangers. Amanda wished she had thought to ask Maria Fernanda about what Isadora had been told. At five years old, surely she could not understand being left behind.

"What's going on?"

Ignoring Alejandro's question as he returned to the room, Amanda reached out with her free hand to try comforting Isadora, but that only caused her to scream and back away into the corner. "Please, Isadora," Amanda tried to comfort her. "Please don't cry." When the crying continued, Amanda felt her own eyes well up with tears. She looked at Alejandro as if he could help. "Say something to her. Please!" she whispered.

He shifted his gaze from Amanda to the child. Amanda could see what he was thinking: without knowing her language, there was little that he could do. He ran his hand through his hair, clearly frustrated and weary after the past twelve hours, which had been so filled with surprises. "Look at your cell phone," he finally said. "Try a translation software."

"A translation software?" Amanda repeated, staring at him in disbelief. Had Alejandro truly suggested that she turn to technology to comfort a terrified child? The noise coming from the child, so distraught and hysterical, tore at her emotions. She wanted to wrap her arms around Isadora, hold her tight, and comfort her with words that meant something to the little girl. Technology could never replace the warmth and reassurance of a maternal embrace. Disappointed with his suggestion, Amanda offered a better solution. "Mayhaps you might want to find a translator, *ja*? A female preferably?"

"*¡Sí, sí!*" He shook his head as he began typing on his phone. "I'm sorry, Amanda. I'm not thinking clearly."

Neither of us are, she wanted to say. Instead, Amanda returned her attention to Isadora, who had pressed her face against the wall as she stood in the corner. Moving closer to her, Amanda continued with a soft "Shh" and reached out her hand to gently rub Isadora's back. She felt the child's skin tremble beneath her hand, and for a moment, she almost withdrew her touch. But she didn't. Whatever Isadora had been through, Amanda knew that love would be the only way to create a bond.

Softly, Amanda began to sing a hymn in Pennsylvania Dutch, something that her mother had done so many years ago. She hoped that the uplifting tune and softness of her voice would calm Isadora. Instead, she cried out for her grandfather.

Alejandro began to pace the floor, his shoulders pushed back as he tried to remain calm. Amanda did not even need to look at him to know that the noise of the child's crying and the tension in the air was breaking down his resolve to remain calm. Focusing on Isadora, Amanda continued singing as she rubbed her back, hoping against hope that it would pacify her.

When someone knocked at the door, Alejandro hurried to answer it. Amanda shifted her weight so that he could open it without knocking into either her or Isadora. A young woman walked into the room, and Alejandro spoke to her in Spanish. And there it begins, Amanda thought. Whatever Alejandro said to the woman would, undoubtedly, be repeated to friends and posted on social media.

How long, she wondered, until the entire world knows about this love child?

The young woman knelt beside Amanda and began to speak to the child in Portuguese. Within minutes, the hysterics turned to soft sobbing and the loud cries to mere whimpers. Between them, the woman and Amanda managed to calm Isadora and even persuaded her to turn around so that they could wipe the tears from her face.

Alejandro spoke softly and slowly in Spanish so that his words could be translated. At one point, Isadora looked at him with her blue eyes, the first time that Amanda had noticed her do so. And then, just as quickly, she turned her gaze to Amanda.

In that moment, as the swollen, tearstained face of the five-year-old girl tilted so that she could get a better look at her, something stirred inside Amanda. It felt like the slow rumble of distant thunder in her heart and grew until she was struck with the realization that she was now responsible for mothering this child. Tears welled in her eyes and she blinked rapidly, hoping that she could stop herself from crying. She forced a smile and, once again, reached out to brush her fingers against Isadora's cheek, touching the outline of a final tear.

Isadora was obedient. That was the first thing Amanda noticed about her. She listened to Alejandro's voice and paid attention to the woman translating what he said into words that she could understand. Those blue eyes did not question the strange man who spoke in a different language. And, to Amanda's surprise, Isadora remained transfixed by her as the woman continued translating. At one point, Amanda held out her hand, palm up, and encouraged Isadora to take it. She did.

"Come with me," Amanda said softly.

The woman beside her translated the words.

"Trust me, Isadora," Amanda continued. "I want to wash your face and then hold you a spell."

The woman hesitated, not quite understanding, before she figured out how to translate.

Quietly, Amanda stood up and walked as slowly as she could toward the bedroom door, holding Isadora's hand. Isadora padded along beside her. Amanda's heart pounded as the two of them left the safety of the large open room with the translator who could help them communicate. But Isadora clutched her hand, and there was nothing more than a sniffle to indicate that, just a few minutes before, she had been crying so hysterically.

In the bathroom, Amanda led Isadora to the sink. She watched as those blue eyes stared at the fancy bathroom with its crystal chandelier hanging over a large bathtub and marble tiles lining the floor and walls. After giving Isadora time to take in the new environment, Amanda placed her hands on the girl's tiny waist, pausing to indicate with a tilt of her head that she intended to lift her to sit on the counter. Without any fight, Isadora allowed her to do just that.

As the silence was broken by the sound of running water, Amanda reached for a white hand cloth. After waiting for the warm water, she wet the cloth and wiped Isadora's cheeks. She tried to maintain eye contact as she silently prayed for help from God. The thought of caring for a child did not overwhelm her. The thought, however, of caring for *this* particular child did.

At home in Lititz, there were always children present at gatherings. Children were a very important part of the Amish lifestyle. Amanda remembered well how her younger brother, Aaron, used to cry and fuss when he was small. Their mother never once lost patience with him. Instead, she would smile and talk softly, comforting him by projecting her own sense of peace. Amanda could only pray that she might imitate her mother's practice and find success in comforting Isadora.

When they returned to the sitting room, Alejandro was standing at the window again. The translator spoke to Isadora. With some reluctance, the girl released Amanda's hand and took the other woman's. They walked over to the kitchen area, giving Alejandro and Amanda some privacy.

"Alejandro?"

He did not move. With his back still turned toward her, he reached out his hand for hers. She crossed the room and took it. For a long moment, they stood there, staring out the window at the city of Rio de Janeiro, no words passing between them.

She rested her head on his shoulder and felt a sense of calm fill her. *What time I am afraid, I will trust in thee.* The verse from Psalms came to her mind as if God spoke to her, his words filling her with the peace that she hoped to project. Amanda knew that, without a doubt, God's plan was unfolding before her eyes. Everything that had previously made little to no sense to Amanda now became clear. He had led her to this very moment, a moment that would undoubtedly change the lives of many people, especially one: Isadora Daniela da Silva.

Amanda knew that Alejandro's decision would have been different under different circumstances. Most likely, he would have dismissed the woman who'd come from the government, and without even setting eyes on Isadora, he would have sent her to live in the orphanage. She would have been destined to live a life of structure and routine, with limited emotional support until the time came for her to be discarded into the streets of Rio de Janeiro.

But turning his back on his own child was the old Alejandro . . . Viper from the past. The new Alejandro knew that he could not just run away from his responsibility. Amanda couldn't help but wonder if that would have been the case if they had not met.

"It's going to be all right," Amanda said. And for the first time since she had awoken that day, she actually meant it.

Chapter Fourteen

Ever since their departure from the hotel, Isadora had clung to Amanda, her eyes widening with fright at everything: from the car that picked them up at the hotel to the crowds at the airport, and then the airplane. Nothing had been easy about that day. In fact, it seemed to get progressively worse with each moment that passed. At several points, Amanda felt that she might break down and cry. She was overwhelmed by the surreal feeling that she was trapped in a bad dream, especially whenever tears welled up in Isadora's eyes.

The photographers had been waiting outside of the hotel overnight. Alejandro tipped Amanda off that they were waiting for Viper's departure. Now the world would know that a child was leaving with them.

"Perhaps Geoffrey should get your publicity people on this?" Amanda had suggested.

But Alejandro merely shook his head. She knew that the shock she felt was just a fraction of what he was experiencing. Her suggestion went ignored as he stood there in the center of the room, perfectly composed in every way except for his worried eyes.

He watched her hold Isadora, who, after an hour of sobbing, had finally fallen asleep in Amanda's arms. Reluctant to release the child, Amanda rocked her back and forth, slowly and gently so that she didn't disturb her. Occasionally, she looked down into the sleeping face of Alejandro's illegitimate child. Her heart broke for Isadora, who by all indications had lived a tough life, if not physically then at least emotionally.

But she wasn't so certain that Alejandro was feeling the same thing.

Despite his strong composure, she saw the truth. He couldn't hide it from her. His eyes gave it away: Alejandro was terrified.

"She's sucking her thumb," Amanda whispered.

Alejandro glanced down at his daughter and then looked away.

"Alejandro?"

He tugged at the sleeve of his shirt and smoothed out the imaginary wrinkles. "We won't make a public statement," he said. "Not yet."

Ah, she thought. So that was what was occupying his mind. "They'll speculate, *ja*? Won't that be worse?"

He looked at her through exhausted eyes. "They'll know." And with that simple explanation, he reached into his pocket for his phone and walked out of the room, his attention on the phone and not on the turmoil unfolding behind him.

Ten minutes later, the knock on the door announced the arrival of security guards. Alejandro returned from the next room and stood before Amanda. "I'll carry her," he said. They hadn't anticipated that the transfer would awaken Isadora, but upon seeing herself being removed from Amanda's arms, she began to squirm and cry. When she reached out her arms in Amanda's direction, her small feet kicking at Alejandro's arms and chest, Amanda couldn't take it anymore.

"Here, let me, then," she said, opening her arms to receive the little girl.

Alejandro did not appear happy with the exchange.

When they had finally calmed Isadora down and managed to make their way to the lobby, the media began snapping photos and asking questions right away. Because of the language barrier, neither Alejandro nor Amanda understood what they were asked, and they walked straight through the crowd to the waiting car. Isadora, however, had understood them, and she wrapped her arms around Amanda's neck, hiding her face from the noisy crowd of people. Even when Amanda tried to get the child into the car, Isadora had refused to release her grip, making it necessary for Amanda to climb in while still holding her.

And then came the scene at the airport.

Amanda hoped that one day she might find humor in the difficulty they'd encountered when they had boarded the private jet. Isadora, her hand clutching Amanda's and her body pressed tightly against her side, had stopped when it came time to ascend the stairs to the airplane. She simply refused to move.

Alejandro was already on board with his phone to his ear, having a teleconference. The security detail stood at the bottom of the stairs, waiting for Amanda and Isadora to follow him, but Isadora refused. She stared at the airplane as if she didn't know what it was. It dawned on Amanda that Isadora had never flown before, so she approached her gently and gestured for her to climb the stairs. But Isadora shook her head and turned, burying her face in Amanda's skirt.

Desperate for help, Amanda looked at the security guard who had accompanied them to the plane. "Please," she said. "Could you explain to her that everything is fine?"

He nodded and, in a gentle voice, translated Amanda's words.

No response.

"Amanda!"

She looked up and saw Alejandro standing in the doorway of the plane, a look of frustration on his face. "I'm trying, Alejandro," she responded, and motioned toward Isadora. "She's afraid."

The muscles in his jaw twitched, and she knew that he was clenching his teeth. Yet he remained composed, probably because he suspected that they were being photographed by paparazzi and fans from the windows in the airport. "Pick her up," he instructed. "We need to get going."

Amanda glanced at Alejandro and sensed his stress. She suspected that it was not just because of the events of the morning, but more due to being behind schedule. Further delays would alter his afternoon appointments. The unpredictable behavior of a small child would not ease the pressure he already felt on tour. Perhaps, she thought, holding Isadora might help alleviate whatever fears the girl had. Gently, she tried to extract herself from Isadora, but the child's grip on her skirt was fierce. Eventually, Amanda sighed and looked at the security guard. "Would you . . . ?" she started to ask, but couldn't finish the sentence.

"*¡Ay, mi madre!*" Alejandro stomped down the stairs and reached down for his daughter. His hands encircled her tiny waist as he lifted her into his arms. The girl began to scream, her fingers still holding Amanda's skirt, unbeknownst to Alejandro. As he climbed the stairs again, Amanda had no choice but to hurry after him, her legs exposed. Isadora reached out to her over Alejandro's shoulder, tears streaming down her face.

The flight attendant took a step back, allowing room for Alejandro to carry the girl into the plane and set her into a seat, the edge of Amanda's skirt still clutched in her fingers. Embarrassed, Amanda quickly slid past Alejandro and took the seat next to Isadora, who immediately crawled into her lap and sobbed against her shoulder.

Alejandro mumbled something in Spanish before sitting down in the seat facing them. He exhaled and rubbed the bridge of his nose, clearly weary from the stress of the day. With the exception of takeoff and landing, Isadora remained on Amanda's lap during the entire flight, while Alejandro simply stared out the window, the lack of conversation between them speaking volumes about his frustration, Amanda's concern, and Isadora's fears.

Fortunately, their arrival at the airport in Salvador was less eventful. Amanda carried Isadora down the stairs, the little girl's arms clutching her neck. Rather than setting Isadora down at the bottom, Amanda continued to hold her as Alejandro led them across the tarmac and toward the airport terminal.

It didn't surprise either of them to find paparazzi already stationed in the main area of the airport, the cameras poised to snap photos of the international sensation known as Viper and his young wife, Amanda. Curiosity regarding the small child in Amanda's arms only increased the value of the photos they were determined to take, despite the security guards pushing them back. Alejandro maintained his composure as he kept his arm around Amanda's waist, his body partially shielding his wife and daughter from the photographers.

No sooner had they managed to escape the crowds by sliding into the waiting car than Alejandro's phone buzzed. Amanda focused on settling Isadora into her seat while Alejandro took the call. More Spanish. When he ended the call, he turned to Amanda and said, "The driver will take the two of you to the hotel."

She didn't think to question him, knowing that abandoning Isadora now would be a terrible idea, one that would do more psychological damage to the child. Still, Amanda knew that the interviewers would question the absence of his wife. And she knew enough about the speed of the Internet and interest of the public to realize that photos of Viper and Amanda with a child would raise speculation. How Alejandro decided to handle those questions was something that she would leave to him. After all, dealing with the public image and the media was part of his world as a professional musician.

He cleared his throat and looked at Amanda. "Carlos arranged for some prospective nannies to be interviewed. He'll ask that you meet those he considers qualified."

Nannies? She frowned at the thought of yet one more change in Isadora's life. The child needed parents, not to be put in the care of yet another strange woman. "I'm not certain I understand, Alejandro," she said slowly. She didn't want to upset him; they were both caught in the same situation. However, the mention of a nanny had unnerved her. "A nanny?"

He lifted one eyebrow as he met her gaze. "*Sí*, Amanda, a nanny to care for the child."

"Your daughter," she whispered as a reminder to him. The rising tension made her feel irritated. She, too, had been blindsided by all this. But she certainly wasn't going to punish a five-year-old child by creating additional emotional stress for her when she had already been through so much. Oh, Amanda knew what getting a nanny meant to Alejandro: the off-loading of his child's care to *another* complete stranger. Even worse, she knew why. "She's *your daughter*, Alejandro, and she has a name. You cannot just transfer your responsibility to a caretaker!"

Again, she saw him clenching his teeth.

"Of that I am well aware." His terse and strained voice hinted at his own rising stress level.

"I am perfectly capable of tending to her," Amanda told him.

"I have no doubt." He pursed his lips and glanced out the window, tapping a finger on the leather seat upon which his hand rested. "Surely you cannot presume that you will be bringing her with you to inter-views and the concerts."

Amanda bit her lower lip. She hadn't thought about how this unexpected addition to their lives would affect the rest of the tour. In truth, she hadn't thought about anything except trying to comfort the child. The entire situation was so unexpected that Amanda hadn't had enough time to sort out her thoughts about anything. What she needed was time alone with Alejandro to understand everything that had transpired since that morning when she learned of Isadora da Silva and signed those adoption papers.

"I presume nothing," she finally said. "But I would think no decisions should be made until you and I have had a chance to talk, *ja*?"

For a moment, he did not respond. Amanda watched him as he stared out the window, his eyes now hidden behind his black sunglasses. She had almost given up on hearing a response from him when he finally said, "Fair enough."

"Just tell me one thing, Alejandro," she said, pressing her hand gently against Isadora's cheek. It was warm and flushed, probably from her earlier temper tantrum and hysterics. "Does she know who you are?"

He tapped his fingers against the leather armrest in the car and stared straight ahead. After a couple minutes, he nodded his head. "*Sí*, Amanda, she knows that I am her father."

In silence, they rode the rest of the way to the hotel, Alejandro deep in thought and Amanda stroking Isadora's hair and praying to God that she would follow his will in dealing with this situation. She fought the urge to pass judgment on her husband and prayed for the strength to do the right thing. The child needed to feel warmth and love from her father and new mother.

But warmth from her father was not something to count on.

When Alejandro dropped them off at the hotel, Amanda lifted her face for him to kiss her. Instead, he reached out and caressed her cheek. "If you need anything, Dali will be over to help you." He glanced down at Isadora, his expression lacking warmth and compassion. "Perhaps some new clothing and shoes, *sí*?"

Amanda felt a moment of irritation. Was that all he could think about? His daughter's appearance?

Amanda realized that he had yet to say Isadora's name or, with the exception of carrying her up the stairs to the airplane, to reach out to her. Her crossness intensified. Had he no sympathy for Isadora's loss, not just today but throughout her entire life? From what little Amanda knew, as a toddler, Isadora had been abandoned by her mother and placed into the care of a sickly grandmother and aging grandfather. Certainly it could not have been easy for the grandfather to tend to his wife and raise a small child.

Amanda had forced herself to swallow her disappointment in his indifference and merely nodded.

That had been over nine hours ago.

And Amanda was exhausted.

She stroked Isadora's hair as the little girl lay beside her on the king-sized bed in the bedroom of their hotel suite. She was curled into a ball with her head tucked under Amanda's arm. Her long black hair, still damp from her evening bath, was splayed out over the pillow. The scent of lavender filled the room, a soft and reassuring smell that emanated from Isadora's skin. Dressed in a new white nightdress, she looked like a sleeping angel, her little hands tucked together and pressed against Amanda's side.

When she heard the suite door open, Amanda glanced at the clock: just after one o'clock in the morning. For a moment, she contemplated waiting for Alejandro to enter the bedroom. But one glance down at Isadora told her that there was no need to remain fearful that the child might awaken. Carefully, she extracted herself from the little girl and slid off the side of the bed. Fortunately, Isadora gave no indication that her slumber had been disturbed, so Amanda quietly tiptoed to the door of the bedroom and opened it so that she could slip through.

Alejandro's tie was undone and hung around the unbuttoned collar of his white shirt. He stood by the wet bar, a drink in his hand, so engrossed in his thoughts that he didn't notice her approach him.

"Alejandro?"

He lifted an eyebrow and shifted his gaze in her direction, peering at her over the rim of his glass.

"Are you all right, then? How was the show?"

At first, he didn't respond. He took a long, slow drink, and then he appeared to savor the taste, swirling the liquid around in his mouth as he set the glass down on the bar. *"¡Buenísimo!"*

"Are you drunk?"

He exhaled and made a face that spoke of irritation. "No, Amanda. That was sarcasm."

"Ah." She walked closer and, standing behind him, put her arms around his waist, her cheek pressed against his back. "And the interviews? Did they go just as well, then?"

"Even better."

She gave him a little squeeze. "I'm so sorry, Alejandro."

"Me, too." Twisting around, he faced her while still letting her hold on to him. After a long moment, he lifted his hand and brushed back a stray piece of her hair. Giving her a soft smile, he asked, "What is it that you always say about God's plans for us?"

She nodded. "He has plans for us, Alejandro. We just don't always know what they are."

"No," he said slowly. "That we do not."

"Tell me about the interviews?"

When he shook his head, Amanda understood that he didn't want to talk about them. She could only imagine the barrage of questions he had faced, and she pictured him doing the best that he could to dance through the answers with a smile on his lips. But she couldn't help wondering what answers he had given to the questions regarding the little girl.

"Tell me about the concert."

He sighed and cleared his throat. "It was fine, Princesa. But there was a lot of fussing about the fact that you weren't there. On social media feeds people speculated that you would show up at the end." He tried to smile at her, but there was sadness in his eyes. He hated disappointing his fans more than anything, and this showed on his face. "At the end of the show, they would not leave. They chanted your name."

"They did what?" She had heard him properly but almost didn't believe him. "Oh, Alejandro!"

"*Sí*, it was not good." He reached behind him for his drink. "I tried to not linger at the arena and told Geoffrey that I had to get back here. He didn't argue."

Amanda nodded, understanding what he meant: Geoffrey knew the entire story, and unlike Alejandro's former manager would have done, he wasn't going to attempt to leverage Isadora's appearance in their lives to create a surge of media interest.

"Have you had a break today?" He stood there, swirling his drink in the glass, the ice cubes hitting against the sides and making a soft tinkling sound. When she shook her head, he sighed. "*Ay, Princesa,*" he said and lifted the glass to his lips for another sip. "What a life, eh?"

"Tell me about what happened yesterday, Alejandro. Please." All day she had been waiting. She needed to know the story, to better equip herself with the necessary tools to deal with what lay ahead.

"What happened yesterday?" He gave a rough laugh, the glass still lingering near his lips. "My world was turned upside down, that's what."

Arguing that both of their worlds had been affected would serve no purpose, so Amanda remained silent. Self-loathing, she thought, is an emotion that doesn't recognize the needs or emotions of other people.

"Geoffrey heard from the courts when we landed in Rio," Alejandro admitted, finally crossing the room to sit in one of the chairs. He yanked at his tie so that it slid away from his collar and then flung it on the ground. "He met with them, realized the validity of the complaint, and spoke with me. What else is there to tell, Amanda?" He shut his eyes and rubbed them with his thumb and finger. "I had to make a decision, *sí*? And I couldn't just throw her into an institution." He took in a deep breath and exhaled. "Maybe the old Viper could have. Just quietly tucked her away."

"Oh, Alejandro!" She caught her breath at his admission.

"It's true." He flung his head back and rested it against the top of the chair. "I contemplated it, Amanda. For a minute, maybe less. Without you . . ."

He left the rest unsaid, and she knew what he wanted to say—or, rather, deny having wanted to say. She hurried to his side and knelt beside him, her hand on his knee as she peered at him. "*Nee,* I can't believe that. You would have felt something, Alejandro."

"You think so, eh?" He laughed again. "I'm not so sure."

"The mother?" she prodded, hoping to shift the focus back on to what had actually transpired the previous day and off his feelings of guilt. "What happened to her, then?"

He stared down at her, sitting by his knee, and reached out to brush a stray hair from her cheek. "You are so beautiful," he said softly. "I do not deserve you, Amanda."

"Alejandro! Don't say such things."

"Ah yes, the mother . . ." He shrugged his shoulders. "I found out she had the baby when she first contacted my lawyers. I don't know how she got their information. She wasn't as much of a *pobrecita* as I thought, *sí?*" He laughed, but in a mirthless way.

Amanda suddenly understood that the word *pobrecita* was an insult. She clenched her teeth, flashing back to the night the women had called her the same name.

"I settled out of court and arranged to send her a modest amount of money each month," he continued. "She didn't come from money, and it must have felt like a windfall. I never heard from her again."

"Never?" The word sounded so cold and heartless. It wasn't a word that she would associate with Alejandro. While he couldn't claim that he'd walked away from this child who'd been born from what she presumed was a very short relationship—if there'd been any relationship at all!—Amanda felt a wave of nausea at the thought that he had never even inquired about his child.

He didn't seem disturbed by the unspoken disappointment in that single word she'd repeated. "Yesterday was the first time that I learned she'd died, this woman," he said.

Again, Amanda found herself wondering at the way he talked about Isadora's mother. How could he have shared something so intimate and beautiful with a woman he did not know or care about? For the first time, Amanda wondered about the things she did not know about Alejandro's past. She had told him that she didn't care and that she didn't want to know about them. But was that true? Not knowing felt almost as bad as she imagined knowing might feel.

"She deserted the family, leaving her baby with her parents, and took the money to return to Rio."

"Oh?"

"And then she died."

"From drugs?"

He nodded. "The woman from the government, Maria Fernanda, said she overdosed on drugs. The family didn't want to tell me, in case I stopped paying the money."

Amanda gasped. "That's awful!"

He reached down and tugged at one of the hairpins that held together her bun. "That's life, Amanda."

"Not my life!"

He slipped another pin out of her bun and then another, until her hair cascaded down her back and over her shoulder. "In my world, it's life."

She shook her head. "*Nee*, Alejandro. I don't believe that. Not anymore. Maybe when you were in Cuba, or maybe when you were starting out. But you don't walk away from family responsibility. That is not the man that you are. Not now." She took the pins from him and held them in her hand as he twisted her hair around his fingers. "Maybe not ever. You just didn't know any better."

The mood for talking seemed over as he twisted her hair into a long, ropelike strand. It wrapped around his hand, and he tugged, just enough, to catch her attention. "I know better now, Princesa," he said, his deep voice catching in his throat. "And I need to show you that I am a changed man."

She didn't need to translate the hidden meaning beneath his words. His insecurities called out to her, loud and clear, through his calm external composure. Like a child who'd been caught doing something wrong, Alejandro needed to be reassured that she forgave him and loved him. She knew all too well that he needed her to comfort him, to hold him, and to let him sleep with his head on her shoulder as she gently stroked his arm. He needed to know that she loved him, no matter what his past sins.

"Come," she said as she stood up and took his hand. "You need some sleep, Alejandro." She helped him stand, and then she walked backward, leading him toward the bedroom where Isadora slept. "Shh," she whispered as she opened the door and guided him inside, one finger pressed to her lips. "Don't wake Isadora."

Chapter Fifteen

In the privacy of her dressing room, Amanda leaned against the cold cinder-block wall, her eyes shut as she waited to be called onto the stage. Her arms were crossed over her chest, her fingers digging into her arms. She took deep breaths, trying to calm her rapidly beating heart. But all she could remember was the folded piece of white paper and the look on her husband's face.

Outside the door, she could hear a commotion. A loud bang, something falling, and then laughter.

Feeling irritated at the noise, Amanda glanced at the door and was confronted by the large ceiling-to-floor mirror on the back of it. Her reflection only caused her more angst, for she wore her least favorite of the dresses that Jeremy had ordered made for her. Red. It wasn't a color that she would ever have chosen to wear, especially decorated with the sparkling sequins on it that caught the light, sending prisms of color in different directions as she moved. The dress was also low-cut. Too low-cut. What was it with men wanting women's clothing to display the top half of their breasts? With a disgusted sigh, she rolled her eyes and looked away from the mirror.

Her dark mood had appeared earlier, during the Meet and Greet. She had quickly learned that the South American women who paid to meet Viper—and there was a long line of them—were definitely not like the women who came to see him in the United States.

No, the South American women were striking and worldly. They were not young girls or older women. Each one was more beautiful than the next and appeared to have one, and only one, thing on her mind: catching Viper's attention. They clung to him, their chests brushing against him as they lingered in his arms, their bodies saying more than any words could, as they waited for the photographer to take their photos. They whispered in Viper's ear and made him laugh. And when they walked away, they looked at Amanda with disdain.

The Argentinean women were the most aggressive of them all.

Amanda tried to remain expressionless as she stood off to the side of the room. But her blood was boiling, especially when she saw Alejandro rub his hand up a woman's arm, his blue eyes flashing as he drank in her beauty. When the woman slipped a folded piece of paper into his hand, not only did he open the note and read it, he slipped it into his pocket and leaned forward to kiss her cheek.

That had been the last straw. Amanda left the Meet and Greet.

Without waiting for anyone to accompany her, she found her way back to the dressing room and locked the door. Her emotions welled up, and she tried to calm herself. Even though she told herself that the man who'd slipped that piece of paper into his pocket was not Alejandro but Viper, she was hurt and angry. These were two feelings that she was not used to experiencing. And she didn't like them.

"Amanda!"

The two loud, sharp knocks on the door did not give her the impression that Alejandro was happy. She had hoped he wouldn't have noticed her departure from the Meet and Greet. But as always, Alejandro knew exactly what was going on at all times. He was the master of seeing everything without appearing to be watching.

And he was not pleased.

She took a deep breath, knowing that no matter how much she wished to pretend she wasn't in the room and to ignore his knocks, she must open the door. Harboring anger and resentment would only make her feel worse. Reluctantly, she pushed off from the wall and walked toward the door.

When she opened it, Alejandro stood with one hand pressed against the doorframe, waiting expectantly with a scowl on his face. "What was that, Amanda?" He didn't wait for her to answer as he pushed his way into the room. "How many times have I told you not to leave without security?"

"A lot."

Hearing her words, he spun around to face her. His angry expression and flashing eyes told her that her insolence did not sit well with him. Yet she didn't want to apologize for it. After the past week and all of the changes that had been thrown at her, she felt that she was owed at least that much.

"We are not in the United States, Amanda. I hire security for a reason. Can we at least get that established, *sí*?"

She didn't respond.

"And you left the Meet and Greet why?"

Oh, she thought. Let me count the reasons.

Ever since the concerts in Rio, the situation had deteriorated quickly. With the concerts over and four days without commitments, Alejandro had kept his promise to enjoy a few days of respite in Argentina. He had rented a private country estate outside of the sea town, Pinamar. What he had neglected to mention was that he and Amanda and Isadora would not be alone. The house was constantly swarmed by different people from Viper's tour as well as Enrique Lopez and his entourage, who'd joined up with the Viper Tour since he, too, was singing in South America.

Amanda had quickly learned that she was not partial to Enrique Lopez.

Unlike Alejandro, Enrique surrounded himself with beautiful women who wore skimpy bathing suits that caused Amanda's cheeks to flush red with embarrassment. Their golden skin glistened in the sun as they strutted around the pool wearing high heels that distorted the shape of their feet. Yet they appeared completely at ease and enjoyed themselves, relishing the attention they received from both Enrique's and Viper's entourage.

Feeling ashamed for those women, Amanda steered clear of the pool area. Instead, for most of the time she was supposed to be relaxing with her husband, Amanda was left to tend to Isadora. The worse part was that Alejandro hardly seemed to notice. He slept late into the day and went to bed early in the morning. Amanda, however, had found herself at the mercy of a five-year-old who cried whenever Amanda tried to leave her with anyone else.

The four days of relaxation had turned into four days of partying, only Amanda never received an invitation. The only time she saw Alejandro was during the evening meal. He didn't appear to notice that she was anything less than her usual, bubbly self. Between arising early with Isadora and lying in bed listening to the noise from the outside courtyard around the pool, Amanda got little sleep and felt increasingly less tolerant toward the scene of debauchery that had crept into what should have been their quiet family vacation.

Yes, she thought wryly as she watched her husband pace around the dressing room with a scowl on his face. *I could make quite the list for you, Alejandro.*

But she said none of this. Instead, she sighed and lifted her hands as if defeated. "I'm tired, Alejandro."

He stopped pacing and looked at her. "Tired? *You're* tired?"

From the tone of his voice, she knew that he wasn't asking her a question but, rather, was mocking her response.

"*Ay*, Dios," he mumbled, lifting a hand to his head. "If you want to know what tired is, Amanda, step into my shoes!"

Immediately, she felt the all-too-familiar wave of guilt. The truth was that Alejandro was working hard, too hard, and she knew it. And with the unexpected situation in Rio adding even more stress to his life, he was clearly at the breaking point. In all fairness, she realized that he was dealing with more than most people could take. But Alejandro wasn't like most people. He thrived on working long hours and pushing himself to the limit. If anything, he challenged himself to continually expand the range of opportunities available to him. His drive to succeed was relentless.

For the first time, Amanda began to wonder if she could keep up with him.

"I'm practically killing myself, Amanda," he snapped. "This is the tour that will push my success to a new level. Geoffrey received a call today; I've been asked to host the international music awards show next year. Do you know what that means? For a Cuban American to be asked to host such an event?"

"That's wonderful," she managed to say.

"But 'wonderful' doesn't happen without the success of this tour, Amanda! And this tour cannot be successful if I am distracted from my duties because I am worrying about your safety!" He began to pace again, his hand back on his forehead. After he turned around, she watched as he clenched his fists and cried out in wordless frustration, sounding like an angry animal trapped in a cage. He spun around and looked at her, his expression still tense, but his tone softening.

"Tell me about the Meet and Greet," he said. "Why did you leave?"

She hesitated to tell him. If he was angry over her leaving without security and even more irritated because she didn't have the energy to keep up, she certainly didn't want to mention her feelings about all of the beautiful women who threw themselves at him, from Colombia to Brazil and now in Argentina. After everything that happened over the holiday season with the tabloids and Maria, Amanda didn't want to even suggest the idea of jealousy. To do so would be to admit the unthinkable: that she had lost her faith not only in Alejandro but also in her own ability to maintain his interest.

"Amanda," he coaxed.

"What do you want me to say?"

"The truth."

She met his gaze and knew that she had to confess. Otherwise, the guilt and the doubt would become a barrier that would break their relationship. "I cannot compete with all of these women," she finally admitted. "Frankly, I'm not certain I would want to. They have no morals, and they certainly don't care that you are married."

She waited, and when her words were met with nothing but silence, she took a deep breath and covered her eyes with her hand. "And I'm starting to worry that there's something wrong with me."

"Wrong with you?"

She nodded, still covering her eyes. "*Ja*, Alejandro, wrong with me." Uncertain how to tell him, she sighed and dropped her hands to her sides. "I . . . I'm not pregnant, and it's worrying me."

Of course, the timing was wrong now anyway, she told herself. With everything in such a state of chaos, Amanda realized how wise God truly was. He didn't want her getting pregnant, not yet. He always had a plan, and she needed to rely on him to determine if she should bear children. After all, he had given her Isadora. Amanda tried to take comfort in that. Even thinking about this hurt her heart. She just had to keep reminding herself that she was not to question God's plans for her life.

Alejandro nodded and glanced at the clock on her counter. "We will discuss this in more detail tonight. For now, I need to go onstage, Amanda. We are already late."

She didn't know how to take that last comment, and she wondered if he blamed her for running behind schedule. If she had expected a look of empathy from him, a word or two that expressed his understanding of her emotional state, she would have been mistaken. Instead, he spun on his heels and walked out the door and down the hallway, ignoring anyone who passed by, even if they paused to ask him a question.

When Alejandro was in a bad mood, people knew to steer clear of him.

"What was that about?" Stedman asked as he walked around the corner. His dark eyes followed Alejandro as he stormed away from the dressing room.

She didn't answer and averted her eyes.

"Lovers' quarrel," he said with a nonchalant shrug of his shoulders. "They always happen midway through tours."

Amanda took a deep breath and swallowed the remark that she wanted to make to Stedman.

"Let's get you warmed up," he said, reaching for her hand. "Shake off the negative energy, shall we?"

He led her to the large waiting area underneath the back part of Estadio River Plate. The open-air stadium was larger than most of the other venues on the South American tour. According to a very happy Geoffrey, it was sold out. Both nights. Given its capacity to seat almost fifty-eight thousand people, Amanda concluded that the Buenos Aires concerts were the highlight of the tour. As the energy of the audience coursed through the air and charged even the atmosphere backstage, Amanda found herself relaxing more in Stedman's company.

Recorded music filtered through the backstage area, and Amanda realized that Viper had not yet started his performance. She glanced around, wondering where he was. When he'd left her dressing room, he had commented that he was already late. Yet she didn't see him anywhere.

"Let's go, Amanda," Stedman said, drawing her attention back to him. Immediately, he began moving his body in time to the music. Salsa. Forgetting about Alejandro, Amanda took Stedman's cue and focused on the dance, her hips swaying to the music. Slowly, she felt the tension leaving her, the music and the movement of their bodies filling her with a slow trickle of happiness.

"Now mambo, 'Manda," he instructed, quickly switching his movements and laughing at her when she stumbled.

"Stedman!" She fell against him, her cheek pressing against his shoulder. "Don't do that!" But she was laughing. Despite his fierce dedication to the art of dance and his focus on perfection when dancing, Amanda had seen a different side of him on this tour. She'd found that his attention to detail, when looked at from a different perspective, could be seen not necessarily as a negative but as a drive to perfect his art.

"You have to be ready for the beat to change," he said, setting her back onto her feet. "Try it again."

She glanced down at his feet, and he clicked his tongue, shaking his head as he lifted her chin with his finger.

"No cheating," he said. Pointing to his eyes, he stared at her. "Keep your attention here, not on the feet."

She tried, but, after she kicked his foot, she started laughing and leaned against him. "I can't!"

The Miami Stedman returned, a frown on his face. "Can't or won't?"

"I'm just not good at those fast dances."

He shook his head. "You are a beautiful dancer, Amanda," he said. He reached out his hand, and when she took it, he spun her under his arm and pulled her close to him so that her back pressed against his chest. "And you should do more of it."

She laughed again as she stepped out of his arms. "I don't foresee that happening," she said lightly and took a step backward. When she bumped into someone, she stumbled once more. This time, she felt a hand slip around her waist and spin her just enough so that she found herself in Alejandro's arms. He wasn't staring at her but over her shoulder at Stedman, a steely and cold look in his blue eyes. "Oh!" she gasped. "You aren't on yet?"

"Go sit on the chair there." He pointed toward the back of the stage, near where she needed to climb up to the platform in another hour. "Dali will be right over."

"She's with Isadora," Amanda said.

"Just go, Amanda!" The way his voice boomed at her, and the way he shouted without looking at her, caused Amanda to question him no further. She bit her lower lip and hurried in the direction he had pointed. But when she paused to glance over her shoulder, she saw him holding Stedman by the shirt, their faces just inches apart. Whatever Alejandro was saying, Stedman wasn't arguing, and when Alejandro released him, Stedman merely backed away and disappeared.

Alejandro brushed off the front of his shirt and took a deep breath, not caring that more than a few people had witnessed the scene.

"Come on, Amanda," someone said, taking hold of her elbow. She turned to see who it was. Geoffrey. He guided her to the back of the stage and motioned for someone to get her some water while she sat down. "Just stay here for now," he instructed as he handed the water bottle to her.

The lights dimmed as the live music started. She didn't need to see what was happening to know that when Alejandro appeared, the spotlight would blast onto his figure as he stood in the center of the stage, his hands crossed in front of his waist and his head bent down.

By now, she knew the entire performance. Rather than watch, Amanda leaned her head back and shut her eyes, trying to figure out where the day had gone wrong.

"Hey."

Geoffrey was watching her.

"Everyone has an off day," he said, and she wondered if he had read her mind.

"Off week," she sighed but said no more. She crossed her legs and stared off to the side, not wanting to talk to anyone who might have witnessed the scene between Alejandro and Stedman.

And that was when something caught her eye.

Normally, she didn't pay any attention to magazines, especially the tabloids. But this one's title was in English, and given that they had been in South America for three weeks, she hadn't seen much English as of late. She leaned over and picked up the tabloid from the top of a black crate. Obviously, someone from the Viper team had been reading it and tossed it aside. Now it was in her hands, and she couldn't help taking in the image on the folded back page.

It was her.

Only it wasn't truthfully her.

"What is this?" She wasn't speaking to anyone around her, merely thinking aloud. When Geoffrey glanced up, Amanda turned her back to him so that he couldn't see what she was staring at. With her mouth hanging open and her breath rising and falling rapidly, she tried to comprehend what she was seeing.

The page showed two images of her. Inside the larger image there was a small inset photo of her carrying Isadora on her hip in the gardens of the rented Buenos Aires house. The clarity of the photo indicated that whoever had taken the picture had done so from nearby, not by using a long telephoto lens. While that concerned Amanda, it was the larger photo that triggered in her a more emotionally charged response. It was a photo of her with Alejandro. He wore a suit, and she wore the same outfit she had been wearing during the pretour photo shoot, the one at which she had felt tired and irritated about the busy schedule that Dali had shown her.

Amanda remembered that day well. She had wanted to go home after seeing the schedule, a schedule that had not included any time for her to spend with Alejandro. Within a few minutes, he had walked into the room and headed directly toward her. In hindsight, she realized that there had not been any fuss from the others regarding Alejandro's unexpected appearance. In fact, she had seemed to be the only one amazed to see him there.

The photograph showed Alejandro, his forehead pressed against hers as he held her by the waist. Her eyes were shut, and the expression on her face did not show her true emotions. Although she had felt joy when he appeared and surprised her that day, in the photo she looked crestfallen. Whether due to the timing of the photograph or the angle at which the photographer had taken it, the photo seemed to portray something very different from what had occurred.

Even worse, the background of the photo was not the white backdrop that had been behind her at the photo shoot. No, this photograph made it look as though they were standing in her dressing room backstage at the Rio arena.

The headline read "Viper Breaks News of Secret Love Child to Amanda."

What her eyes saw, her brain could not comprehend. How was it possible that such a photograph existed, for certainly such a thing had never happened?

Stunned, she began to read the article. With each sentence, her heart began to pound faster and a rage built up, for everything that she read was a lie. How was it possible that a magazine could print an article that was made up one hundred percent of fabricated deceptions?

"Geoffrey!"

She spun around just as he looked at her, and then jumped to her feet.

"What is this about?" she demanded, holding out the magazine for him to take.

His eyes barely skimmed the article, and she knew at once that it was not the first time he had seen it. And if Geoffrey had already read it, certainly Alejandro had, too.

"It's a tabloid, Amanda," he said calmly as he handed it back to her.

"It's all lies," she retorted. "Alejandro didn't tell me about it in the dressing room. Besides, who would have access to this information?" She glanced down at the magazine. "To this photo?" she asked, specifically pointing to the one of her holding Isadora. "And the larger photo is fake! Why, this whole article is fake!" In disgust, she flung the magazine to the ground. "Why the magazines find any of this fascinating is beyond me," she mumbled. She couldn't sit anymore; her nerves made her jumpy and her thoughts were like flames licking away at her self-control. Standing up, she smoothed down the front of the dress, the strands of red crystal beads and sequins glistening under the lights behind the set.

"They just print what people buy, Amanda."

She did not like arguing with anyone; it made her feel empty inside as if part of her deflated and the emptiness filled her with negative energy. "Well, I'd like to know where they got that photo! It wasn't even taken here, Geoffrey. It was taken in Miami and . . . fixed or whatever it is they do to photos!" She began to pace, trying to shake off feelings of hurt and anger. "How would they have gotten that photo?"

He remained silent and glanced down at his watch.

"And that other photo? The one of Isadora and me? Who took that?" She stopped pacing and put her hand on her hip, facing Geoffrey. "That was at the country house, Geoffrey. The media didn't have access to the property. I want to know who took it! And why they sold it to these horrible magazine people!"

"Amanda . . ."

"They must be held accountable for spreading stolen photos and hateful lies."

He reached to grab her arm, and she abruptly stopped walking. "Don't pursue that, Amanda. You won't like what you find out."

"What are you saying?" She pulled her arm free and shifted away from him. "What is that supposed to mean?"

Just then, a stagehand ran over to Geoffrey and interrupted them, frustrating her further. Geoffrey gave a slight shake of his head. "I'll be right there," he said to the man. Turning back to Amanda, he apologized for having to leave her. "Security will help you get up to the top of the stairs, Amanda. I have to go attend to a different matter. Forgive me." Without waiting for a response, he hurried in the direction in which the other man had disappeared.

As the concert continued and the audience responded to Viper, Amanda returned to the chair and sat in it, her eyes roaming over the partially open magazine on the floor. Curiosity got the best of her, and she leaned over to retrieve it again. She took more time to read the article and even flipped the page. Then she caught her breath. There was a photo of Alejandro surrounded by beautiful women; in it, he was looking at one of them with deep emotion in his eyes. The article implied that he had known about the child and that he had married Amanda so that she would tend to the illegitimate daughter while he partied with socialites in Rio.

Have faith, she told herself and shut her eyes to pray:

Dear Lord, please give me your strength to withhold judgment and provide understanding to my husband during these trying days. Please place your hand upon his head and bless my husband with your love and wisdom. We are both in need of your guidance to navigate these unknown waters. Amen.

Almost thirty minutes passed before she heard the music that indicated she should start preparing for her ascent up the stairs. Only one security guard came over to assist her, and since he was Argentinean and spoke no English, Amanda didn't try to engage him in a conversation.

Shake it off, she told herself. Her anger and frustration needed to be compartmentalized, pushed away while she was in front of the fans. After all, they had paid to see a music concert, not to witness a meltdown by Viper's wife.

Taking deep breaths, she waited until the song ended and the lights flashed before the arena was covered in darkness. Only then did she slip through the curtain and stand at the top of the stairs, waiting to descend.

The bright spotlights moved to highlight where she stood, and Amanda lifted her arm in the air in response to the wild cheers from the audience. This time, however, she didn't exaggerate her steps nor did she try to promote playfulness with Alejandro when he met her at the bottom of the staircase.

He took her hand in his and squeezed it, just enough to catch her attention. Their eyes met, and she saw a reflection of herself in him. She realized that they both felt frustrations and irritations: Alejandro with the unexpected way Isadora had popped into their lives, unintentionally separating them. Amanda knew that her eyes told a similar story, though in her case, she wanted to be home, getting Isadora situated. Even though the little girl was genetically another woman's child, Amanda felt a strong attachment to her. She hesitated to call it love, although she suspected that she was indeed falling in love with Isadora.

Alejandro must have been surprised to see his own dark, moody emotions echoing back at him. Certainly, it was not something that he was used to seeing.

He lifted his arm and started dancing with her. But this time, the movements that were usually playful and light were danced with much more force and drama. At first Amanda stumbled, not expecting the deviation in tempo to his steps. But it only took her a few seconds to catch on that it was his emotions that were driving the dance, instead of the opposite. She followed his lead and when she turned from him, she walked down the stage, waiting for him to come after her and pull her back into his arms. He spun her around, and she looked away when she'd finished the turn, instead of gazing up at him. The next time he spun her, he took the initiative to push her away. Angrily, she stomped her foot and glared at him. When he came toward her for the end of the song, she placed her hand on his chest and pushed him away before removing herself from the stage.

The crowd applauded and cheered, thinking the angry dance moves were choreographed.

Despite the crowd chanting her name, Amanda stormed to her dressing room and locked the door behind her. Only when she was ensured of privacy did she release her emotions, allowing herself to cry, her hands covering her face. If she had suspected it before, she now knew that she was not strong enough to carry both of them. Living under the microscope of public scrutiny and media approval was harder than she had imagined. She wished she was secure enough in who she was as a person and as his wife to adapt to Alejandro's constant emotional needs, which conflicted so sharply with the melodramatic desires of Viper.

Chapter Sixteen

"We need to talk," Amanda said.

Five o'clock in the morning. That was the time on the clock when the door to their hotel suite opened and Alejandro entered. He was dressed in white slacks and a black shirt, both wrinkled and reeking of alcohol and smoke. His sunglasses dangled from the front of his shirt and his hair hung over the front of his forehead, casting a shadow over the left side of his face.

Amanda stood in the center of the room, dressed in a navy linen skirt and a light, airy, white-and-navy pin-striped shirt. She was ready for the day—and for the confrontation with Alejandro that she knew lay ahead of her.

When he hadn't shown up at the hotel after the show, she'd known that he wouldn't return until close to dawn. With Enrique Lopez staying in the same hotel and making guest appearances during Viper's concerts, Amanda hadn't needed to ask where Alejandro had been. She spent the better part of three hours trying to sleep, but couldn't do so. She tossed and turned, her mind reeling with thoughts about what she knew needed to be done. Finally, at four o'clock, she had arisen from the bed and showered, then had gotten dressed and prepared herself for what she knew would be a long morning.

Now, Alejandro stood before her, his eyes bloodshot from lack of sleep as well as too much time spent with Enrique. *"Ay,* Amanda,*"* he said. "You know I was out with Enrique."

She nodded. *"Ja, ja* I do."

He started to unbutton his shirt. "Then can we discuss this later? I need to sleep a few hours." He walked toward the bedroom door.

"I'm leaving," she said as he walked past her. She turned and stared at his back. Her heart felt as if it were racing and her skin tingled, each nerve on fire. "Did you hear me, Alejandro? I'm leaving Buenos Aires."

"Excuse me?" His hand was on the doorknob, but he didn't turn it. He remained in that position, waiting for her to repeat herself. When she didn't, he dropped his hand and turned to face her. "What is this about? My firing Stedman?"

Her breath caught in her throat. "You fired Stedman?" This news only made matters worse. After all of those weeks fighting with Stedman during their practices in Miami, she had actually begun to appreciate him and his quirky ways. "What on earth for, Alejandro?"

"You were right about him," he said casually.

"Oh, Alejandro," she said, her voice sad. She knew what had happened and blamed only herself. Hadn't Dali tried to warn her? "Tell me that you didn't fire him because of me. That's not fair."

He thrust his hands into his front pockets and lifted his chin in defiance. "He was becoming too close to one of my investments," he replied.

"'Investments'?"

Remaining defiant, he stood there and stared at her without speaking.

"I've told you before that I'm not one of your possessions, Alejandro. And we have a responsibility to that little girl sleeping in the other room. This is not a life for her, and it's certainly putting a strain on us." She wanted him to say something . . . anything. But he remained silent. "I'm going home, Alejandro, with Isadora."

The cold expression on his face frightened her. He looked at her, emotionless, as if he'd barely heard a word that she said.

"Don't you want to say something, Alejandro?"

"You are not leaving."

She nodded. "Yes, yes I am. And I'm taking Isadora. She needs stability and routine." Pursing her lips, she lifted her hand and placed it over her own chest. "I need stability and routine. Maybe Europe will be different, but I do not care for these South American women."

He lifted his eyebrow at her words.

"I need to go home. This pace that you keep . . ." She shook her head. "It's insane, Alejandro, how you just keep going and going. I can't keep up with you. I'm turning into a person that I don't care for. I want to go home and get away from these people with their cameras and lies and skimpy outfits and immoral desires."

She thought she saw the corner of his mouth twitch, which added to her irritation.

"Besides," she added, "my brand image is not this world. I'm your Amish farm girl, *ja*? Your Amish farm girl cannot adapt to this new world of touring with Viper." She glanced at the open magazine on the table. She had brought it back to the hotel with her and left it open for him to see. "My leaving will just feed the beast, anyway. The media will love to write more trash and lies about what my leaving signifies, and, of course, the fans will devour that news and Viper's image will soar."

"Amanda . . ."

She pointed to the magazine. "How did they get that photo, Alejandro? Both photos!"

He held his hands up in front of himself as if to ward off an attack. "We had to break the story, Amanda."

"We?" Her eyes traveled to the magazine. She felt drawn toward it and crossed the room, her fingers reaching out to touch the inset box with the photo of her carrying Isadora. Tracing the image, she stared at it as she realized what Alejandro had just admitted to her. "You authorized someone to release this photo?"

"It was a controlled burn, Amanda."

Controlled burn? She knew what that meant, but she didn't really feel as if their private lives needed to be aired in such a manner.

"Controlled, *ja*?" She pointed to the other photo. "What's the story behind this one, then? I remember when this photo was taken. And I can assure you that it was not last weekend and not in my dressing room."

"*Ay,* Amanda," he said. "It's just a story."

"It's a lie."

He shrugged, clearly not concerned with the article. "A story to feed the curious."

She shoved the magazine away from her. "Our lives are more than just a story, Alejandro. We need to live them in reality, not in their fantasy."

He ran his fingers through his hair and mumbled something in Spanish.

"Don't do that."

"Amanda, this is our lives," he snapped back at her. "Our reality *is* their fantasy. When are you going to realize that?"

She didn't agree. Living her life for the media, allowing them to take such liberties with her privacy, and now learning that her own husband had permitted his inner circle to leak private photos? "And this is how you want to raise your daughter?"

"I didn't *want* to raise my daughter!" he shouted. "If I had, don't you think I would have been involved from the beginning?"

She gasped at his words. Covering her mouth with her hand, she took a step backward. "You don't mean that," she whispered.

"*Ay,* Amanda." He shook his head. "You know what I mean."

But she didn't. Did he feel nothing for Isadora, despite having accepted responsibility for her? Didn't he see how special she was? His words stung, and she knew in that moment that she had made the right decision.

"I don't know what you mean anymore," she said.

"You are just upset, Amanda," he finally said, breaking the silence. "Emotional over not being pregnant."

"That's not it, Alejandro," she said, although she wasn't certain that there wasn't a glimmer of truth to what he said. She did feel emotional and worried about, once again, not being pregnant. That was not the root of the problem, however.

"You told me earlier, no?" He stared at her with the same void expression. "But you have your *hija* now. You should be happy, not upset."

The coldness with which he spoke hurt more than his words did. Did he actually presume that Isadora's presence eliminated her desire to have a child with him? While she was learning to love Isadora, that didn't mean that she no longer wanted a baby.

"You don't mean that," she said slowly, trying to swallow her pain. "Children are not interchangeable. And loving one does not mean you cannot love another."

He sighed and ran his fingers through his hair. "*Sí, sí*, I know. That's not what I meant. Look, it's late . . ."

"Or early," she said, interrupting him.

"I need to sleep, Amanda. Come to bed," he said. "You will feel better later."

But she knew that she wouldn't. "What I do know is that taking her home is the right thing to do. She needs to be surrounded by love, not resentment."

He stepped toward her and reached out to touch her arm. "Don't be like that, Princesa."

But she moved away from him.

"If she has you," he said, "she has love."

Amanda felt a tightness in her throat. She told herself that he didn't know what he was saying, that his words were not expressing what he truly wanted to communicate. For if he did, he would not insinuate that her love was enough for Isadora. After all, wasn't it Alejandro who had announced to the world on New Year's Eve that he wanted to start a family? Wasn't it Alejandro who had declared his love for her over and over again? What would happen if they did have a baby? Would he be capable of loving the child or would he turn his back on it, too? Was he only capable of loving one person with all of his heart?

"Finish the tour, Alejandro," she said softly. "Focus on the tour now, and we can focus on us afterward."

His eyes narrowed. "You are not leaving," he said one more time.

"Don't do this to me," she said, tears beginning to well up. "Please, Alejandro. I just can't . . ."

"Neither can I." He closed the space between them. "I need you with me. You know that." Despite her protests, he wrapped his arms around her. "I can't do this without knowing you are here . . . with me."

She lost the fight to hold back her tears. A sob escaped her throat, and she clung to him. She just felt so tired. Her body ached from the reality of Alejandro's travel schedule, and her heart ached from the fantasy of Viper's busy life. Now that there was also the added responsibility of Isadora, she had a choice to make. She had wondered before about the reasons behind God's plans for her, but she at least knew what he wanted her to do now. Everything in the past year . . . everything since Aaron's death . . . had led up to this moment. A responsibility and a choice.

"Just two weeks," she whispered, her tears staining his shirt. "We've survived much worse, Alejandro."

Later that afternoon, after the car had arrived to take her and Isadora to the airport, Alejandro stood in the center of the suite and watched her walk toward the door.

They had slept for five hours, wrapped in each other's arms, his gentle breath warming her shoulder and neck. When she'd awakened at ten o'clock, she had carefully slipped from underneath his arm and hurried to the bathroom to change. She hadn't wanted to wake him; he needed more sleep. With it being Saturday, he had fewer obligations before the show, and her and Isadora's flight wasn't scheduled to leave until four in the afternoon.

When he had awoken and she was not beside him in bed but sitting with Isadora and reading an English picture book, Alejandro's dark mood had returned. No amount of consolation on Amanda's part would appease him.

Now that it was the time for her to depart, he simply stood there, his jaw tense and his eyes sharp. His displeasure with her decision was apparent. He had said little since he had awakened, and she could see that he was trying to maintain his temper.

Two security guards had already taken her luggage downstairs, and another stood outside of the door to escort them down to the lobby. With the tickets having already been booked and the car outside waiting, there was nothing more for anyone to do but say good-bye.

Without being asked, Dali reached out toward Isadora. During the time they'd spent at the country estate outside of Pinamar, Isadora had come to trust that going somewhere with Dali did not mean that Amanda would not return. So when Dali said, "Come, Isadora," and took the little girl's hand, she willingly followed her. Together, they walked out the door. "We'll meet you in the car," Dali said over her shoulder before the door shut.

Amanda waited until she heard the click of the door handle. She needed this moment with Alejandro, a chance for one final explanation. The last thing she wanted was for them to part on such terms. Despite everything—the photos, the women, his feelings about his daughter— she loved him. And she knew that their wounds would eventually heal. They just needed time to adapt as a family. Even more important: he needed time to get to know his daughter outside of this fantasy world, immersing himself in the only reality he needed: his family.

But he simply stood there, his legs slightly apart and his hands held before his waist. It was a cold stance, one that he usually used at the beginning of his sets. But he wasn't singing and she wasn't his fan, at least not today.

"You could at least say good-bye to us," she finally said.

He lifted an eyebrow and stared at her, his dark hair casting a shadow across his forehead.

"It's two weeks, Alejandro."

Oh, she knew that she sounded stronger than she felt. Being separated again wasn't something she wanted to happen. However, she didn't see any other solution to the situation. He still had tour dates in Chile, Paraguay, and Uruguay ahead, followed by the last two concerts in Mexico. While Alejandro claimed that he needed her by his side, she knew that Isadora needed her more. He would be busy almost every day with appointments, recordings, and concerts. Dragging Isadora to all of these different events was not responsible, she reminded herself as she stood there, waiting for him to say something. Anything.

But he remained mute.

"You asked me to take on this responsibility," Amanda said calmly.

"I wanted to hire a nanny."

Amanda took a deep breath. Arguing with him frustrated her. "A five-year-old needs a home, a place to run and play. She needs a place where she can learn routine and responsibility." She walked toward Alejandro and placed her hand over his chest, pressing it against his heart. "She needs to trust love, Alejandro. That's a lesson we all must learn. I trust our love enough to do this. You need to trust our love enough to let me."

He covered her hand with his and pulled her into a warm embrace. He held her tightly, his one hand still over hers, and rocked her back and forth. "I love you, Amanda," he whispered. "And I will learn to love Isadora. I trust that you will show me how."

With her cheek pressed against his shoulder, she inhaled, trying to capture the scent of his cologne and the feeling of his warm flesh beneath his shirt. Two weeks would go quickly, she told herself. And when he returned, they'd have time to regroup and come together as a united front to tend to his daughter's needs.

As she extracted herself from his embrace, she reached up and gently kissed his cheek. This pain of leaving was part of the responsibility that she had agreed to take on when Isadora was signed over to their care. Time would soothe that wound, and just as Alejandro said, she would teach him how to love his daughter. If she had already taught him the depth of his love, he now needed to learn its breadth. A lesson she felt certain he *could* learn, but one that she knew he was not likely capable of learning while he was on the road.

Chapter Seventeen

On Sunday afternoon, Alecia arrived at the condominium, her arms heavily laden with wrapped packages stuffed into bags. As she hugged both Amanda and the child in the foyer of the condo, she wept, appearing overwhelmed to be meeting her granddaughter for the first time.

Amanda waited until the jubilance and tears ended before she escorted Alecia into the sitting room off to the side of the kitchen. It felt odd being in Alejandro's house without him. She chastised herself. Our house, she corrected herself. Still, as she sat on the white sofa by the sliding doors that led to the tiered patio and pool, Amanda did not feel that she was at home.

"*Ay,* Amanda." Alecia's eyes drank in the sight of the five-year-old who sat quietly by Amanda's side, a stuffed white unicorn under her arm. "*¡Qué linda!* She's just beautiful, *sí?*"

Like any proud Amish-raised parent, Amanda fought the urge to nod her head and agree. Vanity was a sin; she did not want to teach it to Isadora. Still, she couldn't help but feel that Alecia was right. "She has been blessed by God, that is for sure and certain. But the life she has lived . . ." Amanda shook her head. "And to think that she's so sweet of nature!"

"And Alejandro arranged this?"

Amanda didn't miss the tone of disbelief in her mother-in-law's voice. "He had a choice, Alecia," she admitted slowly. "He chose the right option."

"*¡Gracias a* Dios!" Alecia clutched her hands together and lifted them to the ceiling.

During their visit, Amanda kept the attention on Isadora and away from any discussion about the tour or Alejandro. She didn't mention their last twenty-four hours together or their argument at the arena and then later at the hotel. She didn't tell Alecia that he hadn't even accompanied them to the airport, instead sending them off in a car and barely saying good-bye. Amanda knew that this detachment was a self-defense mechanism intended to keep his emotions in check. Despite her frustration with him, she had sent a text message to him the moment that the plane landed in Miami. By the time the driver arrived at the condominium, it was well after two in the morning.

It had taken her almost an hour to get Isadora settled into one of the guest rooms. Although quite tired, Isadora didn't want to sleep. Amanda had softly sung songs to the child and had rubbed her back until, finally, sheer exhaustion took over and sleep claimed her. Only then did Amanda leave the room, shutting the door before quietly walking down the hallway toward the master bedroom. She, too, quickly succumbed to her fatigue and fell asleep without having heard back from Alejandro.

When she awoke in the morning and checked her phone, he still had not answered. He was angry, she told herself, mad that she had left. He simply did not understand how painful it was for her to watch those women flinging themselves at him and to see how he responded—regardless of his " brand image"! Added to that was the stress of the travel and the work of caring for Isadora. No, she consoled herself, she'd had no choice but to leave, for the direction in which their relationship had been headed would have led to a much sadder outcome had she stayed.

"*Gracias,* Amanda. " Five hours after her arrival, Alecia finally stood at the door, ready to leave. "When I met you, you told me that my son saved you." She rested her hands on Amanda's shoulders and gently rubbed her upper arms. "Truly, *hija*, it is you who saved him."

Amanda lowered her head and blushed.

"All of his life, Alejandro was one who walked away from responsibility. But it was always his choice to do so, and no one could convince him to do otherwise," Alecia said. "Now, for once, he has corrected a wrong, putting his responsibility before his career. You, Amanda, made this possible. You are a blessing to Alejandro." She paused. "And to me."

Long after Alecia left, Amanda thought about her words. While Isadora slept in her own room—a room already littered with more toys than Amanda had acquired in her lifetime, thanks to Alecia's packages—Amanda curled up in the comfy armchair in the bedroom. She gazed out the window and stared at the moon's reflection in the pool. She knew by the time display on her phone that Alejandro was already at the Meet and Greet before the Sunday concert. She also knew that he had still not replied to her text.

By Wednesday, having received no word from Alejandro, Amanda had made up her mind to return to Lancaster. What difference did it make, she had told herself, if she waited in Miami or at her parents' farm? With the weekend approaching, Amanda knew that Alejandro would be busy traveling to three different countries in just as many days. There was no point in sitting around Miami, waiting, when she could take Isadora to her parents' farm, where spring was dawning and her family would welcome them with open arms.

"Look, Isadora!"

Amanda pointed out the window as the hired car drove by a field with horses in it.

"*¡Cavalos!*" There was a look of genuine joy on Isadora's face.

"That's right. Horses," Amanda corrected her, saying the word slowly. "Can you say that, Izzie?" she asked, using the nickname she had given her stepdaughter. "Horses?"

After more coaxing, Isadora finally said the word in English.

It was their game, a private game that Isadora loved. She was an eager learner, and she shone under the attention that Amanda showered on her. And as much as Isadora was a willing and appreciative learner, Amanda was equally enthusiastic about her progress.

"Horses," Isadora repeated, turning to press her nose against the window, her small hands resting on the car door. "Horses."

Laughing, Amanda reached over and hugged Isadora. "Very *gut!*"

During their time in Miami, Isadora had picked up new words every day. Now, however, she seemed to understand something even more important: she was learning a new language. Amanda's constant approval seemed to inspire Isadora even more. She was like a sponge, soaking up the words while feeding off Amanda's praise. The more she learned, the more she wanted to learn. Every day she tried to expand her vocabulary by exploring the world around her, pointing to things and asking Amanda to teach her the words.

Now, as the car approached the farm, Amanda watched as Isadora morphed from a tiny caterpillar into a beautiful butterfly. As the scenery became more and more rural, Isadora became more and more excited. If Amanda had suspected that the tall buildings and urban environment of Miami had gotten in the way of Isadora adapting, now she knew that she had been correct. What the little girl needed was one-on-one time away from the city and back in the country: the place that was, undoubtedly, most familiar to her after the time she'd spent living with her grandparents.

Amanda's sister and mother were waiting for them when the car pulled into the driveway. Amanda had told them what time they would be arriving in a letter posted just four days before. So seeing them waiting on the front porch, sitting on the bench with their coats wrapped tight around their bodies, made her feel that she was being welcomed back. She could hardly wait to share with them all that she had experienced over the past few weeks. Even more important, she couldn't wait for Isadora to finally have the home life and nurturing environment she needed.

"Mamm! Anna!" Amanda called out to them as soon as she opened the car door. She stepped outside and reached down for Isadora's hand. She wasn't surprised when the little girl lunged into her arms and hid her face. Strangers, Amanda realized, felt dangerous to Isadora. The presence of strangers had often meant that she was leaving the people who she knew and cared for. "Don't worry, Izzie," she said softly, rubbing Isadora's back. She hugged her tight and kissed her warm cheek. "This is home. Home." She said the word slowly and made certain to give her an extra squeeze.

Carrying Isadora in her arms, Amanda walked as fast as she could toward the house. She felt different from the way she had the last time she had visited the farm with Alejandro. Perhaps his presence had made her feel different then, more removed from her family. Or perhaps it was the joy of introducing Isadora to her old life, one that was more comfortable and familiar to both of them, that made her feel different now. Regardless, she felt happy and giddy, excited to share all that she could with the little girl she held in her arms.

"It's so *gut* to see you!" Amanda gushed, shifting Isadora in her arms before she hugged her mother and sister. "It's been such a long few weeks."

When she said that to them, Amanda experienced a moment of disbelief. Weeks? It felt like months to her. Still, any stress that she felt disappeared when she took a step backward and turned so that they could see Isadora.

"Oh help!" Lizzie said, smiling as she saw Isadora peek up at her with her sky-blue eyes. "What an angel!"

Anna reached out and touched Isadora's arm. "Oh, Amanda. What an amazing gift God has given you."

Amanda felt her cheeks flush as she clung to Isadora. "Izzie," she said, enunciating each word. "My mother and sister." Then, hoping that she was translating the words correctly, she said it even more slowly in Spanish, hoping that it was close enough to Portuguese. *"Mi madre y mi hermana."*

"She doesn't know any English, then?" Lizzie shook her head and clicked her tongue.

"Nee, nor Spanish." Amanda caught the disapproving look that flashed in her mother's eyes and knew exactly what her mother was thinking. She had always been too critical of the demands Alejandro made on Amanda's life. Tending to a small child that didn't speak English was just added to the list. "Mamm . . ."

"I didn't say a word, Amanda," Lizzie said defensively, holding up her hand as if warding off an attack.

"You thought it."

"I'll pray for forgiveness later." Lizzie returned her attention to Isadora. "Now bring that precious child inside, Amanda. I have cookies made. Cookies will fill any child's stomach, as well as warm her heart."

Anna held the door open for Amanda as her eyes took in the small girl. "We want to hear everything, Amanda. What interesting stories you must have to tell." As Amanda walked through the doorway, Anna lifted her hand and gently rubbed Isadora's arm. "Especially your stories about Isadora!"

Once inside, Amanda paused and shut her eyes, inhaling the smell of freshly baked sugar cookies and bread. It smelled like home, and she smiled. "Mamm! That's just a *wunderbar gut* smell!"

"Don't you bake in this Miami of yours?"

The disapproving tone in her mother's voice was not lost on Amanda. How could she explain the ways that life in Miami differed from Lititz? Even more important, why should she have to? Choosing to ignore her mother's question, Amanda set Isadora down on the bench at the table and immediately sat next to her. "I'm sure we can get quite a bit of baking done during our stay," Amanda said, watching as Isadora looked around the room, her eyes filled with curiosity. "Izzie will love that, for sure and certain."

"And how long exactly will that be, Amanda?" Her mother placed a plate of sugar cookies on the table and, with a gentle motion, pushed it toward the little girl. "Go on now," Lizzie urged softly.

While Isadora reached out for a cookie and happily began munching on it, Amanda shared the details of how Alejandro's daughter had come into her care. Both Lizzie and Anna listened intently, interrupting her only to shake their heads and comment about how the little girl had gone through so much already during her short life.

"I can hardly imagine a sadder story!" Anna exclaimed when Amanda had finished.

Lizzie remained silent.

Protectively, Amanda leaned over and put her arm around Isadora's shoulders, sliding her body down the bench so that she was tucked tight against the girl's side. "None of this is her fault," Amanda said defensively. "She just needs time to adapt, that's all."

Anna smiled, reaching over to hand Isadora a second cookie. "*Ja vell*, it's *gut* you brought her home, then. Some *wunderbar* food, chores, and God fixes everything!" When Isadora took the offering, Anna's smile broadened. Her eyes never left the little girl's face. "Oh, I think she'll do right *gut* here, Schwester."

Right away, Amanda felt at home. Yes, she definitely felt different returning home without Alejandro. But the difference, she realized, was the changes in her. Despite the fact that only a month had lapsed since her last visit, her experiences in South America had expanded her perspective on the world. And she realized that the outside world wasn't anything like Lititz, Pennsylvania, a place for which she had suddenly gained a finer appreciation.

Despite their questions, however, she found herself reluctant to share her observations with her family. How could she explain the endless days and nights? The women? The tension that had so unexpectedly developed between Alejandro and her? Even if she knew how to explain it, she wasn't sure if she'd want to, for fear that her observations might ruin their peaceful view of the world.

The one thing, however, that she found herself happy to discuss was the child sitting next to her on the bench. She'd neglected to mention the history between the deceased mother and Alejandro, choosing to relate only that they had taken on a child who'd been headed for an orphanage. And she certainly avoided any discussion about why she had left her husband thousands of miles away on a different continent.

While Anna might have accepted her explanation of the child's origins, Amanda noticed her mother's eyes suspiciously studying Isadora's face.

Rather than dwelling on the truth of the child's background, Amanda focused more on the time she had spent with Isadora. She didn't need to say how much she loved her new daughter; that much was apparent just from the way she talked.

"Oh, and Alecia!" Amanda laughed. "She might be one tough cookie, but she sure did melt when she met Isadora."

Perhaps because she had heard her name, Isadora looked up, first at Amanda and then across the table at Lizzie and Anna. Her blue eyes seemed to absorb the warmth of the kitchen. When she smiled at Anna, Amanda felt as if her heart would burst. Amanda could tell that Isadora felt more comfortable at the farm, even without being able to communicate it through words. The change in the environment was exactly what they both needed.

"You were in Miami, then?" Lizzie asked.

Amanda nodded. "*Sí* . . . I mean *ja!*" She laughed at the slip of her tongue. "We arrived last Sunday."

Lizzie raised an eyebrow. "On a Sunday? You flew?"

"The plane left Saturday afternoon, Mamm. It's a nine-hour flight."

"Ah."

Amanda continued with her story. "Alecia came over that afternoon. Alone." She smiled at the memory. "This woman never travels alone. But she took one look at Isadora and I didn't think she would ever leave!"

"Oh help!" Anna covered her mouth as she tittered; she knew about Alecia from Amanda's letters.

"*Ja vell*, she has no other grandchildren," Lizzie said, shaking her head. "That she knows of, I reckon."

Amanda's mouth opened, and she pulled Isadora closer as if sheltering her from words that the child couldn't understand. "That's unkind, Mamm."

Lizzie pressed her lips together and turned her back to the table, redirecting her attention to another task and removing herself from the conversation.

The truth, however, was that Amanda was guilty of wondering that same thing. While she had never questioned Alejandro's past, she knew that the one-night stand he had shared with Isadora's mother was not the only one he'd had. Certainly his past was tainted by other women, and not just the ones that had been occasionally hinted at in the tabloids. Whenever Amanda met new women, there would always be a lingering question in the back of her mind as to how well her husband had known them in the past.

Hadn't it been at the awards dinner in Los Angeles when she felt the angry glare of women watching her? Another young woman, Celinda Ruiz, girlfriend of Justin Bell, had told Amanda to ignore the talk and to accept that if she was going to be with Alejandro, gossip and glares would be part of the deal. Of course, Celinda had also informed Amanda that her relationship with Justin was rock solid, despite the tabloids stating otherwise. Only two weeks ago, however, Amanda learned that the power couple had broken up. The rumor about their relationship, the very one that Celinda claimed had been planted by the paparazzi and gossip reporters, turned out to have had more than a grain of truth to it.

"Tell us all about South America, Amanda," Anna said, diverting her attention from the unpleasant to something more upbeat and cheerful.

"*Vell,*" Amanda started, eager for the change in conversation. "I'm not quite sure where to begin . . ."

On Saturday morning, Amanda awoke extra early and wrapped her arm around Isadora, who was snuggled beside her in the bed. Outside the window, the sun began to warm the sky. Amanda watched as the darkness of dawn faded away, as if God were painting a canvas, dragging a brush with lighter paint over the horizon in a long, slow, sweeping motion. The birds began to chatter, their morning songs chipper. Winter had been long and hard, full of snowfall and twenty-degree temperatures, and spring was eager to arrive. The mornings started earlier now, and the chill was less apparent.

Amanda pulled the little girl tight against her chest and kissed the top of her head, smiling when the child sighed in her sleep. It was a sound of contentment. Amanda knew that Isadora was beginning to relax. She suspected that Izzie had never had so much attention paid to her before. It didn't sound like her mother's lifestyle would have allowed for a baby to be given much more than the basics for survival. And by the time Isadora had found her way to her grandparents' care, her grandmother had most likely already been ill while her grandfather tended to her needs.

Praise, laughter, and lots of attention quickly won over Isadora's trust. Even now, as she slept in the bed beside Amanda, Isadora appeared to sleep peacefully, as if she knew that when she awoke, Amanda would be there to take care of her. Something as simple as stability was all that the child needed in order to blossom, and Amanda suspected that a week in Lancaster would bring balance back not just to Isadora's life but also to hers.

It had taken her a while to admit that. She had wanted to be there for Alejandro, to support him like a wife should. But after what she had experienced in South America, Amanda knew that his life on the road was not the place for a wife. She had felt lost and unstable, unsure of herself in the arena and insecure with herself when dealing with his fans. She had lost her equilibrium and couldn't think of a place better than Lancaster to go to, to focus on regaining balance in her life. The peace and quiet of the farm would heal Isadora's old wounds while giving Amanda a chance to recover from the weariness of life on the road.

And she needed to recover.

She heard her cell phone vibrate, the side of the device hitting the edge of the oil lantern on her nightstand. As quietly as she could, she reached over to grab it, both to silence it so that Isadora would not awaken and also because she knew that only one person would be texting her, especially at this hour: Alejandro.

```
Why are you in Lancaster?
V.
```

Amanda frowned. After almost a week, *that* was his first communication with her?

Pulling her other arm out from beneath Isadora, Amanda repositioned herself so that she could sit with her back against the headboard. She stared at the cell phone, wondering how to respond. A quick glance at the time display on the phone made her frown. It was not quite six thirty in the morning. If she recalled correctly, he had performed in Chile on Friday, which meant that he had then caught a late-night flight to Montevideo, Uruguay. Chances were likely that, upon landing in Uruguay, he had not gone directly to the hotel. There was an hour time difference between Lancaster and Montevideo, and she doubted Alejandro had just awoken out of a sound, restful sleep. Besides, he had no reason to get up at seven thirty in the morning.

She could picture him standing in his hotel room, probably looking out the window at the lights of the city. He would be wearing his usual outfit: black slacks and a black shirt. Surely, he had gone out after the concert and spent the early-morning hours dancing and laughing and drinking. The adrenaline rush he felt after performing was not something that he could just push down and ignore. Without her there to tame him, Alejandro was not about to sit in his hotel room, a remote control in one hand and a mug of decaf coffee in the other. She hadn't expected him to, but she was struck by the reality that she was just beginning her day while his was just ending.

At least he had texted, she told herself. Finally.

```
When are you coming home? We miss you.
<3
```

Not even a minute passed before the phone vibrated again, this time with his name flashing across her screen. Amanda scrambled out of the bed and hurried to the bedroom door so that she could answer his call without fear of disturbing Isadora.

In the quiet of the small kitchen, she answered the phone.

"Alejandro!" She smiled as she leaned against the counter, the phone pressed against her ear.

"Amanda, what is this I hear?" His voice sounded far away, but no amount of distance could hide his irritation. "Why are you not in Miami?"

"I . . . I was lonely and thought to come home."

"Miami is your home," he said curtly. After a brief pause, he added, "Our home."

She cringed at her mistake. "Of course, I know that, but . . ."

"And I learn this news from Geoffrey?"

From the tone of his voice, Amanda felt his hurt. She took a deep breath, wondering why it would bother him that she had taken Isadora to Lancaster. He still had a week of touring and partying ahead of him, if that was what he wanted to do when they were apart. The memory of Argentina awakened, and she quickly counted to five while biting her tongue. Instead of responding to his anger with irritation of her own, she directed the conversation elsewhere.

"Alejandro, I've missed hearing your voice."

He remained silent, just for a few drawn-out seconds. She waited, hoping that he might calm down. After the way they had parted in Argentina, the last thing she wanted was to stoke his ire any further.

"The tabloids are claiming that you left me." His words sounded flat, void of any emotion. "Do you know what that is like? To read that in the paper?"

"Oh, Alejandro!" She could hear the pain in his voice. Learning that the tabloids had pounced on her departure did not shock her. His reaction, however, did. He knew the truth, so she wasn't quite certain why it had bothered him to read the exaggerated rumors printed in the tabloids. After all, he was the one who always reminded her about brand image and giving the public the story. When she had been upset by the leaked photos and lie-filled stories, his level of empathy hadn't extended beyond a mere shrug.

"Meet me in Mexico," he said.

She felt as if her heart had stopped. "I can't just do that, Alejandro."
"I need you with me."

She shut her eyes and bit her lower lip. *Please, please don't do this to me,* she prayed. "We've only just arrived here, Alejandro. And once you get to Mexico, you'll be busy with interviews. I can't uproot Isadora again."

There was a slight pause on the other end of the phone. She guessed that he was pacing the floor, his free hand in his front trouser pocket. "How is she, anyway?"

"Oh, she's just blossoming, Alejandro!" Amanda couldn't help but gush over the way that Isadora's spirits had improved in the one week since they'd left South America. "And she loves the farm. She was ever so curious about watching Jonas and Harvey milking the cows last night." She laughed. "Of course she's still sleeping now, not offering to help with the morning chores so early."

He didn't respond and, for the briefest of moments, she wondered if the line had disconnected. When she heard the noise of running water, she knew that he was still there.

"Isadora is a beautiful little girl," Amanda said, hoping that he might respond with something positive to say about his daughter. "You will love her very much, Alejandro, when you are finished touring and can see for yourself what she is like."

He didn't respond right away, and she gave him a few seconds to collect his thoughts and find his words. "*Sí, Amanda,*" he said. His voice was soft and missing the edge it had in it when she first answered the phone. "With you loving her, she is sure to blossom. That is your gift, no? Making others blossom." Another pause. "Think about Mexico, *Princesa.*"

Long after they had hung up, Amanda stared at the phone in her hand. He was pressuring her to make a choice, a choice she didn't feel prepared to make. She couldn't uproot Isadora and take her to

Mexico City. And to make matters worse, Amanda didn't want to go. She needed time to heal and time to bond.

There was no other choice to make. She simply could not leave Lancaster.

Chapter Eighteen

Outside the window, a small flock of sparrows clustered at the hanging bird feeder. The birds fluttered back and forth, coming and going, appearing to work in sync with one another. After one snatched a few seeds, it flew away, leaving room for another bird to come and feed. The sun shone against the backdrop of the blue sky, a few scattered clouds lingering far above the fields. In the distance, Jonas stood on the manure spreader, driving the mules across the field as the machine fertilized the ground.

"Red bird!" Isadora shouted.

A male cardinal landed on the feeder and plucked at the seeds with his orange beak. His vibrant red feathers contrasted sharply with the plain brown of the sparrows and gave Isadora something to cheer over.

"Cardinal," Amanda said. "That's a cardinal. Can you say 'cardinal'?"

Obediently, Isadora repeated the word, and Amanda hugged her when she said it correctly on the first try. The entire family had quickly learned that praise and hugs worked magic on Isadora. The more they gave her, the harder she tried.

The sound of the door opening interrupted their excitement, and Isadora, still wrapped in Amanda's arms, turned toward Lizzie and Anna as they walked into the small kitchen of the *grossdaadihaus*. Isadora squiggled free from Amanda's embrace and, smiling, ran to them, her arms spread wide as she grabbed Anna's legs.

"Oh help!" Anna laughed, stumbling backward. "What a greeting!"

Standing up, Amanda pointed to the bird feeder. "What is that, Izzie? Can you tell Mammi Lizzie and Anna? What is the name of the bird?"

"Cardinal."

The past week had seemed to fly by. Each day, Amanda saw the world in a fresh way, through the eyes of Isadora. The child's energy was as endless as her willingness to learn. She loved to laugh and run, always looking over her shoulder to make certain that Amanda was nearby. In the afternoons, Isadora insisted on helping in the dairy barn. Both Jonas and Harvey found small jobs for her to do, such as sweeping up stray straw or dumping grain into the horses, and mules' buckets.

Harvey had taken a special interest in Isadora. Amanda often caught him carrying Isadora in his arms, walking her down the aisle of the barn so that she could rub a small hand across the back of every single cow. And with everyone's support, Isadora's English improved. While she was not yet able to string words together into sentences, she could certainly get her point across.

"Harvey's fixing to go to the store, Amanda." Lizzie had set down a large bucket of milk on the counter. She had announced earlier in the morning that she wanted to make cheese before the planting season began. Once the fields and gardens began to grow, there wouldn't be as much free time to devote to cheese making, and her inventory was depleted.

"Oh *ja*?" Amanda brightened at the news. "Do you think he'd take me along, then?" She wanted to stop at the fabric store to purchase some material to make more dresses for Isadora.

Lizzie nodded. "He already said that was fine."

Anna excused herself to lie down for half an hour, and Amanda hurried to fetch her wallet. Since her return to Lancaster, she hadn't left the farm. After three weeks of the constant hustle and bustle of travel that went with touring, a week of calm had been more than welcome. But after days of worrying, Amanda was grateful for the opportunity to take a small trip.

During the past week, she hadn't heard from Alejandro again. She blamed his silence on his schedule and on inadequate cell phone signals in South America. Each night when she prayed, she made certain to ask God to bless her husband and help him see his way home. She pretended not to fret during the day and merely smiled when Anna inquired after him. But she did worry, especially since, after curiosity got the best of her and she checked her smartphone to see what the social media was saying, she learned that Enrique Lopez was still traveling with him. In the past, Enrique and Alejandro had been a bad mix. Now that Amanda wasn't by Alejandro's side, she couldn't help overthinking what the two men were doing after the shows.

"You ready then, Amanda?" Harvey greeted her at the car and opened the back door for Isadora. He reached inside and buckled her into a child's car seat.

"You bought a car seat for Izzie?" Amanda asked. She shouldn't have been surprised. Harvey's affection for the little girl was more than apparent. Still, his thoughtfulness about Isadora's safety touched Amanda.

"State law," he said. "Can't drive little ones around without them."

Isadora stared down at Harvey's big hands as he checked the car seat straps. When they proved sound, he smiled at her. She rewarded him with a big grin and reached out to pull at one of his suspenders.

"Well, I reckon that's fair," he said to her. "I checked your strap; you check mine."

Amanda laughed and reached over the back of the front seat to wiggle her fingers at Isadora. "I just can't believe how well she is adapting."

"These little ones are stronger than we give them credit for, that's for sure and certain." Harvey shut the car door and walked around to the driver's side.

The roads were empty, except for the occasional horse and buggy that passed them going in the opposite direction. Isadora squealed with delight each time she saw one. Amanda would ask her the horse's color, and Isadora would shout out the answer. When they passed a herd of ponies standing by a fence along the road, Isadora cried out and started speaking rapidly in Portuguese.

"English, Izzie," Amanda said softly. Sometimes she needed to remind Isadora, and Isadora—frustrated that she couldn't speak the language or make herself understood—would cry. This time, however, Isadora found her words.

"Pony! White pony!"

Astonished, Amanda looked at Harvey. "Did you hear that?"

"I sure did."

Turning around, Amanda applauded Isadora's effort. "Well done, Izzie. That was a white pony!"

"Mayhaps we can stop there on the ride back," Harvey offered as he put on his blinker and pulled into the parking lot of the fabric store.

Isadora needed no translation for that. She began to squiggle in the car seat, trying to look out the window in the direction of the pony. "Now? Now?" she insisted in a loud, animated voice.

"Shopping first, Izzie. Always work before play, *ja*?" Amanda said gently, trying to calm down the overexcited five-year-old.

Harvey carried Isadora to the store, ignoring Amanda's offer to do so. She hadn't insisted, as she knew full well that Harvey doted on the child. As she walked beside Harvey, Amanda pointed out pretty purple pansies planted along the walkway and the yellow daffodils blooming in ceramic planters by the door. She said different words and waited for Isadora to repeat them, cheering whenever she did so properly.

A long time had passed since Amanda had been in a fabric store, and she lingered longer than she'd expected to. The possibilities were as endless as the fabrics. When she was growing up, she'd worn only three dresses: two for work and play, one for Sunday. As she grew older and taller, she rarely had anything new added to her limited wardrobe, since most of her dresses were replaced with hand-me-downs from Anna. But the year she had turned sixteen, Mamm had let her pick out a fabric for a brand-new dress. The possibilities weren't as varied for her at that time, five years ago. She was allowed to pick from only certain colors. But Amanda hadn't cared. She knew what she wanted, and that was blue: her favorite color, one that most young Amish girls did not wear since it was the color of the dress they would wear on their wedding day.

Now, for Isadora's dress, Amanda could choose any fabric. She was no longer limited to just the colors and the plain style favored by the Amish. She could make floral dresses or use striped fabrics. She finally settled on the more subtle prints, knowing that once Alejandro returned to the United States and sent for them, the handmade dresses would most likely be left behind, replaced by fancy dresses gifted to her by designers who hoped that the papers would print photos of Isadora wearing their fashion designs. Dali had warned her about that after their return to Miami.

The thought of Dali gave Amanda a moment of pause.

Despite her stoic nature and her determination never to cross the line between the professional and the personal, Dali had turned out to be a pillar of strength for Amanda. Her advice was always given with the best of intentions and, as Amanda had learned too late, was usually spot-on. During the nine-hour flight back to Miami, while Isadora slept on Amanda's lap, Dali had given one more piece of advice to her.

"Your strength is given to you from God, Amanda," she had said. "He will not lead you anywhere that you should not be."

Dali had kept silent for the remainder of the trip, but her words had stuck with Amanda as she'd stared out the dark window and prayed to God for help. Now, almost two weeks after she had left Alejandro in South America, she didn't know what to think. Like clockwork, Amanda texted him each morning and each evening. She knew that he was now in Central America and would return to Miami by midweek. The only problem was, she didn't know when he would come to fetch her.

"You ready, Amanda?" Harvey asked as she walked out the front door of the fabric store.

"*Ja*, I think I am."

As they walked down the wooden steps, Amanda held on to the handrail. Harvey waited on the sidewalk at the bottom of the stairs, turning around just as the heel of her shoe caught on a rusty nail that stuck out of a board. She stumbled and missed the next step. Harvey shifted Isadora in his arms and reached out to steady Amanda.

"Oh help," she muttered.

"Careful there, Amanda." Harvey helped her to stand up and then glanced over her shoulder, eyeing the nail suspiciously. "It's a wonder that didn't get fixed before now."

"Must've been from all the snow, you think?"

He nodded. "Take her, and I'll fix it."

Amanda took Isadora from his arms and watched Harvey, feeling a mild curiosity about what he would do. With his big, heavy work boots, he stomped on the nail until it lay flat against the board. "Well, that was easy!" he said.

"You're a good man, Harvey Alderfer," Amanda said. And she meant it. How many other people had passed by that nail, not one of them thinking to fix it before someone, possibly an elderly woman leaving the fabric store, lost her footing and fell? All it had taken was a good heart and a strong boot to fix the problem.

As they walked back to the car, it dawned on Amanda that the same could be said about Alejandro. Although he didn't like her leaving, her heart was in the right place, and she took comfort in the fact that he knew that. His requests for her to join him in Mexico were hard for her to turn down. But like Harvey, she needed to use a firm boot when putting down her foot. And as Dali had said, God would not lead her to a place where he did not want her to be. And as much as Amanda struggled with being apart from Alejandro, she knew that being together on the European tour would be even harder. The schedule was grueling, even worse there than in South America, with concerts every Tuesday and Thursday night as well as on weekend evenings. There were even dates that overlapped, meaning that Viper and his crew would travel to multiple countries in one day, doing an afternoon performance in one country and an evening performance in another.

No, she told herself. The impossible logistics of touring with a family would have to be faced when he returned from South America. Isadora could not go on the European tour, and without her stepdaughter, Amanda would not go either. The rusty nail needed to be flattened, she felt, in order to preserve Isadora's progress—as well as her own sanity. It was a decision she had made on her own. The hard part would be helping Alejandro to see the wisdom of it.

Chapter Nineteen

The message on her voice mail sounded urgent: Dali demanded to know when Amanda was returning to Miami. Amanda knew it wasn't polite to ignore the message, but she didn't have an answer for her assistant. She felt no obligation to return to Miami during a time when she had been scheduled to accompany Alejandro in South America. Her schedule was empty, so Dali had no reason to make such requests, Amanda told herself. Besides, the weather had finally turned for the better and the last thing Amanda wanted to think about was leaving the farm.

She sat at the picnic table with Anna, helping her fold the dry laundry. Overhead, the warm afternoon sun shone in the vibrant blue sky. A gentle breeze kept the air cool, and the birds darted back and forth over the fields, hunting for small bits of straw and grass to use for their nests.

Amanda's phone sat on the edge of the table as she waited for a message from Alejandro. She knew that the tour had finished over the past weekend, and she figured he had certainly flown home on Monday, Tuesday at the latest. But it was now midday on Wednesday and she still had not received any word from him.

An orange barn cat strutted by, its tail waving in the air, and Isadora jumped down from the picnic table to chase it. Her bare feet ran through the grass, carrying her in the direction of where the old tomcat had disappeared.

Amanda watched her daughter turn the corner of the house. "Spring is the best season on the farm," she said, more to herself than to Anna. "God's gift for us having survived the winter, *ja?*"

"Oh, *now* you say that, Amanda," Anna replied, a teasing tone to her voice. "But I don't recall that you were the one shoveling snow from the walkway or driveway!"

"Mayhaps not this year," Amanda laughed in response. "But I've still shoveled enough to make me appreciate the springtime."

Setting down the dress in her hands, Anna sighed and stared at Amanda. There was a wistful look in her eyes, one that displayed a mixture of emotions. "It has been nice having you home these past weeks," Anna said. "Such a shame you must be leaving again."

Amanda placed the shirt she had just folded on top of the laundry in the basket and reached for another, smoothing out the fabric before starting to fold it. "And when I return to the farm, you'll have your *boppli!*"

The mere mention of her baby caused Anna to lay her hand on her protruding stomach. It was hard for Amanda to believe that there was a baby inside her sister's belly. When she was growing up, she learned from an early age that pregnancy among the married Amish women occurred so frequently that some were pregnant every year for a decade. But this was her sister, not just *any* woman in the church district. After all that their family had been through, Amanda couldn't help but feel protective of her.

As if reading her mind, Anna changed the subject. "It's hard to believe that it was round about this time last year when Daed wanted us to leave for Ohio."

"No!" Amanda gasped when she realized her sister spoke the truth. "It *is* hard to believe. So much has happened. For both of us!"

"Oh for sure and certain, for both of us," Anna agreed. "But more so for you than for me." She put down the dress she had been folding, letting it fall onto her lap in a crumpled heap. "What an adventure you have lived, Amanda. And I'm truly not surprised. You always did have a touch of wanderlust."

"Wanderlust? Oh, that's not so!" Whether her sister spoke the truth or not, Amanda couldn't say. But she didn't like hearing such things said about her.

Anna laughed. "Oh *ja*, you did. Why, you always thought traveling would be right *gut* fun!"

"Oh, Anna!" Amanda shook her head. "To Harrisburg, *ja*! But not to foreign countries that I didn't even know existed!" They both laughed, knowing that there was a bit of truth to both their claims. "Besides, I was always happy on the farm."

Anna shook her head. "*Nee*, that's not so. Especially after Aaron passed . . ."

The sound of Isadora's laughter rang out from the barn. Amanda looked in that direction and saw that she had found Jonas, who now accompanied her as they left the dairy barn and headed toward the house.

"But we all know that you've sacrificed so much to help Daed," Anna continued. "Even before Aaron passed. You never should have felt guilt over Aaron's death or about . . ."

Amanda knew why her sister couldn't finish the sentence. While Anna loved Jonas, she still felt the pain of being abandoned by the man she had thought she'd marry, just weeks before their wedding was to be announced.

"And now," Anna said, changing the subject, "you have a man that you love and a daughter that you adore!"

This time, Amanda smiled. "I do, Anna. I truly do."

"And the travel!"

Making a face, Amanda rolled her eyes and pretended to collapse on the picnic table, which made Anna laugh again.

"Speaking of Daed," Amanda said, glancing up at the sky as she tried to gauge the time. "They should be back from physical therapy soon, *ja?*"

"I reckon so, unless they stopped at the cafeteria at the hospital. Does Daed some good to get out of the house a spell. Mamm, too."

Just then, they heard the sound of car tires on the gravel. Amanda looked up. "Must not have stopped after all." She glanced at her sister. "You going to finish folding that dress? That's the third time you started and stopped!"

Anna looked up, realizing that Amanda spoke the truth, and they both laughed as Anna quickly folded it and tossed it into the basket.

A black car pulled around the side of the barn. Amanda squinted at it, wondering who might possibly be pulling in. After all, her parents had left in a wheelchair-accessible van that morning, Lizzie fussing over Elias as the driver helped secure his chair in the vehicle. The car that now parked in the driveway was clearly not transporting her parents.

And then it dawned on her.

"Alejandro!"

She tossed the shirt onto the picnic table and slid out from the bench. Running as fast as she could, she practically jumped into his arms when he emerged from the car's backseat. She threw her arms around his neck and clung to him, laughing and crying at the same time. With his arms around her waist, holding her tight, she felt as though she could finally exhale, as if she had been holding her breath for the past two and half weeks.

He placed his hands on her cheeks and stared into her face. "You are radiant, Princesa," he breathed. "As beautiful as the sun in the sky." Not caring that Anna could see them, Alejandro kissed her lips and Amanda let him.

"Oh, I've missed you so much." When he tried to pull away, she wouldn't release her hold on his neck, and he laughed, swinging her around. "You never contacted me. I didn't know when you were coming!"

"I'm sorry. You know how busy it gets," he said. "Besides, you were rather diligent about letting me know how you were doing." He gazed into her face, his blue eyes flickering back and forth as if he was studying her every feature. "And I am here now."

"I see that." Amanda laughed through her tears. Absentmindedly, she wiped at them, still finding it hard to believe that he was there, on her parents' farm, and holding her in his arms. "I was worried when I didn't hear from you."

"Worried?" He didn't have any time to inquire further about this as they were interrupted by the sound of laughter coming from the barn. Alejandro looked over his shoulder toward the doorway, just in time to see Isadora follow Jonas and Harvey outside. The two men shouted their hellos as they approached.

"Just in time for afternoon chores, I see," Jonas joked, reaching out to shake Alejandro's hand.

Before Alejandro could respond, Isadora ran to Amanda, a small orange kitten in her hands. "Look," she demanded.

"Oh help, Izzie! That kitten is too small to be away from its mother. Let's go put it back, *ja*?"

Harvey held up his hand. "Permit me." Without waiting for Amanda's response, he reached down and scooped Isadora into his arms, talking softly to her about the kitten as they headed back into the barn.

It was only when Amanda glanced at Alejandro that she realized Isadora had not only neglected to greet him, she hadn't even noticed he was there.

The look on his face said it all.

She didn't have time to say anything, to explain that Isadora hadn't known that he was coming and probably hadn't seen him because her excitement about the kitten had been too great.

Jonas and Anna invited him inside. They were eager to hear about the rest of his South American tour, as the stories of the different countries were fascinating to them, despite their vow to shun worldliness. As Jonas and Anna escorted Alejandro inside, Amanda trailed behind them, eager to have a moment alone with him and to reassure him that all was well, but knowing that, given her family's emphasis on togetherness, that moment would not come anytime soon.

Chapter Twenty

Isadora leaned against Amanda's leg and stared, wide-eyed, at the cow. Her long hair was tied in a messy bun just above the nape of her neck, and she wore a tan dress with small green flowers on it. Lizzie had made it for her from the fabric Amanda had purchased in town just a few days prior. The dress quickly became a treasured possession for Isadora. She insisted on wearing it every day, forcing Amanda to wash it at night if Isadora had dirtied it. One morning, when it hadn't dried yet, Isadora had refused to budge from where she waited on the porch in her nightgown, and she'd sat there, cross-legged, until it was ready for her to wear.

Now, Isadora was absorbing everything that Amanda did to the cow. It wasn't the first time that she had clung to Amanda's side and watched the way cows were milked. But today was different. Today Amanda had promised to let Isadora try to milk the cow herself.

"Me now?"

Amanda nodded. "*Ja*, if you want."

She opened her knees so that Isadora could stand between them, and Isadora braced herself against Amanda's right leg. Leaning forward,

Amanda guided Isadora's hand to the udder of the cow and helped her to wrap her small fingers around the teat.

Squealing, Isadora quickly withdrew her hand and pressed against Amanda.

"Feels funny, *ja?*" She tickled Isadora's neck. "Try again, Izzie?"

The next attempt resulted in the same reaction. Giving up on Isadora's hands getting any milk flowing, Amanda took over. "Like this. Rolling the milk down with your fingers, not squeezing."

Harvey walked by and glanced over the back of the cow, looking first at Amanda and then at Isadora. Because Jonas had taken Anna to a doctor—At last! Amanda had thought—Amanda had offered to help with the afternoon milking.

"Not working for you, now, is it?" he said with a wink at Isadora. "Might be that she's broken?"

Amanda pretended to look surprised, gasping dramatically at Harvey and turning to look at Isadora. "A broken cow? Oh help! We'll need lots of Band-Aids, don't you think?"

She felt, rather than saw, Alejandro watching her, his presence too large to go undetected. She wondered how long he had been standing there, leaning against the wall, hidden by shadows. After his unexpected arrival the day before, and his obvious disappointment in the greeting he had received from both her family and his daughter, Amanda had done as much as she could to shower him with attention after Isadora went to bed.

But when the sounds of crying filtered down the staircase and into the main room of the *grossdaadihaus*, Amanda had excused herself and gone to calm Isadora, who wasn't used to sleeping in the small upstairs bedroom by herself. By the time Amanda finally returned downstairs, Alejandro had already gone to bed and fallen asleep. He hadn't even stirred when she slipped under the covers, curling her body around him. The sound of his deep breathing gave her enough satisfaction, for she knew that sleep was the one thing he needed more than anything else. Amanda pressed closer against him, putting one arm around his waist and her cheek against his shoulder, and listened to the sounds of Alejandro sleeping. She vowed to make it up to him the following day.

He hadn't awoken until almost noon, a fact that had not escaped Lizzie's attention.

"Sure knows how to sleep," Lizzie said while she washed garden dirt from her hands at the kitchen sink.

"Mamm!"

Lizzie raised an eyebrow and pursed her lips, that all-too-familiar disapproving look on her face. She'd said no more as she merely walked over to Elias and unlocked the brakes on his wheelchair so that she could take him outside for a breath of fresh air.

Nothing more had been said about Alejandro sleeping late. Amanda knew better than to make excuses for her husband; her mother wouldn't understand, and the rest of her family didn't particularly care. But when he had finally risen and entered the kitchen for coffee, Amanda could tell that his mood was not greatly improved from what it had been the previous day.

Now, as she continued to milk the cow, her cheek pressed against the bovine's rump, Amanda pretended not to know that he stood there watching her. She felt her heart race, anxiety coursing through her body, as she hoped that his silent surveillance meant that his mood had improved. Usually, it meant that he was deep in thought, the act of observing others a mask that obscured whatever else was going through his mind. He'd address her when he was ready, and Amanda knew that there was no point in pushing him.

Beside her, Isadora draped her body over Amanda's knee and giggled when Amanda squirted a little milk toward her bare toes.

"She should wear shoes out here," Alejandro said, finally making his presence known.

Amanda looked up, feigning surprise at seeing Alejandro leaning against the rough-hewn wall, his arms crossed over his chest. *"Gut nochmidawk!"* she said, a happy smile on her face. "It's a beautiful afternoon, *ja?*"

Isadora grabbed at Amanda's skirt, swinging back and forth as she sang *"Gut nochmidawk! Gut nochmidawk!"*

Amanda laughed and reached over to embrace the child. "That's right! Good afternoon to your *daed, ja?*"

At the mention of her father, Isadora glanced over to where he stood, and Amanda followed her gaze. He hadn't laughed at his daughter nor did he smile at Amanda. Instead, he seemed deep in thought, his eyes focused on them, but his mind centered elsewhere.

"Come, Alejandro," Amanda said, gesturing with her hand for him to join them. "Show Izzie that you know how to milk the cow. Maybe then she won't be so afraid, *ja?*"

To her surprise, he did as she asked. Amanda stood up and motioned toward the stool and was even more surprised when he accepted it.

Amanda knelt down and gently leaned against him, her side pressed against his thigh and Isadora quickly settling into her arms. Amanda watched the girl's face as she peered up at the man she knew as her father in name only. There was a mixture of curiosity in Isadora's eyes as well as a yearning to feel love and a tendency toward fear. With the comfort of Amanda's arms around her, Isadora leaned against Alejandro's leg, too, and let herself relax just enough to watch what he was doing.

The stream of milk hit the side of the metal pail, the little tingling sound causing Isadora to jump a little. Amanda thought she saw a hint of a smile on Alejandro's lips. When Isadora realized what had happened, she clapped her hands and demanded more.

"Let her try, *ja?*"

Amanda took Isadora's hand and placed it in Alejandro's, pausing just long enough for the three of their hands to be united. She held her breath, waiting to see what Alejandro would do, especially when she withdrew her own fingers, leaving father and daughter hand in hand.

He coaxed Isadora to touch the cow's teat one more time, only this time he left his hand on top of hers and helped her to roll her fingers downward so that milk streamed into the bucket. Isadora did it again, this time needing less pressure from her father. Delighted, Amanda watched as Isadora lifted her blue eyes and sought his.

But if she sought approval, she received none.

Instead, Alejandro cleared his throat and stood up, his abrupt action almost knocking Amanda to her knees.

"Alejandro?" she asked, questioning him with her eyes. "What's wrong?"

He pointed toward Isadora's feet. "Shoes," he said and turned around, walking away from both his wife and his daughter, giving no reason for his sudden departure.

Amanda watched him leave, wondering what she could have possibly said or done that upset him. She had noticed his quiet mood, a mood that felt heavy and oppressive as it lingered between her and Isadora, like a heavy fog in the fields behind the barn on a muggy spring morning.

"*¡Vaca!*" Isadora cried out, reaching toward the cow.

"*Nee,* Izzie," Amanda said, redirecting her own attention to where it belonged: on the five-year-old. "Cow. Can you say 'cow'?"

"*¡Vaca!*" she insisted to Amanda, a mischievous gleam in her blue eyes.

"Cow!"

Isadora giggled again and buried her face in Amanda's leg, mumbling "cow" into her skirt.

Forgetting about Alejandro and his moodiness, Amanda started to laugh and wrapped her arms around the little girl. Only, she didn't think of her as a little girl; she thought of her as her daughter. "Aren't you the sneaky one, *ja*? You knew exactly what you were doing, didn't you?" To her delight, Isadora threw her arms around Amanda's neck and hugged her. "Oh, Izzie!" she said as she inhaled the sweet scent of innocence in her arms. "I just love you so much!"

"Mammi," Isadora whispered, squeezing Amanda as tightly as she could.

The word took Amanda by surprise, and for a second she thought she had misheard the little girl. After all, over the past month, Isadora had not called her anything at all. To Amanda, the sound of that word was sweeter than any other. If her heart had swelled with emotion for Isadora before that moment, now she felt as if it would burst open. In that moment, Amanda knew that she felt more love for Izzie than ever before.

Fast on the heels of that realization came another: Alejandro.

A chill ran through her body, and her arms felt tingly and cold. Amanda looked over Isadora's head and stared at the place vacated by Alejandro less than five minutes before. She could still visualize his eyes, the expression on his face as he observed them interacting with each other by the side of the cow. He had watched them, and he had known exactly what Amanda had just learned.

"I'm leaving for Los Angeles," Alejandro said, his voice flat and emotionless.

"When?"

He hesitated, darkness clouding his face.

"Alejandro?" Amanda had just tucked Isadora into her bed and returned to the kitchen. Her body ached, and she felt tired. Juggling Isadora's clinginess and Alejandro's dark mood had simply worn her out. Now this announcement? Just one more thing to worry about, she thought.

"Tomorrow." The muscles tightened in his jaw. He was clenching his teeth, another indicator that his black mood from earlier in the day still lingered.

"When will you be back?"

This time, he frowned. "I have obligations, Amanda. The European tour starts in two weeks." His words were stilted and curt, as if he chose them carefully.

Europe. She had forgotten about Europe. The idea of leaving Lancaster to travel around another continent, of being chauffeured from one place to another, and of living off barely a few hours of rest at each hotel was less than appealing to her. Added to that was the advent of spring, which was just around the corner. The days were already warming up, and life was returning to the farm. She wanted to share those moments with Isadora, to show her the first crocuses and let her watch the newborn kittens grow and play.

Clearly, her lack of response spoke volumes. Alejandro's eyes never left her.

"I expect you to join me, Amanda."

The fact that he had not called her Princesa was another hint of his displeasure. He normally only used her given name when discussing serious matters, especially when she accidentally did something wrong. But she simply couldn't imagine why he spoke so firmly now. What had she done that could possibly have upset him? "I thought we agreed . . ."

His eyes narrowed, and the anger in his expression caused her to abandon her sentence.

"No, Amanda. We agreed not to be apart, no? We said 'never again.' Yet you are the one who unilaterally decided to leave Miami, to return to Lancaster. You are the one who wants to stay here rather than travel with me to Los Angeles."

She gasped at the hard tone in his voice. "I didn't . . ."

He held up his hand. "Stop, Amanda. Don't say that you did not do these things, because you did."

"That's not fair!"

"No!" His voice boomed in the small house, and he took a step toward her. "What is not fair is this," he said with more control in his voice. He gestured in the air, making a wide sweep of the room. She glanced in the direction he indicated and saw the wooden toys on the floor near the sofa as well as the pieces of a chunky puzzle that Isadora had not finished.

"She's your daughter," Amanda said, lifting her chin as she met his eyes. "And mine, too. You had me sign those papers, Alejandro. You asked me to become her mother."

"Mother, *sí*! But not convert her to Amish!"

She gasped, her hand instinctively covering her chest as if suddenly wounded. "Alejandro!"

He pressed his lips together and took a deep breath. Running his hands through his hair, he looked upward as if searching for something. "Amanda," he finally said. "I need you." She could see that he struggled to remain calm. "I *need* you with me. And you know that."

"And I want to be with you." She stepped forward and touched his arm. "You are all that I want, Alejandro. I love you so much that I have to remind myself that God must come first." She tried to smile. "And God does not want our daughter to be abandoned while we traipse around the world. Nor does he want her growing up in the spotlight with late nights and sleeping on planes." She paused. "She is just a child, and she needs stability."

Pulling his arm free from Amanda's touch, he glowered at her. "Stability?"

His reaction surprised her. "She lost her *mother*, Alejandro."

"You are being condescending," he retorted, the anger rising in his voice. "I know that she lost her mother, Amanda. I am not an ignorant *pobrecito*! But I did the right thing, and that shouldn't mean that I must now lose my wife!"

"You're not losing your wife!"

"If I leave here without you," he said, his eyes narrowed and lips pressed tightly together, "what, exactly, do you think will happen between us?" His expression told her that she traveled down a road full of hazards. His next words told her that there would be no recovery if she took the wrong turn. "I can assure you, *Princesa*, there will be no happily ever after."

The sarcastic tone in which he said her nickname did not go unnoticed, and without warning, tears began to well up in her eyes. The way that he looked at her, with such contempt and anger, frightened her. Why couldn't he see that touring on the road was no place for a child? The situation was not ideal; she could admit that much. But this was not something that they had planned. All of their plans had changed overnight when Isadora entered their lives. But responsible parents put the needs of their children ahead of their own.

"Do not cry," he warned and pointed a firm finger at her. "*You* are making this choice. You have no right to cry."

As soon as he said those words, Amanda lifted her hands to her face and covered her eyes and cheeks. She turned her back to him and let the tears fall. Even if she were able to speak, she wouldn't respond to his words, which were so cruel and out of character. This ugly side of Alejandro threw her off. How could this man who she loved so much speak to her in such a way?

She moved away from him and started to head toward the bedroom to collect herself and her thoughts. Words spoken in anger create wounds that cannot heal, she reminded herself. This was just one more of the wise adages she had been taught by her mother. The harshness with which Alejandro had spoken to her just now would take a long time to forget.

As she walked away from him, she suddenly felt Alejandro's firm grip on her upper arm. In one fluid movement, he spun her around and pushed her backward so rapidly that she gasped in surprise. Her tears immediately stopped as he pinned her against the wall and, maintaining a firm grip on her wrist, held her arm so that she could not escape.

"Alejandro!"

She tried to push him away, pressing her free hand against his shoulder. He responded by tightening his hold on her other wrist. Her surprise turned to anger. She had caught glimpses of his temper before, but it had always been directed elsewhere. She had never thought that he would treat her in such a rough manner. In hindsight, she knew that the tension between them had been building, and that it had created a divide that neither one of them knew how to cross.

This, however, is not the way, she told herself.

"Don't," she snapped at him. She tried to free herself, but it did no good. When she realized that her determination was no match for his physical strength, she stopped fighting him. She looked up at him, ready to say something else when she saw that his blue eyes no longer held rage and fury. No, those emotions were gone and had been replaced by a new one: panic.

"Amanda," he said. The softness in his voice contrasted with his sharp tone from moments before. "I cannot leave here without you."

"Let me go. You are hurting my arm, Alejandro."

Immediately, he loosened his hold on her, but kept her pinned against the wall. She didn't like the feeling of being restrained but knew better than to fight him.

"You don't know what it was like," he whispered, lifting his hand so that he could wipe the remnants of tears from her cheeks. His fingers paused at her mouth, and then he brushed his thumb against her lower lip. "Knowing you were here. Knowing you didn't need me." He shut his eyes as if pained by the memory. "Maybe you don't, Amanda, but I need you. Even if you are only back in the hotel, I need to know that you are there."

The rapid shift in his tone, anger turned to anxiety, was almost as startling as the way he was restraining her against the wall.

"Who are you?" she whispered.

"I am your husband," he responded, his voice trembling just enough so that Amanda knew that he was holding back his emotions. "Bring Isadora, Amanda. Bring your family. Anything you want. I'll provide for them all." His thumb fell from her mouth, and he cupped her chin with his hand. "Just come with me," he said, lowering his eyes and looking at her lips. "Be with me, not because you want to but because you need to."

She shut her eyes and pictured the scantily clad dancers onstage with Viper, the screaming women in the audience, the workers swearing behind the scenes whenever things went wrong. She felt the weariness in her body caused by traveling from country to country and the weariness in her soul caused by the barrage of fans, paparazzi, and reporters. How could she do all that with Isadora? How could she help this child adjust if change was the only constant in her life? To uproot her from the farm, especially after the past few weeks, would be to shatter her trust in all people. Amanda knew that she couldn't do that to Isadora.

Just as important, Amanda realized that she couldn't do it to herself.

"I . . ." She opened her eyes but could not finish speaking. The words wouldn't come, and she knew, as he surely must, what her answer would be. Neither of them wanted to hear her say it.

"Shh," he whispered, pressing a finger against her lips. When he released her hand, slipping his own down her back and cupping her waist, she felt the warmth of his skin through the material of her shirt. Her body relaxed a bit as she leaned against him.

"Don't say anything, Amanda." His eyes sought hers, but there were no answers there. The answers remained unspoken, and as if to ensure that it remained that way, he relaxed his hold on her and kissed her, gently at first but then more intensely, until she felt the full urgency of his driving need to possess her: mind, body, and soul.

She realized that his urge to possess her had always been there. While she often let him take control of situations and her, she hadn't permitted him to change who she was as a person. And lately she had been standing up to him more frequently, especially now that she was responsible for Isadora. Amanda wondered if her increasing independence was the driving force behind him coveting both her attention and her affection: he couldn't have one without the other. The only problem, she realized, was that neither could she. And, as of late, she wasn't getting either.

In the early-morning hours of dawn, she felt Alejandro get out of bed. The mattress shifted under him, and she heard his bare feet on the floor. She rolled over, tucking the sheet under her chin. The sun wasn't up, and she had no idea what time it was. Certainly long before he should have arisen.

"You are awake?" he whispered, his voice soft in the quiet of the room. She could see his silhouette in the darkness as he stood by the side of the bed, looking down at her in the gray-blue glow of morning. "Go back to sleep, Princesa."

She stretched her hand toward him. "Come back to bed, Alejandro. It's cold here without you."

He shook his head and held a finger to his lips. She heard him slip on a pair of pants and bend down to retrieve the rest of his clothing that was scattered across the floor. He tried to be quiet as he slipped out of the bedroom. Moments later she heard the water running in the bathroom.

Sighing, she reached over and retrieved his phone to check the time. Four thirty. He never got up this early. Amanda wondered why he had gotten dressed. Surely he wasn't planning on helping Jonas and Harvey. Alejandro needed his sleep, and everyone on the farm knew it.

She got out of bed and pulled on her robe, padding across the floor and opening the bedroom door. The cold air chilled her, and the floor felt like ice under her bare feet. She hoped that Isadora had enough blankets covering her, and for a split second, she contemplated checking on her.

"Go back to bed," her husband said when he saw her standing there. He buttoned the front of his shirt and avoided her eyes.

"What's going on, Alejandro?" She took a step toward him and covered his hand with hers. The warmth of his skin caused her to remember the previous night and his words of love. She felt light-headed and wanted nothing more than to linger in his arms, to feel his heartbeat against her back and to smell the musky scent of his skin as he held her. "Why are you up? You need sleep."

He shook his head, one of his dark curls, still damp with water from the sink, falling over his forehead. "My car is picking me up at five."

"Your car?" She removed her hand and stepped backward. "What do you mean your car?"

He finished buttoning the shirt and began tucking it into his waistband. "I told you yesterday, Amanda, that I am leaving. I meant it."

"But . . ." She couldn't even form words to speak. He was leaving? It was the furthest thought from her mind, especially after his declarations of love to her during a magical night spent in each other's arms.

His shirt now tucked in, Alejandro tightened his belt. "I need to be in Los Angeles for the weekend."

"What about us?"

He paused and looked at her. "I told you once that my world was not like here. That it is ugly and not good. That you would find reasons to hate me for bringing you with me."

"It's not all ugly," she said. "Look at the good that you do. The people you touch."

He made a scoffing noise.

"It's true. You bring so much joy to so many people, Alejandro."

"Amanda," he said sharply. "This is where you belong. This is where your life is. It is not with me. Not on the road, not with the paparazzi and the fans." He gestured toward the staircase that led to Isadora's small bedroom. "And that is certainly not the life for her."

"You're leaving us?"

He gave her a noncommittal shrug. "You already left me, Amanda. Remember? The tabloids announced it to the world."

"I left you for two weeks," she retorted. "To take care of your daughter."

"It was your choice to do so."

Her heart began to race, and she felt a sense of panic build inside her chest. "It wasn't my *choice*, Alejandro. It was my *responsibility*. Let me wake her. Let us come with you to Los Angeles."

He lifted his hand, stopping her. "You left me and you returned to Lancaster," he said. "You are happy here, Amanda, and so is she."

"I'm happy where you are, and she'll be happy anywhere. We just need to be together."

Alejandro leaned over to kiss her. "I'm headed to Los Angeles and then Europe. It's clear we have a lot to think about, Amanda. Choices to make. It's better to not procrastinate."

She stood there, stunned that he was actually leaving. She realized that had she not awakened, he would have left her without saying good-bye. That wasn't like her Alejandro, the man she had fallen in love with and married. Even though South America had ended on a bad note, she knew that it was because of the stress and not because of lost feelings on either side.

"You're pushing me away on purpose," she said. "Don't do that. Please, Alejandro."

He paused and for the slightest moment she held out hope that he would change his mind. He reached out his hand and brushed his fingers across her cheek. Feeling desperate, she clasped his hand and clung to it, her eyes shut and her heart aching.

"I love you, Amanda Diaz," he said softly. "And I'm leaving because of that very reason. You once asked me if there was any part of me left for me." He squeezed her hand. "There is, and that is the part of me that loves you. But I love you enough to know that there will be no part of you left for you if I let you change my mind. It is better here, on the farm, for you and Isadora. What happens later, time will tell." He kissed the back of her hand and then, abruptly, released it. He turned his back to her. "We have choices in life, Amanda. You chose to leave the tour with Isadora *despite* your love for me, and I . . ." His shoulders lifted as he took a deep breath. "I am choosing to leave you here *because of* my love for you."

Without another word and without looking back, he walked out the door. Amanda stood in the center of the room, feeling as if the walls of her world were caving in around her. She ran to the door and flung it open just in time to see him approach a waiting car. Not once did he look back. She saw the headlights of the car turn on as he opened the passenger door and disappeared inside. And then, as quietly as it had slipped into the driveway, the car rolled away, turning before it disappeared around the side of the barn. The illumination of the headlights faded away, and she knew that Alejandro was gone.

It didn't make sense. None of it made any sense. He loved her, yet he had left her under the cloak of darkness, having not even intended to say good-bye. He had spoken of choices, for both of them . . . decisions that had to be made that would be best made apart and not together. He had spoken of the happiness she felt being back in Lancaster, not realizing that she could not be happy without him.

A wave of panic washed over her once she realized that Alejandro had just left. The idea of not seeing him for six weeks was more than she could handle. She leaned against the doorframe and slid down to the floor, her heart racing and her mind whirling as she replayed everything in her head, from the moment Isadora had been turned over to their care until the night before, when he had told her that he was leaving.

And she realized that he had been right, that she *had* made a choice: a choice between him and Isadora. She would not doubt her decision, not now or ever. What she did doubt was his ability to realize that she had done the right thing for the sake of his child.

The sound of little feet running down the wooden stairs and across the linoleum floor of the kitchen redirected her anxiety. She wiped at her eyes, hoping that in the darkness of the early morning Isadora wouldn't notice that she had been crying.

"Gut mariye, Mammi!" Isadora whispered, wrapping her arms around Amanda's neck and sliding onto her lap. *"Gut mariye!"*

Amanda shut her eyes, feeling the warmth of Isadora's skin against hers and inhaling the scent of lavender from her hair. She held the little girl close to her heart and rocked her back and forth, just enough so that Isadora fell back asleep within minutes. As Amanda sat in the doorway and watched the sun rise over the field, Isadora sleeping in her arms, Dali's words echoed in her ears: *Your strength is given to you from God. He will not lead you anywhere that you should not be.*

Pushing thoughts of Alejandro's departure out of her mind, Amanda focused on those words. She had put too much worldliness before God over the past few weeks. It was time to return to him and let his plan unfold. She realized that if Alejandro was part of that plan, God would make that known.

Still, her heart ached as she took a deep breath and watched the sky change from the dark of night to the orange-red of morning. *Protect him, God, and keep him safe,* she prayed, shutting her eyes and letting her head fall against the doorframe. *Bring him back to me if that is your will. Bring him back to me . . .*

Glossary

Pennsylvania Dutch

ach vell	an expression similar to *oh well*
boppli	baby
Daed, or her *daed*	Father, or her father
danke	thank you
dochder	daughter
Englische	non-Amish people
Englischer	a non-Amish person
fraa	wife
g'may	church district
grossdaadihaus	small house attached to the main dwelling
gut mariye	good morning
gut nochmidawk	good afternoon
ja	yes
kapp	cap
kinner	children
kum	come
Mamm, or her *mamm*	Mother, or her mother
nee	no
schwester	sister
vell	well
wunderbar	wonderful

Spanish

ay, mi madre	an expression; literally *oh, my mother*
buenísimo	excellent
bueno	good
buenos días	a greeting; good day
claro	of course
dígame	talk to me
Dios *mío*	my God
gracias	thank you
linda	pretty
listo	ready
mamacita	little mama
mi amor	my love
mi hija	my daughter
mi querida	my dear
pobrecita, probrecito	an insult, literally "little poor one" or "poor baby"
qué	what
sí	yes
vamos	let's go
ven conmiga	come with me

Plain Choice

Book Five of the Plain Fame Series

Sarah Price

Waterfall
PRESS

Chapter One

Amanda stood at the crest of the small hill at the back of the property, wiping the sweat from her brow. The sun had barely crested the horizon—the full impact of its powerful heat still hours away—but she still needed a moment's break to catch her breath. Her dress, a simple floral pattern on cotton fabric that brushed against her knees, did not keep her cool enough, given the work that they were doing.

Up ahead, she saw her brother-in-law, Jonas, and their hired man, Harvey, working the team of Belgian mules as they plowed the fields in preparation for the planting of corn. As the mules pulled the plow, the earth parted behind the moldboard. It was like watching the ocean as it rose up in gentle waves, the only difference being that the footprint of the plow left behind neat rows of tilled soil, whereas the ocean continued to roll onto the sand and then back to the sea.

The ocean.

She wondered if Alejandro was in Miami or Los Angeles since she knew that he had not yet departed for Europe. Less than two weeks had passed since he had left her on her Amish parents' farm in Lititz, Pennsylvania. Almost two long weeks in which she had done her best to remain unemotional and calm, knowing that her five-year-old adopted stepdaughter, Isadora, needed stability, not more drama, in her young life.

But on the inside, Amanda's emotions churned, switching from heartbreak to humiliation, from angst to anger, a constant roller coaster of different depths of despair that she had never before experienced.

As much as she tried, Amanda could not erase from her memory the image of Alejandro leaving her on that morning. The coldness with which he had spoken to her, the dismissive way in which he had merely turned and walked away, conflicted with everything else that she had learned about the man she called her husband. Wrapping her mind around the fact that she had been deserted was impossible. Not her, she thought, and certainly not by *her* Alejandro. Where had everything gone wrong? she wondered.

"You all right, then?" a deep voice said from behind her.

Amanda shifted her attention from her inner sanctuary to the man who approached from the other side of the hill. She tried to smile as she turned to face Harvey, the Mennonite farmer hired by Alejandro to help with the farmwork. Without Harvey, Amanda knew that she never could have balanced working the dairy barn while helping her mother with her father after his stroke. Thankfully, her sister and her husband were now taking over the farm, although neither one of them seemed in a great hurry to sever the work relationship with their hired hand.

When he stood before her, his tall, willowy frame blocking the sun from shining in her face, Amanda wrapped her arms around her waist, as if that would help hold everything together. Amanda nodded her head in response to his inquiry. "*Ja*, I'm just fine," she said.

He reached out and placed his hand on her shoulder, a gesture that caused Amanda to look away. "You don't have to be out here, Amanda," Harvey said. "We'll do just fine the two of us. 'Sides, Izzie will be looking for you shortly."

Again, she nodded her head. "I know" was her simple response.

"But you do what you have to," Harvey said, a soft expression on his tanned face.

She managed to smile at him, a way of letting him know how much she appreciated his compassion.

Two weeks, she thought as she watched him walk back to Jonas, who was adjusting the harness on one of the mules.

It was hard for her to face the truth, that her husband had left her in Lititz and gone off to continue his own life, separated from her and their daughter, Isadora. After all that they had been through, she could not comprehend that their marriage might actually be over. So much had happened in the past year, from the accident in New York City to the onslaught of paparazzi in Lancaster County to the whirlwind romance that took her to Las Vegas, Los Angeles, and Miami.

And then they had gotten married.

She had known that marrying Alejandro would not be easy. It wasn't that she didn't love him. That had never been the question. But the clash of their lifestyles merging together had been the final cut to the ties that had bound them together.

The South American tour had been especially hard for Amanda. On a continent where she did not speak the language, both linguistically and culturally, their differences had begun to emerge. From the women with their sophisticated mannerisms and exotic beauty to the arrival of Alejandro's friend, Enrique Lopez, Amanda had watched as Alejandro transformed into Viper, the womanizing international sensation who charmed everyone he met. His nights began to stretch into the morning hours, and with all of his interviews and obligations, she rarely saw him. Their time alone disintegrated until she found herself alone more than with him.

Neither one of them had been prepared for the arrival of Isadora, his five-year-old daughter from a one-night stand with a Brazilian woman. Amanda had known about the daughter since Alejandro had told her about the child when they first met. But because he maintained no relationship with either the mother or the child, Alejandro never mentioned them again.

So when the Brazilian government worker arrived with the child, explaining that Isadora was headed to an orphanage if Alejandro and Amanda did not take her, the shock of suddenly becoming parents had overwhelmed both of them.

"Amanda?"

She looked up at the sound of her name carried on the morning breeze. Jonas was waving to her, beckoning her to help them.

Obediently, and grateful for the interruption to her racing thoughts, she hurried down the field and joined the two men.

Her brother-in-law stood by the larger of the two mules, examining a piece of leather. "Ach, it's broken, I reckon."

Amanda peered over his shoulder at the tie strap. The ring that held it to the trace carrier, the piece of leather that lay across the mule's rump and kept the plow attached to the harness, had indeed torn off. "That's not *gut*," she said. "I don't think I remember Daed having an extra one."

Harvey took off his hat and wiped his brow with the back of his arm. "I can run over to the harness shop, fetch a new one." His offer would save them time since, as a Mennonite, he drove a car. It would be much faster than Amanda or Jonas hitching up a horse to a buggy and riding over. "Amanda, you want to ride along?"

She was about to decline, but Jonas nodded his head. "You haven't left the farm since Alejandro left. Might do you some good."

Surprised that Jonas had mentioned Alejandro, she could not respond to turn down Harvey's offer. It was the first time Jonas, or anyone besides her sister, Anna, had said anything about her husband.

The morning that he had left, her family quietly accepted Amanda's explanation for Alejandro's abrupt departure. She tried to tell them that he had meetings and she hadn't wanted to leave yet, especially with Isadora's progress adapting to her new life in the United States. Despite her puffy eyes and tearstained cheeks, they simply listened to her, nodded, and never asked another question about him.

Later that morning, in the privacy of the *grossdaadihaus*, where Amanda stayed with Isadora, Anna had inquired further. When Amanda burst into tears, sobbing into her hands that covered her face, she shared the entire story. She told her sister about the South American tour, the truth about Isadora's appearance in their lives, about Alejandro's rebuffing the child and leaving her in Amanda's care, and about the final hours of their time together.

As any good sister would do, Anna listened and then embraced Amanda, holding her while she cried. Afterward, the rest of the family seemed to look at her with a sense of pity. But they never asked any questions. When it came to matters of the heart between husband and wife, they wouldn't interfere or even probe for more information.

While grateful for their support, Amanda found the cautious way that they treated her, as if she were a fragile doll ready to break at any moment, hard to bear. Only one person ever asked about Alejandro's absence and that was when Isadora asked where "Papa" had gone. When Amanda explained that Papa had gone away on business, Isadora hadn't mentioned him again.

"Ready, Amanda?" Harvey asked, the broken tie strap and trace carrier in his hands.

She nodded and followed him as he walked across the field toward his car parked behind the barn.

The number of paparazzi that camped out by the entrance to the farm had declined since Alejandro's leaving. With Amanda staying on the farm and no news to report, most of the photographers moved on to somewhere, and someone, else. A few remained, and when Harvey drove past them, they eagerly snapped photos of Amanda riding in the car with him. She ignored them, oblivious to their intrusive lenses and knowing that at least one of the photographs would make the tabloids and social media news.

"You'd think they'd give up," Harvey said as he drove down the road.

Amanda shrugged. "They hardly bother me anymore."

He nodded as if he understood.

Feeling as if she should fill the silence in the car, Amanda continued explaining. "Those few photographers are nothing like the paparazzi at the airports and arenas. The Englischers sure do have a propensity for enjoying gossip about their favorite celebrities, I reckon."

Harvey chuckled under his breath. "Like the Amish grapevine?"

She smiled. "*Ja*, I reckon so."

Even though the Amish community shunned all worldliness, allowing only what the bishops of each church district permitted, they were human beings who spread stories as often as the non-Amish people. Amanda remembered when she had returned to Lancaster to help her mother when her father first fell ill. Women in the community had known about her leaving with the famous singer known as Viper in the media. The younger ones might have stared at her in awe, while the older ones scowled and scorned her. On more than one occasion, the bishop had arrived with a tabloid in his hand, angry that so much attention was focused on their community.

"Just worse, I imagine," Harvey added.

"Much worse."

Harvey cleared his throat and glanced at her. "Ever think about calling him, Amanda?"

She shook her head. Harvey knew better than to ask that question. Only once had she gone against the unspoken rule from her upbringing about a woman reaching out to a man. That had been when Alejandro first left her after the accident. He had accompanied her back to the farm, and they had spent a week together: she was curious about his world, and he was eager to disappear into hers. When the paparazzi discovered he was there, he left. The only problem had been that the cameras didn't.

When the bishop wanted her to leave the community, perhaps to return to Ohio to stay with family, Amanda resisted. She didn't want to be shuffled from community to community. So she had approached the media that lingered by the driveway and spoke to them, hoping against hope that Alejandro would get the message.

He had.

And he had come for her.

She leaned her head against the headrest and watched as they passed farm after farm. With everything turning green at last, she couldn't help but take comfort in the fact that at least she was not in Los Angeles, surrounded by tall buildings and busy highways. She'd probably be spending her days alone or, at best, sitting in the studio as Alejandro recorded new songs. She thought about her friend, Celinda, a young singer who she had met last autumn. Amanda wondered if, had she gone to California with Alejandro, they would have caught up for lunch or shopping like they had one day so long ago. Of course, according to the tabloids, and confirmed by Alejandro, Celinda, too, was in the midst of a separation from her longtime love, Justin Bell.

Amanda couldn't help but wonder how Celinda had coped with the devastating discovery of his indiscretions.

At the harness store, Harvey got out of the car and hurried around to open the door for her. She hadn't realized they'd pulled into the parking lot.

"I'm so sorry," she said as she started to get out of the car. He held out his hand for her and she accepted it, looking up at him and managing to thank him with a soft smile.

She knew that it was a fortunate day when Alejandro had arranged for him to work on their farm. He had become like a brother to her and an uncle to Isadora. Without Harvey, Amanda knew that the farm would have fallen into disarray before Jonas arrived. Now that Jonas was fully entrenched in the community after moving there from Ohio, the two men managed the farm without need for much assistance. Still, when the four walls of the kitchen felt like they were closing in on her, Amanda often escaped to the outside to lend a hand.

"You all right?" he asked.

She nodded her head and looked away. The sting of holding back tears forced her to blink several times. She would not cry, she told herself. Do not cry.

"I'll go in. Why don't you just take a seat on that bench yonder?" He pointed toward the shade of a large overgrown tree.

With misty eyes, she nodded her head and obediently walked to where he had pointed. Sitting on the bench, which was long overdue for a fresh coat of paint, Amanda stared into the distance, watching a car pulling out of the parking lot. But her mind was elsewhere, across the continent, lying in the arms of her husband. She smiled, her first genuine smile in weeks, as she shut her eyes and remembered the feel of his touch on her bare skin.

It was a memory that she was beginning to fear would fade over time.

When Alejandro awoke, the sun had not yet risen. He had an appointment with the recording company first thing in the morning and then needed to work with the choreographer and dancers on some new routines for the European tour. With only one week until his departure, he felt as though he were on autopilot, simply moving through the day and responding to the reminders from both his smartphone and his manager, Geoffrey.

Shuffling from the kitchen to the bedroom of his condominium, he stretched his arms over his head, feeling the tightness in his neck and shoulders. The stress of the upcoming tour combined with the added strain of his separation from Amanda weighed heavily upon him. While he almost dreaded the former, being busy kept him from thinking too much about the latter.

He missed her. That was something he had anticipated when he made up his mind that space was what she needed. Leaving her had been the hardest thing that he had ever done. Her face, her tears, and her pleas haunted him at night, and he found himself taking a strong nightcap each evening to avoid struggling with sleep. Many times, especially at night, he longed to pick up his phone and call her.

But he knew that he couldn't.

For all the awful things that his former manager, Mike, had done to disrupt his relationship with Amanda, Alejandro was now starting to see the wisdom behind the actions. How could he have anticipated that Amanda would adapt to his lifestyle? With her Amish upbringing, she had handled it as well as anyone could have expected. And when Isadora was thrust into their lives, she had taken to the role of mother better than any other woman would have.

The only problem was that he didn't want children. Not yet. And dragging a small child on tour with them was not only taxing, it was also inappropriate. When Amanda left Rio de Janeiro, his first feelings of anger at her abandonment were soon replaced with enlightenment at the situation. His alter ego, Viper, would always be a playboy in the minds of the fans, even now that he was married to Amanda, the princess of social media. Just as Mike had predicted, the fans quickly devoured any controversy over love. And as Justin Bell had played the media with his relationship to Celinda Ruiz, the social media gobbled it up, so Alejandro realized that they wanted the return of the old Viper.

Perhaps they merely wanted to see how that played out, a philandering Viper with innocent Amanda. At first, he had no intention of giving the public what they wanted. His love for Amanda was unquestionable. Even before his rise to fame, people always wanted something from him. Always people surrounded him with ideas and schemes, trying to become a part of the story. His story. Alejandro had learned

Sarah Price

long ago to proceed with caution and to ensure that his own reward far outweighed anyone else's.

With Amanda, he had finally learned how it felt to be loved and supported with no expectations in return.

He ran the faucet to fill the Keurig water reservoir. Coffee. That's what he needed. Something strong to jump-start the day.

As he waited for the liquid to pour into his mug, he leaned against the counter, rubbing his forehead and wondering what Amanda was doing at that moment. Perhaps sharing breakfast with Isadora? Or milking the cows with Jonas and Harvey?

He grimaced as he thought of Harvey. For the past two weeks, he had tried to abolish the memory of Harvey carrying Isadora and hearing the soft banter between Harvey and Amanda. When the media published photos of Harvey protecting Amanda from the paparazzi a few months earlier, he had never given it a second thought. The photographers hadn't wasted any time before speculating about a possible relationship between the two, a thought that Alejandro easily dismissed.

But when he saw them together and the ease with which they worked side by side, Alejandro saw something that made the pieces of the puzzle come together: What if Amanda was not meant to be his wife? What if all of this was God's plan for her to return to the Amish community and find a husband more aligned with her past?

His phone vibrated, and Alejandro broke free from his thoughts. He looked around the kitchen to locate his cell phone; it rested on the counter near the stove. He hadn't remembered placing it there. When he glanced at the clock and saw that it wasn't even six thirty yet, he sighed. Probably Geoffrey confirming that a car would be waiting downstairs for him in forty-five minutes.

He reached for the phone and answered the call. *"Dígame, chico."*

"Alex! You're up already?"

"Sí, sí," he responded. *"Claro*, Geoff. *¿Qué pasa?"*

There was a brief pause on the other end of the phone. For a moment Alejandro wondered if the call had dropped. When he heard Geoffrey clearing his throat, he knew something was going on, something that his manager hesitated to tell him.

"You asked me to alert you if there was . . . uh . . ."—another hesitation—"any word from Lancaster. My guys just saw photos hitting the social media circuit. I wanted to alert you."

Alejandro took a deep breath. If Geoffrey was calling him, the photos were not good news. Geoffrey would not bother him with photos of Amanda hanging out the laundry or sweeping off the porch.

"You want me to send you copies?"

Alejandro nodded, even though Geoffrey could not see him. Behind him, he heard the hissing noise of the coffeemaker finishing the brew for his coffee. He didn't need it anymore: he was wide awake.

"Send it to my private e-mail, *sí*."

"There are more than one, Alex."

Bracing himself for the worst, Alejandro hung up the phone, set it on the counter, and started pacing. He kept his hands clutched behind his back, his thumbs tapping nervously. Other than that, he tried to maintain his composure as he waited for the digital photos. Geoffrey's voice said it all. Whatever was being sent would most likely be the one thing he did not want to see: his wife assimilating back into the life of the Amish. Still, he knew that it was her choice. He had given that to her: the gift of choosing which life she wanted.

When his phone made a noise, Alejandro picked it up and prepared himself for opening the e-mail. One tap of his finger on the link, and the images began to display on his screen.

His heart fell.

The photos confirmed his suspicions. As he swiped through them, seeing Harvey Alderfer talking with Amanda on the crest of a hill, Harvey opening the car door for her, and Harvey guiding her through the parking lot of a store, Alejandro knew what her choice would be.

When he saw the final image, the one of Amanda staring up at the Mennonite man, with that look of innocence on her face, he shut his eyes.

Maybe he had known from the beginning that she belonged there, with her family and community. If it wasn't Harvey, it would be someone else to accept her for who she was and who she should become: a hardworking farmer's wife and doting mother. He had fooled himself to think that he could settle down into the role of loving husband.

"*Ay,* Dios *mío,*" he muttered, clicking the phone so that it shut down. He shoved it into the pocket of his robe and stood at the counter, both hands pressed down on the granite top. With a lowered head, he took several deep breaths. He didn't want to leave her. Losing Amanda would be the single most difficult thing he would ever do. He knew that. His fans would greet a divorce with mixed feelings: some supporting the decision because they missed the old Viper, and others hating him for leaving Amanda. But she deserved better. She deserved happiness.

Alejandro needed time to think through the decision before making a final choice. He knew she loved him. There was no reason to doubt that. The only problem was that he loved her more, and from the look on her face in that final photo, he knew that his love was just not enough to maintain her. Not with his lifestyle. Now, if he could only get Amanda to arrive at the same realization.

About the Author

The Preiss family emigrated from Europe in 1705, settling in Pennsylvania as part of the area's first wave of Mennonite families. Sarah Price has always respected and honored her ancestors through exploration and research about her family's Anabaptist history and their religion. For over twenty-five years, she has been actively involved in an Amish community in Pennsylvania. The author of over thirty novels, Sarah is finally doing what she always wanted to do: write about the religion and culture that she loves so dearly. For more information, visit her blog at www.sarahpriceauthor.com.